A NOVEL

RIPPLES

JASMINE O'HEA

RIVER GROVE
BOOKS

Published by River Grove Books
Austin, TX
www.rivergrovebooks.com

Distributed by River Grove Books

Design and composition by Greenleaf Book Group
Cover design by Greenleaf Book Group
Cover images: ©iStockphoto/Sayan_Moongklang; ©iStockphoto/arfo; Unsplash/Philippe Schrettenbrunner

Publisher's Cataloging-in-Publication data is available.

Print ISBN: 978-1-63299-704-3

eBook ISBN: 978-1-63299-705-0

First Edition

For Katie
My sister, my first reader, and my best friend

1

NOLAN

I met my uncle for the first time at my mom's funeral. His hair was the same light blond color as mine and my mom's, which sort of annoyed me. He was wearing a slick, black suit that probably cost more than my entire wardrobe. When he shook my hand, he told me he was sorry for my loss. Good. He should be sorry.

When Bailey invited me to live with him and his wife, Trish, in their Eastside mansion, I figured it was just a guilty conscience, or maybe that he had some weird savior complex. It obviously wasn't because he felt it was familial duty. The guy didn't step in when his sister had practically been living on the street, so keeping his sixteen-year-old nephew out of foster care couldn't have been high on his priority list.

Trish didn't even show up to the service, but Bailey made sure everyone there knew what a big deal it was that they were taking me in. "Such an upgrade this will be for my nephew," he said loudly. "I'm paying to send him to the prep school my daughters attended. He'll want for nothing."

As if wanting my mom to be alive again didn't count. As if I'd be excited about going to the school that had expelled my mom when she'd been my age.

We packed up my five boxes of possessions and old mountain bike, then drove a half hour across the city to northeast Morley. After we parked in the sprawling driveway of Bailey's house, I got out of the car and grabbed one of the boxes.

"Oh, don't bother," Bailey said dismissively. "I hired some people to take care of that."

I used to think, in those rare moments she talked about Bailey, that my mom had been exaggerating. Now, I could tell why my mom used to say that Bailey was the second-biggest ass she knew.

The first biggest ass was my dad. My mom hadn't kept in touch with him after he'd ditched her seven months into her pregnancy. I knew practically nothing about him, but Mom said I was better off that way. Because there wasn't much to remind me of my dad, I didn't really think about him. It was different with Uncle Bailey, though. He lived in the same city as us.

Once, on a long bike ride, my mom told me, abruptly, to stop. "We're getting too close to Eastside," she said, her fingers grasping the handlebars tightly.

"What's Eastside?"

"The neighborhood where Bailey lives. With all the other entitled morons of this city."

I wasn't about to let myself become one of those morons. I rolled my eyes and carried the box inside.

Bailey led me upstairs to my room. "What do you think?" he said, clearly impressed with it himself.

It was nice, in a generic hotel way. I didn't like the fake evergreen scent coming from the oil diffuser on the nightstand. The room was bigger than any I'd slept in before, but I suddenly felt suffocated and desperate to get outside. Somewhere that wouldn't smell like a department store.

"I need some fresh air," I said, dropping the box on the queen-size bed.

"Wait," Bailey said, and something that looked like embarrassment crossed his face. "I . . ."

He sighed.

"Nolan, I'm sorry I wasn't there for Liz, er, your mom before. Really, I am. I hope I can . . . make it up to you now."

You can't, I thought resentfully, though I wanted to say it out loud. Instead, I just repeated that I wanted to go outside.

Bailey sighed again, and for half a millisecond, I felt bad for him. Then, I pictured my mom on the couch where I'd found her, and all sympathy vanished.

"Yes, well, I'll show you the backyard," he said and led me downstairs to some sliding glass doors. "The yard is a dream. Especially now in late summer. We have a hot tub, a barbecue island, a custom-built doghouse for Duke—he's our Corgi—"

I slid the door open, stepped outside, and slammed it shut. I don't think I'd ever been so rude to an adult before, but I couldn't bear to hear another word.

I paced around the backyard, growing antsier by the second. I wanted to be anywhere but here. I wanted to go home to my own bedroom, or ride away into the woods on my bike. I paced faster as I began to feel more trapped. Just then, I spotted a gate behind the barbecue and headed over to see what lay beyond the yard.

The city of Morley, Maine, sits in the middle of a vast forest. I was relieved to discover the familiar sight of trees, untouched by expensive landscaping, at the bottom of the hill that Bailey's house sat atop. It was a small comfort to think that a few miles away, this same forest encircled the neighborhood where I'd lived my whole life. This was the forest of bike rides and camping trips. It was the last place I'd be bothered by Bailey. Or anyone, for that matter.

I jogged down the hill, stopping when I got to the trees. It was already early evening, and I was wearing the suit Bailey had bought me for the service. He'd insisted on buying it after looking through my closet of secondhand t-shirts, jeans, and hoodies. This probably wasn't the best time to explore the area. Still, the prospect of returning to the house and suffering through a dinner with Bailey and Trish was bad enough that even the potential of getting lost in the forest was preferable.

I started walking, but after a few minutes I realized how tired I was and sat down at the base of a tree. Finally, away from the fancy house and my uncle, I could breathe a little easier. Now, the air smelled like real pines. I let myself sort through the memories that were still jumbled in my mind.

An ambulance barreling through the narrow alleyway.

The way all the kids at school tried not to stare when the news spread.

My mom unconscious on the couch.

My mom teaching me to ride a bike.

There, sitting alone in the forest, I let myself do what I hadn't done all week. Cry.

There was a scuffling noise in the distance. Instinctively, I jumped to my feet, scared it was a bear or some other animal. I thought about the stories my mom used to tell me about vagrants who lived in the woods. I listened hard, my heart pounding.

The rustling gave way to the faint sound of someone humming, and I relaxed a bit, sinking back down to the ground. The humming didn't sound menacing. Maybe I should have been more afraid of meeting a stranger in the woods by myself, but I was too drained to care. I just hoped that whoever it was, they would walk by without noticing me.

The hummer probably *wouldn't* have noticed me had a squirrel not scampered up the tree I was leaning against. I looked up at the same time she turned toward me. It was a girl, around my age. When we locked eyes, she gasped, froze, and stared at me nervously. It struck me that she couldn't have been expecting to come across a guy lying in the dirt, and I should do something to let her know I wasn't dangerous.

"Hey," I said as I stood up. "Sorry, I didn't mean to scare you."

She exhaled and adjusted the straps of her purple backpack. "No, it's okay." Giving me a curious look, the girl pushed a long lock of brown hair behind her ear and inched closer. "Are you all right?" she said. She seemed genuinely concerned.

I'd gone from potential threat to a charity case in two seconds. I guess I had my gawky frame and chin acne to thank for that.

"Yeah, fine," I said. My initial relief that this short girl wasn't a burly, axe-wielding murderer gave way to annoyance that she wasn't leaving me alone. I didn't want anyone else feeling sorry for me today.

She continued to assess me thoughtfully, her eyes narrowing. "You're sure you're not lost?"

Who did this girl think she was, my mom? Immediately, I cursed my thoughts for taking me there. Why did everything have to remind me of my mom? Even this nosy girl?

"Yeah," I said. "I'm not lost. I live just up the hill."

The girl frowned. "You do?"

"Yes." Now she was really getting on my nerves.

"Oh. I've never seen you around."

I brushed the dirt from my pants. "That's 'cause I just moved in today."

"Really?"

"Yep," I said, trying to end the conversation. I hated small talk on normal days, but today it felt impossible.

"Where are you from?"

"From here."

"You're from Morley?"

"Yeah."

"So, your family just moved to Eastside?"

I should've let this girl think I was some weird drifter. She might have left me alone.

"No," I said, seeing no way out but the truth. "I moved in with my uncle."

"Oh, I see." She was quiet for a moment. Probably she was wondering why I was suddenly living with someone who wasn't my parent. "Who's your uncle? I might know him."

"Bailey Fredericks?" I offered.

"Oh, no way," she said, her eyes brightening. "He lives next door to me. His kids used to go to my school."

"Cool." I was getting more and more irritated by this girl and her stupid happy demeanor. Humming through the woods and trying to make a new friend like a fairy-tale princess. I decided to add something I thought might get her to stop asking me uncomfortable questions. "I've never met his kids."

I watched her struggle to find something polite to say.

"You've never met your cousins?" she said carefully.

"No. And today's the first time I met Bailey."

She nodded. "Well, I think you'll like living here."

Her optimism was grating on me. The last thing I needed was another person chattering on about how special this neighborhood was, and how lucky I was to be here. I knew she was only trying to be nice, but the more she forced the conversation to continue, the more I wanted her to get lost.

"Well, my choices were Uncle Bailey's or a group home."

The girl's smile disappeared. "Oh," she said with way too much sympathy. "That's just . . . um . . ."

Her fair skin started to redden, and she glanced to where our houses lay in the distance. It kind of amused me that now *she* was the one who was uncomfortable.

"I almost went with the group home," I said bluntly, to put her out of her misery. "I don't think it would have been so bad. I could've stayed at my school. And I'd be living with people who would sort of understand what I'm going through. Instead, I'm here with a rich stranger who thinks my mom was a junkie loser and wants to change pretty much everything about me."

To my surprise, the girl didn't flinch. No pitying smile, no pointing out some silver lining that didn't exist, nothing. She just stood there, nodding slowly as though absorbing what I'd said.

"Yeah," she said after a long pause, "that makes sense."

"It does?" I said, looking at my feet.

"Yeah." She sighed. "I'm sorry. I didn't mean to pry."

"No, no you didn't," I said, feeling guilty for acting like such a jerk. "I was being stupid." What was happening? Just a few minutes ago I was trying to get rid of this girl, and now I was worrying about hurting her feelings.

"*Stupid* is a bit harsh," she said, a small smile slowly returning to her face. "But I think someone in your situation has the right to be stupid. At least, for a little while."

That made me laugh. "I guess."

We were quiet for a moment until her cell phone dinged.

"It's my dad," she said, looking at the text. "I better go."

"Yeah, sure." I felt an unexpected twinge of disappointment.

Instead of leaving, though, the girl gave a thoughtful glance toward the sky. "It's getting dark," she said. Her green eyes flickered back to meet mine. "Maybe you want to walk back with me?"

Yes, I did. But I tripped over my words, something that happens when I get flustered. "Oh, um, yeah, good idea."

"I come out to Mountain Pass Trail when I need some time to myself," she told me as we walked. "I rarely come across anyone else. Most people like to use the landscaped trails in the neighborhood, or the forest trail that loops back to the city. This one just leads one way out. It's peaceful."

"Yeah," I said. "That's what I was thinking."

"Sorry I interrupted you," she said, turning to look at me for a second.

"No problem, really."

We reached the top of the hill just as the sun was setting.

"I'm Harlow, by the way," she said.

"Nolan."

"Nice to meet you, Nolan."

"Thanks. I'll . . . I'll see you around?"

"Yeah, for sure."

She went through the gate next to Bailey's. Going from the meandering path of the forest to the perfect lines of the backyard made me remember how irritated I'd been earlier. I wasn't looking forward to living in Bailey's world any more than before, but it was nice to know that I might be able to escape to another world just beyond the gate.

2

HARLOW

"*There* you are!" my dad said as I punched the code into our gate's keypad and slipped into the backyard. He was standing in front of the barbecue grilling and—from what I could tell from the thick smoke in the air—burning dinner. "I was starting to get worried." My dad wiped the back of his hand against his forehead and adjusted the heat. "Everything okay out there?"

"Yeah, sorry, I lost track of time," I said. That was true, but I knew I was being evasive, which is not at all like me. For some reason, I wasn't quite ready to tell Dad about meeting Nolan. Usually when I get home, I talk in paragraphs before my dad can get a word in. We like to joke that all he has to do is ask one innocuous question, and we're set for conversation for the rest of the day. Losing track of time isn't like me either. I despise being late.

My dad's eyebrows raised expectantly.

"*Really?*" he said, flipping one of the burgers over. "That's all the story I get?"

I toyed with the zipper on my jacket. I came home with reports about people I met around town all the time. You can't be the mayor's daughter without shaking a few new hands every week. Normally, I'd just tell him about meeting someone new. *Not* telling him was making it a big deal. Dad and I don't keep secrets from each other.

"Yep, that's all." Then I added, "For now, anyway."

My dad nodded. "I can be patient. But in the meantime, why don't you tell me about the rest of your day?"

~~~

Later that night, I tossed back and forth in bed, unable to fall asleep. I was thinking about Nolan, the way his pale blue eyes had lit up when he laughed. At first, his terse answers made me regret starting a conversation, but after his guard slipped, he told me about his mom. I understand how sore a subject moms can be.

There was something sort of sweet about him, but more than that, Nolan was . . . refreshing. He didn't have a clue who I was, and he wasn't trying to be friends with me because he thought my dad could help him land a cushy summer internship at his law firm or city hall. To Nolan, I wasn't a network connection or the lab partner you could count on to do all the work. I was merely a girl he'd met in the woods.

~~~

When my alarm went off, I was groggy from too little sleep. It was one of those days I was thankful to have a uniform to put on. Even after I got to school, it felt like I was still waking up. I was heading inside when, from the corner of my eye, I spotted Nolan on the sidewalk a ways back, ambling toward the main doors. At once, my sleepiness was gone.

"Hey, Nolan," I called out. I was almost as surprised to see him now as I had been yesterday. Although, this was an excited surprised, not a scared surprised.

"Harlow!" he said, a wave of relief visibly washing over him. His sandy-blond hair was coiffed to the side like it had been yesterday. I waited while he jogged to catch up.

"I didn't know you'd be going to school here," I said. "I would've offered you a ride."

"Oh, it's okay," he said. "I rode my bike. It's only like four miles."

"Your uncle didn't drive you?" Bailey Fredericks was no poster child for generosity—Dad tried, unsuccessfully, to get him to volunteer at the holiday food drive every year—but it still seemed strange to me that he wouldn't drive his own nephew to school.

"He offered to *hire me a car*, but . . ." Nolan trailed off, his voice thick with disdain.

"Well, do you want to drive to school with me?" I said as I started walking up the steps. Nolan followed me, but he didn't answer right away. I was suddenly self-conscious, realizing how much I was hoping he would accept the offer. "I leave at 7:45. The only thing is that after school I usually have something going on, so you might have to find a ride home."

"Yeah," he said. "That would be cool. Thanks."

I smiled, and our eyes met like they had yesterday on the path. "So . . ." I said, trying to think of what to say next. It was rare that I couldn't think of something to say. "What's your first class?"

Nolan pulled his phone out of his pocket. "Uh, English. In room 211. But I think I'm supposed to check into the office first."

"The office is over there," I said, pointing down the hall. "C'mon, it's on my way."

We started toward the office when a voice called my name from behind. It was Amaya. Her softly curled black hair, still damp from her morning swim practice, bounced from side to side.

"Harlow! Can I borrow your chemistry textbook? I forgot my backpack this morning; I must have left it in my mom's car."

I laughed at her brown puppy-dog eyes. *Typical Amaya.* She'd been forgetting her books or backpack from the time we were in kindergarten. "Sure," I said. "But wait—does that mean you also don't have your notes for our English presentation?"

"Yeah, it's okay though," Amaya said, with a wave. "My mom's gonna drop my backpack off as soon as she can."

I exhaled. "Okay, good." Now it was Amaya's turn to laugh a little at me. *Typical Harlow*, I could see her thinking as I handed her the book.

Then I noticed Amaya eyeing Nolan.

"Who's this?" she asked me, grinning.

"This is Nolan," I said. "It's his first day here and I'm helping him find the office." The warning bell rang. "We gotta go, but I'll see you later, Amaya."

Quickly, I turned and walked down the hall with Nolan. I could feel Amaya watching us and I knew she'd have a hundred questions for me later.

"Can I give you my number?" I asked Nolan when we got to the office.

He looked startled, which made me worry I was coming on too strong.

"You know," I added, "that way you can text me at lunch if you want to sit with me and my friends."

"Okay, yeah," he said, handing me his phone. "That would be cool."

What I really wanted was the chance to talk to him without my phone going off, or the bell ringing, or other people listening in, but for now, I'd have to wait. Hopefully, I'd only have to wait until the morning when we could drive to school, just the two of us.

At lunch, I waited for Amaya at our spot by the bell tower. I was with the rest of our regular lunch crew and checking my phone to see if Nolan had texted when Amaya walked up, Nolan straggling behind her.

"Hey guys," Amaya said to everyone, "this is Nolan Fredericks. Today's his first day here."

"Hi," Nolan said quietly. I tried to catch his eye, but he was looking shyly down at his feet.

"But I guess *some* of you already knew that," Amaya said, giving me a mischievous smile. I rolled my eyes, a bit annoyed at the way she was corralling Nolan. "Nolan and I just came from History. I thought he could have lunch with us."

Introductions were made, and we sat down at our table. Nolan let everyone settle in before squeezing himself into a space at the end of the bench. He crossed his arms and put his elbows onto the table.

"Don't you have a lunch?" Amaya asked in her straightforward manner. It's not that she's oblivious to social cues, she's just always been very direct. Whatever Amaya does, she does it boldly. Whereas I started wearing mascara and lip gloss last year, Amaya hasn't gone a day without neon eye shadow or shimmer blush on her olive skin since we were eleven. It's something I really admire about her, the confident and easy way she carries herself. Today, however, when I was feeling so *un*confident, I was finding it a little tiresome.

"Um, no," Nolan said. I wondered if he'd refused lunch from his uncle like he had the ride to school.

"Here, take my pretzels," I said before anyone could offer him a few bucks for a school lunch. Nolan, I guessed, wouldn't accept money, but he might be *just* hungry enough to take a few snacks.

He hesitated, eyeing the pretzels I held up. "Well, okay. Thanks." I tossed the bag over.

Amaya offered Nolan some almonds, and a minute later he also had a banana and a homemade brownie. My friends' conversation took off, but I didn't listen to much of what they were saying. I was too distracted trying to gauge how Nolan was doing. He remained quiet, but by the time lunch ended, the creases in his forehead had softened and his posture had straightened. I relaxed a bit too.

"Nolan," I said before he got up from the table. "Where are you headed next?"

"Study hall."

"That's on my way to math. You can walk with me, if you want."

He nodded, so we said goodbye to the others and I led the way inside.

"Your friends are really nice," he said.

"Yeah," I said, glad he hadn't been too overwhelmed, especially by Amaya. "You should sit with us again tomorrow." He nodded again and I glanced at my watch. Only three minutes until the bell. "That's your class on the left," I said pointing out the study hall room. "I'll see you tomorrow? For the ride to school?"

"Actually, about that—" Nolan said suddenly, then stopped.

I looked at him, alarmed. Had he changed his mind?

"It's just," he said, "I was thinking maybe we could hang out after school today, like maybe we could meet up on the trail again if that would be okay, just to talk or go for a walk or something, but no problem if you're busy or don't want to, I get it."

It was the most words I'd heard him string together all day, and he seemed almost out of breath once he'd finished. I didn't bother fighting the smile that had made its way to my face.

"Yes!" I said. "But it can't be right after school. I have a student council meeting, so I could be there by six. Does that sound all right?"

"Yeah," Nolan said, "that sounds good."

When I sat down at my desk in math, I told myself that my heart was beating so fiercely because I'd sprinted to make it to class on time. But that wasn't true. My heart had begun racing when Nolan asked me to meet him, and it showed no signs of slowing down.

~~~~~

After my student council meeting, I told Amaya I had too much homework to hang out. She didn't argue with that. Amaya knew when we "did homework" together we rarely ended up getting anything done.

I hated to tell a lie, even a small one, but I was afraid that if Amaya knew I had a crush on Nolan, she'd let it slip. That's what's happened in the past. It was never a huge deal though because none of those crushes had been serious. The way I was feeling about Nolan seemed important, somehow. I wanted a better idea of *how* important before I told her.

At home, I made a few sandwiches, grabbed two flashlights and a picnic blanket, then headed down the hill behind my house to wait at the edge of the woods. I pulled out my phone to distract myself from my nerves. Soon, I heard footsteps. Nolan almost lost control of his lanky frame as he stepped around a mushy spot in the grass.
~~~~~

"Hey," he said, shoving his hands into his jacket pockets.

"Hey. I'm glad you're here," I said. My obvious happiness seemed to put him at ease.

"Yeah, me too," he said. "Sorry, have you been waiting long?"

"Nah, just a few minutes. If you ever arrive somewhere before me, you'll know something's the matter."

"Okay, I'll remember that," he said.

"How was your bike ride home?" I asked.

"Pretty good. Light wind today, so that helps."

Nolan looked like he was going to say something else, but didn't.

"There's a small clearing not too far away," I said. "We can hang out there if you want. I brought some sandwiches."

"Yeah, that sounds good."

As we walked side by side, I did most of the work keeping our conversation going, same as the day before. I asked him how the first day of school went and what he liked to do for fun. I learned ours was smaller than his old school. Physics is his favorite subject. He worked in a bike shop before moving to Eastside. Normally, I'd be annoyed at his reticence, as I believe in expressing oneself fully, but I got the sense that his matter-of-fact answers and lack of questions in return weren't because he was uninterested, but rather because he was being overly cautious. Was he intimidated? At school I have a reputation among both students and teachers for being "intense." But Nolan had just met me. If something about me was already making him uncomfortable, I worried what he might think when he found out my dad was the mayor. We're a whole family of "intense."

We veered off the path to the clearing. I spread out the picnic blanket I'd brought and handed Nolan a sandwich. He must have been starving, because by the time I had unwrapped my sandwich, half of his was gone. I offered him another one, and he protested politely. "Oh, come on," I said. "Just take it."

"Okay," he said. "Thanks."

After a few minutes, Nolan asked, "So, what's it like being on student council?"

"It's fun for the most part," I said, "but it can be stressful sometimes. It's impossible to make everybody happy."

Nolan nodded. "Have you been on student council for long?"

"Since it was an option to join in 4th grade," I said, laughing. "I'm basically a career politician."

"Ugh, the worst kind," he teased. "I've never really been into politics. It just seems like even good people with good intentions end up getting bogged down by the system. They become what they set out to get rid of." His eyes grew wide. "Not that I'm saying that about you. *At all.*"

"No, I know," I said. People often said this kind of thing to me, but, like my dad, I'd learned not to take it personally.

"I think you're really cool," Nolan said before I could speak further. "Not that I know you that well yet, but sometimes you can just tell about a person, you know?"

"Yes," I said, grateful that he'd put into words what I'd been feeling all day. "I think I know exactly what you mean." Nolan avoided eye contact, but even though his head was down, I could tell he was smiling. All of this was beginning to feel like something truly important. I didn't want to ruin the moment, but I felt that now was the time to tell him who my dad was. The longer I delayed addressing it, the harder it would be later.

"Maybe I was destined for politics," I said. "You may not follow Morley politics closely, but you probably know who Mayor Matt is."

"Yeah," he said. "I think my mom voted for him."

"Right, well, now you know his daughter."

Nolan looked up and I watched him process what I'd said. He nodded slowly. "Wow," he said, "that's . . . cool." I was relieved that the news didn't faze him.

"Yeah, it is pretty cool. *Most* of the time, anyway. My grandpa was actually the mayor before my dad, so sometimes I wonder if people are expecting me to follow in their footsteps. I'm not entirely sure I want to." Then, I caught myself. "But I know whatever complaints I may have about being the mayor's daughter absolutely *pale* in comparison to what you're going through. I don't mean to sound ungrateful."

"You don't," Nolan said quickly. "And yeah, it's been tough for me, but that doesn't make me some kind of martyr. I think everyone's life is hard, in its own way." Then, his serious mood lightened a bit. "Except maybe for Uncle Bailey's."

"I think *blissful ignorance* protects some people," I said.

"But I'd rather know the truth," Nolan said. "I'm glad you told me about your dad."

"Me too," I said. I wondered then if I should tell him about my mom, and how she had left me and my dad years ago. Nolan was a good listener and sharing the story might bring us closer. But I decided I didn't want to get into all that right now. The story was long and complicated, and I was enjoying things exactly as they were.

We chatted for a few more minutes, until the late afternoon sunlight was replaced by shadows and the first layer of nighttime fog.

"Ah, dang it," Nolan said as he pulled out his phone and turned on the flashlight. "I guess we're walking back in the dark."

I reached into my backpack and retrieved the two flashlights I'd packed, holding them up with a smile.

Nolan laughed. "Jeez, do you think of *everything*?"

"Guess you'll have to stick around to find out."

3

TOPHER

When I was young, I became a photographer by trade. Today, I remain a photographer out of necessity. I don't trust the images that only exist in my head. At least, not the ones from before Arizona.

Life became less confusing, less muddled when Jojo and I moved from Morley to Scottsdale sixteen years ago. My parents were understanding when we told them we were moving. Jojo's parents didn't debate our decision either.

"A change of scenery will do us good," she explained to them all, and they agreed.

I packed up my studio with meticulous care. Each photo featured the smiling faces of people I was sure I'd never met, let alone photographed. "It's one of the effects of generalized dissociative amnesia," the psychiatrist assured me. Still, it felt like I wasn't being asked to retrieve erased memories so much as replace the memories that I did have. If my memories were simply gone, then why did I sense I was missing a photo? One of a red-faced young man, his fingers digging into his screaming baby's rumpled blue dress.

I asked Jojo about it, and she said she hadn't seen it.

"But look at this place," she said, gesturing to the clutter around her. "There are boxes and stacks of paper everywhere. I'm sure it will turn up."

"And if it doesn't?" I said, a strange feeling rising in my gut.

Jojo pressed down hard on a suitcase and wrestled it closed. "Then it doesn't."

So, the photo was real. Did that mean the memories I had of the man and baby were real too?

I banished the thought. I had to, for the sake of my own child. Moving wouldn't change anything if I dragged Morley along with us. I didn't want to mess up our chance at living a semi-normal life, especially with the baby due in just three months. I didn't ask about the photo again and we left without it.

The longer I was away from Morley, the easier my new life became. I took pride in my work as a photographer and was caught up in the day-to-day busyness of raising a family. It seemed that Jojo and I had moved on as much as we possibly could. As a precaution, we never traveled to Morley. Our parents made the trip to visit us in Arizona. At first, they understood the arrangement and respected our desire to leave what they referred to as my "mental lapse" behind. But after a few years, they found our position unreasonable. Wasn't it time to let the wounds be fully healed? Shouldn't Cate see where her family was from?

Cate started asking about it too. What situation was so traumatic that we couldn't set foot in that city again? Why were we being so evasive? What were we hiding?

Sometimes, when special occasions like birthdays or holidays came up, Jojo and I discussed what it would be like to visit Morley.

"Do you think you could handle it now?" she asked hopefully.

I wished I could tell her yes, but Jojo must have seen the fear I wasn't doing a great job of hiding. "We won't go then," she said. "It's not worth upsetting the good thing we have here."

The older Cate got, the trickier it became to come up with satisfying answers about our aversion to visiting Morley. We never promised to talk about it later like it was something she couldn't understand yet; we just said it wasn't up for discussion, now or ever. "We had a bad experience and decided the best thing for our family was to leave," Jojo would say. "It's all in the past," I'd add.

It's incredible, though, how the past can reach out and snatch you back after it's been buried for so long.

When my mom called to tell me my dad was sick, Jojo and I debated the wisest way to handle the situation. Not going was callous and would be unjustifiable in Cate's eyes, but going meant . . . well, we weren't entirely sure what it meant. We'd never tried.

"Sixteen years," Jojo mused. "I think it's been long enough. I think you'll be okay."

"Everything that happened . . . it seems like a dream now," I said. "One I woke up from long ago."

Jojo nodded. "I think you should go. You need to see your dad."

She was right. I bought my plane ticket.

There was heavy fog on the morning I landed, and it wasn't until I was in the rental car driving toward my parents' home in the Eastside neighborhood that I had a clear view of my surroundings. I saw the green, sky-high trees stretching out before me. Then, I saw my wife's face. But it wasn't Jojo.

Jody?

As the memory continued to play, I saw a woman with golden skin stand by a door—our front door?—and wave. I think she'd been waving goodbye. Now it was like she was welcoming me back, back to Morley, back to where I belonged.

Overcome, I yanked on the steering wheel and veered to the side of the road. I sat with my hands pressed firmly against my eyes. The musky forest smell slipped in through the windows. How wrong I'd been when I'd told Jojo—when I'd told *myself*—that Morley had only been a dream. How foolish I'd been to try and forget that this, the forest and the trail and the pond, was what was real. It was our life in Arizona that was the dream.

I had to keep going though, and so I drove on, not knowing if the road led to the future or the past.

4

NOLAN

As I settled into my new life, I began to feel guilty about how well things were turning out. I was the new kid who'd shown up a few weeks into the semester, but by the end of September, I already had a group of friends. While my old friends checked in on me from time to time, things felt pretty strained with them. I'd been evasive all summer because I hadn't wanted them to know what was going on at home, and neither had my mom. She'd said everything would be back to normal in no time, so there was no use in worrying people. When my friends found out my mom had died, they were shocked. They said I should have told them what was happening, that they would have done something to help. Maybe they could have. There was no way of knowing now.

Aside from stirring up regrets, talking to my friends also reminded me of how stifling my old routine had been. I'd come home from work completely spent and walk into the apartment afraid of what I'd find. I didn't realize the stress I'd been under until I moved. But then I felt bad for thinking that way, like it was a betrayal of my mom. I tried to tell myself she'd be happy to know I was doing okay. Besides, it was no thanks to Bailey and Trish.

It was because of Harlow.

Seeing Harlow instantly put me in a better mood, even if I just passed her in the hallway on the way to class. Her green eyes would brighten whenever they met mine, and the dimples in her cheeks would deepen. I'd forget whatever I'd been thinking about. Harlow was very busy though, and finding time to hang out was difficult. During our car rides to school, she invited me to sit in on student council and debate team meetings or join her at community service events. I didn't feel up to trying any of those things. I wanted to see Harlow more, but not necessarily in places where there would be a lot of people playing by rules I didn't know. At first, I made up excuses, like I had too much homework or chores to do. Unsurprisingly, Harlow saw through those pretty quickly.

"Nolan, it's okay if you don't want to go," she said one morning. "You can tell me the truth."

Even before the summer, I'd never been totally open with my friends, but with Harlow, I believed her when she said I could be honest. "I *do* want to hang out with you," I said, "but I'm trying to get used to everything here. Sometimes I feel like this is all a strange dream and I'm going to wake up in my old apartment."

She nodded. "Do you feel homesick?"

"Yeah," I said, still a tad self-conscious that I was so easy to figure out. "I'm basically living with two strangers. Besides asking me if my homework's done, Bailey and Trish barely talk to me. Most of the time they just look at me with an expression that's half pity, half irritation."

"That sounds lonely," Harlow said softly.

"It can be," I said. "Back at my apartment, I could be by myself without feeling lonely. But here, even when Bailey and Trish are home, the house still feels empty somehow."

"You can always come over to my house," Harlow said. "You're going through *so* many changes right now. You shouldn't do it alone."

She glanced at me, just for a second, but I felt a knot form in my stomach.

Every day, it was becoming clearer that the feelings I had for Harlow were different than anything I'd experienced before. But like she'd said, I was in the middle of a lot of changes, and what I needed more than anything was a friend who understood that. I felt caught. I was comfortable with the way things were, but I also needed Harlow to know that she was important to me, and I really did want to see her more. We were only moments away from school, but I made myself say what I had on my mind before doubt got the better of me.

"Harlow, have you ever been mountain biking?"

"No," she said. "I don't have a mountain bike."

"Would you . . ." I fought back the nerves that were creeping in. "Would you be up for trying it?"

Harlow kept her eyes on the road, but she smiled. "Yeah, that'd be great."

It somehow didn't register in my head that Harlow had said yes, and I kept babbling. "Mountain Pass Trail only takes about an hour one way, but we don't have to go that far if you don't want to. A path in the neighborhood is good too."

"Nolan," Harlow said, a little louder. "Mountain biking sounds fun."

<p style="text-align:center">~~~</p>

On the second Saturday of October, Harlow and I met at the top of the hill.

"What do you think?" Harlow asked. "Is my bike okay to go on the trail?"

I leaned down to look at the thin tires on her city bike. "I think so," I said. "Mountain Pass Trail is pretty flat, so this bike should be able to handle it."

We walked our bikes down to the trail and started riding. I set a leisurely pace so that Harlow wouldn't feel rushed. It felt strange to pedal slower than I was used to, but even stranger to be biking side by side with a girl.

"I hope we have time to make it to the end of the trail," Harlow said. "I just have to be home by two o'clock. Today's my dad's birthday."

"That's cool," I said. "What are you guys doing?"

"Mini golf, then dinner with my grandparents."

"No big party at city hall?"

"No," she said. "My dad doesn't like to make a fuss about his birthday. Besides, he spends enough time at city hall. He needs some time away from it all."

Although I hadn't met Mayor Matt yet, hearing this made me like him. Harlow told me this month was keeping him particularly busy, but usually he was around more. "I've told him a *little* bit about you," she said, grinning. "He wanted to know who I was going biking with today. You'll meet him soon."

Harlow talked all the time about her dad, but she never mentioned her mom. If it was a painful topic, I wanted to be the last person to bring it up. I hadn't said more about my own mom to Harlow since we'd met. In some way, it felt like I was protecting Mom, saving her from being remembered as a drug addict by someone who'd never met her. I didn't want to remember Mom as a drug addict either, but my memory of her lying limply in a hospital bed was much more vivid than the ones of us riding bikes or eating cereal together in the mornings. I wondered then whether talking about those good memories might make them a little stronger. If I was going to confide in anyone, it was Harlow.

I was just about to tell her about the Italian restaurant we'd gone to once a year for my mom's birthday when Harlow's front tire swerved. She gave a short scream as she toppled off and hit the dirt.

"Harlow!" I cried, jumping from my bike in a panic. She'd landed on her side, the bike on top. I practically threw it off her and knelt down.

"Are you okay?"

"Yeah," she said, her voice a bit strained. "Totally fine. I think I just hit a rock or something."

I felt as guilty as if I'd placed the rock in her path myself. "I am so, *so* sorry. I shouldn't have said your bike was fit for this path, I—"

"Really, Nolan, I'm fine," Harlow said as she propped herself up.

"No, you're not," I gasped. "You're bleeding."

"What?" Harlow said. A bright patch of blood was forming on her knee where her yoga pants were torn.

"Oh," she said, touching it gingerly. "Well, it's not that bad."

She was so cool about it, but I was growing more alarmed each second. "I'm sorry, Harlow. Do you want to just stay here and rest a while?"

"No need," she said. "I've got some antiseptic and Band-Aids in my back-pack. If you don't mind grabbing it from the basket?"

I sprang to my feet and retrieved her backpack. She winced briefly as she cleaned the wound.

"Are you sure you're okay?" I said. "If you feel like you can't make it back—"

"Nolan," Harlow laughed, "you're almost as bad as my dad. He goes into panic mode when I get a paper cut."

"Oh," I said, a little embarrassed. "Sorry."

"There's no need to apologize," she said.

There's no need to apologize. I heard the words again in my head, but in my mom's voice. "Actually," I said, "my mom used to tell me that a lot. She said I apologized when I didn't really need to."

Harlow carefully stretched the Band-Aid over her wound. "My dad says something similar, that you should only say sorry if there's really something to forgive." She crumpled the Band-Aid wrapping and looked at me, a pensive expression on her face. "Apparently, my mom used to tell him that he apol-ogized for little things that didn't matter, but wouldn't own up to the bigger stuff, the more important stuff."

I hadn't expected Harlow to bring up her mom and couldn't think of what to say. No words felt delicate enough for the questions I wanted to ask.

"They're divorced," Harlow said, probably sensing my awkwardness. "It happened a long time ago."

"I'm sorry," I said instinctively, before catching myself a second later. "I mean, no, I . . . " Only then did I realize I was holding my breath. I exhaled slowly and the end of my breath unfolded into a soft laugh. Harlow laughed too.

"I'm ready to keep going," she said, climbing to her feet.

I peered down at her knee, just to make sure it was okay. "I hope it doesn't leave a scar or anything."

Harlow shrugged. "Even if it does, it'll just be a way for me to remember my first time mountain biking."

I held my breath again. "You . . . you mean you'd go mountain biking again?"

She smiled. "Yes. I would."

⌇

After Harlow and I got back from biking, I went home and sat on one of the chaise lounges next to the hot tub. Bailey and Trish were entertaining inside, and I didn't want to get involved. They didn't say so, but I knew they preferred it that way, too.

I played some games on my phone for a while but grew antsy. I got up from my seat and looked out at the woods. Even though I'd spent all morning there, I already wanted to go back. I opened the gate and left.

I lost track of time as I walked, replaying the morning with Harlow over and over in my head. I'd never had much luck with girls in the past—any luck at all, really—and I was a little surprised at how well things were going. I still got jittery around her, but it was hard not to; Harlow was so pretty, and smart, and good at everything. When we were together, it always took a few minutes to remember that I could simply be myself. She had asked me to hang out again tomorrow, and as excited as I was, I was hoping her dad wouldn't be home. I wasn't sure what a high-powered lawyer and politician would think of someone as average as me.

Then I wondered what my mom would have thought of Harlow. Probably, she would have poked fun at her, calling her a goody-two-shoes and making snide comments about how privileged her life is. Even though it was only in my imagination, I found myself arguing with Mom about this assessment of Harlow. Soon, I was thinking back to the real arguments I'd had with her over the summer. She'd grown moody and irritable and started lashing out at me like she'd never done before. I've never had much of a temper, but whenever she raised her voice at me, I raised mine back, and louder. The worst argument happened when I discovered she'd stolen money out of my backpack.

"Mom!" I shouted. "That was my lunch money for the week. I need that!"

"You have a job," she said, staring at me with accusing eyes. "I don't."

"Yeah, because you got fired for going to work *high*."

After that, my mom started avoiding me as much as possible. That suited me fine. I didn't know how to handle her when she was around, and I was exhausted by our constant fighting. When she wasn't in the apartment, I could partway believe her lie that she was going to NA meetings. I'd wait in my room, dreading the moment she'd stumble home with her purse full of something she wouldn't let me see.

"Mom," I'd practically beg, "you need to get help. Why won't you let me help you?"

"I don't need help."

That was always the worst lie.

I trekked deep into the woods until I reached the end of Mountain Pass Trail. It was as far out as I'd ever gone. Beyond it lay what was basically no man's land. I turned around to look back at the path. As I brooded more about all the mean things my mom and I had said to each other, the suffocating feeling I'd had before descended. I hadn't felt it since my first day at Bailey's, but suddenly, it was like if I didn't move now, I'd be trapped. Without another thought—I was sick of so many thoughts—I charged off the marked trail, zigzagging between trees and snapping twigs with each step. Eventually, I had to stop for air. For a minute, all I could do was stand there and pant. At least the suffocating feeling was gone.

Once I could breathe again, I realized how thirsty I was, but I had no water with me. There might be a creek nearby, I thought, but retracing my steps was going to be hard enough without taking a detour for water. I pictured Harlow, prepared as ever, with her purple backpack full of supplies. My only option was to hurry up and walk back.

I was turning to leave when the bushes behind me rustled. I froze. It was quiet and I listened more closely. My heartbeat sped up as I waited. A minute went by. The longer the quiet lasted, the more stupid I felt. I was scared of nothing.

Then I heard the rustling again. This time, it was more distinct. I whipped back around, but saw nothing out of the ordinary. I was telling myself that rustling noises were normal in nature when I heard something that definitely *didn't* belong to the woods.

A cough.

At first, I was more surprised than anything else. I wondered who was out here, and what they were doing.

Then, my inner wimp spoke up. *Are they watching me? If I run, will they chase me?* I clutched my phone tightly. There was no service out here. Part of me wanted to sprint away as fast as I could, but the other part was afraid to take my eyes off the patch of bushes where the cough had come from.

The person coughed again. As the coughing continued, whoever was in the bushes seemed less threatening. Then I wondered if they needed help. If Harlow was here, she'd probably make sure they were okay. I pictured my mom in our kitchen, clutching her purse defensively. I should have done something to help her instead of waiting to be asked.

"Hello?" I called out. "Are you all right?"

The coughing grew muffled, like the person had hidden their face in a coat.

I decided to give it one more try. "Do you need any help?"

No response. I took this to mean that the person in the bushes didn't want to be found. I was going to leave, but then I noticed a pair of eyes looking at me from above one of the bushes. I nearly screamed as I stumbled backward. My stomach fluttered wildly, but I regained my balance and forced myself to remain still. I'd wanted to help a stranger, and here was my chance.

"Sorry," I said, "you scared me."

The person—a man—raised his head a bit higher over the bush. His eyes were watery.

"Do you need help or something?" I said.

He frowned and scratched his stubbled chin. This guy didn't fit my stereotype of a vagrant in the woods. Even though he was tucked behind some plants, I could see the top of a nice windbreaker jacket. His dark hair was sort of long, almost touching his collarbone, but it wasn't unkempt. This was getting weirder by the second.

"Um, well, I'm going to go now, but do you want me to send somebody to help? It might take a while . . ." My words drifted away. I couldn't think of what to say with him *staring* at me.

The man coughed again, giving me a chance to scoot a few more feet away. He sounded old, and I was sure I could outrun him, if it came to that.

When he finished coughing, the man stood up. His posture was stooped, but he was taller than I would have guessed. And younger. I tripped over my own feet in a frantic attempt to run away. What had I been thinking? This wasn't brave or heroic. It was stupid. I scrambled back up and turned to run.

"Wait," a weary voice said. "Wait."

I jumped behind a tree and looked toward the bushes where he stood.

"No," he said, "no, no, no." He shook his head and his shoulders hunched forward.

I wondered if this was a trick. If it was, the man was a good actor. He was full-on crying.

Not wanting to leave my spot, I called out to him. "I'm here. What is it?"

The man wiped his eyes. He looked around the trees until he saw my head peeking out. We watched each other for a few seconds. Then, in a trembling voice, he said, "Have you seen my ID?"

"What?" I said, confused.

The man pointed at the forest. "I think I lost it out here. Have you seen it?"

This guy was crazy. Had to be. I saw that his clothes were wet and smudged with dirt. "Yeah, sorry, I haven't seen it," I said, inching away from the tree in preparation to run.

"I left it at the pond," he said, more agitated. "I need to find it. I really need to find my ID. We should look for it at the pond, that's where it has to be. Please, I want to go home." The man continued blubbering nonsense as he sank down to the forest floor.

This time when I started running, I didn't stop.

I reached Uncle Bailey's at seven. He and Trish must have been out somewhere because the house was empty. In the kitchen, I guzzled a bottle of water. Then, I grabbed a box of crackers and two protein bars from the pantry. I was going to take a shower, but ended up falling asleep on the living room couch next to Duke as he scrounged through the wrappers.

～～

"*This* is how you spend your Saturday?"

Trish's voice was shriller than any alarm clock. And there was no snooze button.

"Filthy, *covered* in dirt and sweat, sprawled out on *my* couch, trash piled everywhere—" She stopped herself and I mumbled that I was sorry.

This was the first time Trish had been upset with me since I'd moved in, but as I collected the trash, I realized this was only because I'd been making myself scarce.

"Tell us, Nolan," Bailey said, "what were you thinking?" He crossed his arms tightly over his suit. "You deliberately disobeyed our rule about eating in the living room." He glanced at my shoes. "*And* you're wearing muddy sneakers."

"Yes, um, sorry," I said. "I didn't mean to."

"It doesn't matter if you *meant* to," Trish said.

"I'm sorry, really," I said, hoping that sounded more earnest. "It won't happen again."

"Whatever. Clean up this mess. Duke could've eaten something to make him sick." With that, Trish turned on her high heel and left.

"What *were* you up to?" Bailey said, like it just occurred to him that he should be keeping up on my whereabouts more closely.

"I went for a hike," I said as evenly as I could. "The trail was longer than I thought, so I was starving when I got back."

"I see. Who were you with?"

"No one."

"I thought you'd made friends," he said.

"I *have*," I said, growing impatient. "I just like to be alone sometimes."

"Your friends are your network," Bailey said matter-of-factly. "I know you're spending time with the mayor's daughter. I doubt she *or* her father would be impressed with your slobbish display here."

And I doubted Harlow would call eating snacks on the couch slobbish.

I thought he was going to lecture me more, but Bailey uncrossed his arms and chuckled. "I'm just looking out for you," he said, like he was suddenly bored of playing the stern parent and wanted to go back to being Mr. Nonchalant. "They're a key family to know, the Stevensons. You're too young to remember, but Mayor Matt's father, Patrick, was the mayor a few years back. Good for you for establishing a connection so quickly. That's a real skill."

"Sure it is," I said, then shut my mouth before I could add anything else. If only Bailey knew what Harlow thought of people like him.

Still, irritating as this was, I was glad to find out that Bailey approved of my friendship with Harlow. "Actually," I said, trying my luck, "Harlow and I were planning to hang out tomorrow. If that's okay with you and Aunt Trish?"

"Of course. Is she coming over here?"

"No, I'm going to her house." I'd been to Harlow's house several times already and although it was just as big as Bailey's, it didn't have any of his pretentious style. In a lot of ways, I felt more comfortable there.

"Very well," Bailey said, eyeing my old sweatshirt. "But don't wear *that*."

<p style="text-align:center">~~~~</p>

I got a bad night's sleep, despite my exhaustion. I kept thinking about the strange man I'd met in the woods. He was probably delusional, but I felt that I was starting to understand him, at least a little bit. Grief recognizes grief. "I want to go home," he'd said. Wherever his home was, I thought he must be missing someone there. Someone he couldn't get back.

<p style="text-align:center">~~~~</p>

Harlow texted me at two on Sunday afternoon letting me know she'd finished her homework. I was hit by the normal bout of anxiety I get right before I see her, but when she answered the door wearing sweats and a t-shirt like I was, I felt better. We sat down at the kitchen counter.

"How was your dad's birthday?" I asked.

"It was really fun," she said. "But, like usual, he beat me at mini golf."

"You felt okay to play?"

Harlow looked confused for a second. "Oh, you mean because of my knee?"

"Yeah," I said, worried her dad might be angry at the person who took her mountain biking.

"I'm totally fine."

I nodded, relieved. "Okay; that's good."

"I'd offer you some leftover cake," Harlow said, "but my grandparents took it home." She laughed a little. "Not that it was anything special; I used a box."

"There's nothing wrong with that," I said. "My mom always used a box."

"She did?"

"Yeah. I think it's the best kind."

Harlow smiled. "So," she said, tucking a stray lock of brown hair behind her ear, "what else did you do yesterday?"

I hesitated. I wanted to tell her about the man I'd seen because the whole thing had been pretty weird, and it was still bothering me. I just wasn't sure how to explain to Harlow why I'd strayed so far from the trail. It might be a bit much to tell her I'd been arguing with my dead mom in my head, and that had made me so frustrated and panicky that I'd taken off running and gotten myself lost.

"What is it?" Harlow said, and her expression grew serious.

"It's just . . ." I said, trying to find the right place to start. "Okay, so yesterday afternoon I went on a hike, or well, kind of a run. I ended up going beyond Mountain Pass Trail and getting slightly . . . turned around."

Harlow raised her eyebrows but stayed quiet.

"Anyway," I said quickly, "I heard a noise in the bushes and at first, I thought it was an animal, but it turned out to be a person. And not a hiker, but a guy, maybe in his forties, dressed in nice clothes—nice but dirty. I asked him if he needed help, but he just wanted to know if I'd seen his ID. He told me we should look for it at some pond. And he was crying. Like, a lot."

I shrugged, trying to seem casual. I didn't want Harlow to think I'd been afraid of a guy crying.

Her eyes were wide. "Nolan!" she said. "That's *terrifying*. You were out there alone? There's no cell service. What if something had happened?"

I looked down, embarrassed by her concern, but secretly happy that she cared so much. "It was *kind of* scary," I said, remembering I didn't have to put on a show for Harlow. "But I didn't want to abandon the guy if he was injured. Turns out he was just crazy."

"He didn't try to hurt you, did he?"

"No," I said, enjoying her attention more now. "I think he wanted to talk to me. He was obviously upset. But I had no idea how to help without following him deeper into the woods, so I ran back."

"It's good you got out of there when you did. He sounds pretty erratic." She crossed her arms, looking more nervous than I'd seen her before. "Did he try to follow you?" Harlow went out to the woods for peace and quiet, and suddenly, I felt like I'd ruined that for her.

"No, don't worry, he didn't," I said, hoping that sounded reassuring. "I don't think he'll come anywhere near here." She still looked uncertain, so I added, "If I see him in the woods again, I can call the police or something."

"Actually," Harlow said, "if the man was out in the middle of nowhere, I don't think a call to the police would make a difference. Morley's jurisdiction ends with Mountain Pass Trail, so the police would have to call some county agency, or maybe even a state agency, if they thought something illegal was going on."

"Oh," I said, feeling a little defeated. I tried to think of another way to make Harlow feel better. "The thing is, I don't think this man was doing anything wrong. Maybe he was just . . . camping?" Immediately, a hundred memories of camping trips with my mom flooded my mind.

"That could be," Harlow said, not sounding convinced.

"Actually," I sighed, "my mom and I used to go camping out in the woods all the time."

"Really?" Harlow said. She leaned in a bit closer.

"Yeah," I said. I told Harlow a few of my favorite stories from our camping trips. Talking about the trip we'd taken last April during spring break, I was hit with a feeling of wistfulness, even though, really, the only notable thing about the trip was that it turned out to be the final one. I recalled little details that hadn't seemed terribly important at the time, like how it had rained on the first night and that my mom had packed mismatched socks.

Then, Harlow told me about the trips she'd taken with her dad. She'd been to eight countries, and I couldn't hide how impressed I was by that kind of traveling.

"I know I'm lucky to have gone to so many places," Harlow said, "but *who* you travel with is just as important. The camping trips with your mom sound like they were really fun." She always seemed to know just what to say.

We kept talking, and the man in the woods didn't come up again. In fact, I couldn't have spared another thought for him if I'd tried. Now I was only thinking about Harlow.

5

HARLOW

I glanced over at Nolan, who was sitting with me at our lunch table. Although he was quiet, Nolan had obviously become more comfortable with my friends over the past few months. He smiled more easily and didn't apologize as often. I think he was getting the idea that we genuinely liked him.

I, however, wanted to know how much he liked me, and in what way. Nolan had told me a while ago that he thought I was "cool," but he used that word to describe a lot of things. We drove to school together most mornings and hung out a lot, but I was getting impatient to know if we were ever going to be more than just friends. I'd been too nervous to bring it up with Nolan directly, but I was reading too much into every little thing he said and did, like noticing that he slowed down and smiled whenever we passed each other in the hallway. I liked knowing things for certain, and I wished Nolan would tell me how he felt instead of leaving me to guess.

The warning bell rang, and I stood up from the lunch table. Nolan and I were almost inside when Amaya stopped me.

"Harlow, wait," she said. "I forgot to ask: Can I come over tonight? My sister's wilderness troop is having dinner at my house and there'll be like a billion eight-year-olds. I'd love to not be there."

I laughed. "I won't be home. There's a town hall meeting and I promised my dad I'd go."

"Wait, is that tonight?"

I looked at her, bemused. Amaya was the last person I'd expect to care about a town hall meeting. "Yeah . . . why, are you suddenly interested in politics?"

"*Hardly*," she said, "but I have this history project that's forcing me to go to some kind of political event and write about 'democracy in action.'"

It could be fun to have Amaya at the meeting—it was usually just me and a bunch of angry old people. "Come with me. It won't be *that* bad. I go all the time."

"Yeah, but you *like* that kind of stuff." She sighed. "I guess it's better than finding another event to go to alone. Hey—Nolan, you're in my history class! You've *got* to come with us."

"Yeah, okay," he said. Then he turned to me with a shy smile. "That'd be cool."

I could feel redness moving across my cheeks. When I looked back to Amaya, she was watching us with raised eyebrows. Quickly, I tried to think of something to distract her.

"You'll have fun tonight," I said. "Town hall meetings are like a comment section come to life. People have a lot of feelings."

She snickered. "They do, don't they?"

The redness bloomed into a full scarlet.

Amaya loves drama more than anyone I know, which is why I still hadn't told her about my crush on Nolan. But after that little exchange, it was clear she knew *something* was up.

<div align="center">~~~</div>

That night, I picked up Amaya at her house. Nolan was already in the car, but he insisted on letting Amaya have the front seat. I wondered if he was just being polite, or if he didn't want to give Amaya anything to joke about.

We got to city hall just before seven and sat at the back of the auditorium.

Up on the stage, my dad sat in the center of the long table, neat piles of papers stacked around him and a desk plate that read, "Mayor Matt Stevenson." He ran his fingers through his chestnut-colored hair then scanned the crowd. When he found me, I gave him a small wave. Subtly, he waved back.

I watched, with a surge of pride that never got old, as my dad welcomed everyone to the meeting and thanked us for being there.

"Oh, the honor is all mine," Amaya whispered, rolling her eyes.

Within ten minutes, Amaya had lost her snarky tone. She may as well have been watching one of her favorite soap operas. Her knee bounced up and down, and I could hear her muttering commentary under her breath, agreeing and disagreeing with the various statements made by the people of our city.

Nolan sat on my other side, pen in hand jotting down notes. He gave fewer clues as to what he thought. I was so used to Morley politics that it was hard to imagine what the long string of complaints and concerns sounded like to a newcomer's ears. The way my dad was able to smooth ruffled feathers always astounded me. I know some people complained he was too "charming" and "suave," but if they were honest, they'd have to admit that although those traits certainly *helped*, it was the sincerity, patience, and good sense behind my dad's smile that made him so popular.

At 9:10, Amaya tapped me on the shoulder. "I gotta go, my curfew's 9:30. You know how my mom is." The three of us grabbed our stuff and shuffled out of the auditorium.

"Damn," Amaya said at full volume as soon as the door had shut. "That was crazy. Who knew that Morley was full of so many pissed-off people?"

"Does that mean you want to come with me next time?"

Amaya sucked in her breath. "Nah, probably not. I've got enough of my own problems to worry about." She elbowed Nolan. "Back me up here!"

"Um, yeah," he said.

I noted the noncommittal answer. I'd ask him what he really thought later.

Amaya chattered the whole way back to her house. While normally I had fun listening to her rant, Nolan's palpable discomfort put a damper on the car ride for me. I wondered if something at the meeting had upset him.

"I seriously don't get how your dad does it, Harlow," Amaya said. "I mean, he has to sit up there and pretend to care about all these people's complaints for, like, a million hours."

"Actually, my dad really likes these nights. He says they're more honest and straightforward than council meetings."

"Still, his job is basically dealing with an endless line of people saying, 'Can I speak to your manager?' And him being like, 'Well actually, I *am* the manager.' And then he has to watch them lose their minds or storm out of the room making lame threats. That's why I could never work in politics. Or customer service."

"At least now you have plenty to write about for your history paper," I said, stealing a glance in the rearview mirror at Nolan. He was looking out the window.

"Yeah, that's for sure," Amaya said. "I'll write about how one night at city hall basically turned me into a monarchist. This guy's in charge. Shut up and deal with it."

"Oh yeah, Mrs. Cooke will *love* that," I said.

"Hey, she's always saying the most important thing is to back up what we're arguing. I've got plenty of reasons."

"Are you really going to write that?" Nolan said, startling us both. His voice was quiet, wobbly even. Clearly, something was up.

"No," Amaya said after a few seconds. "Not really. I was just kidding."

When Nolan didn't respond, Amaya threw me a sideways glance. She mouthed the words, *What's wrong?* I mouthed back, *I don't know.*

"So, Nolan," I said, hoping I wasn't about to upset him further, "what are you thinking of writing about?"

"Um, I . . ." he mumbled.

"It's okay; you don't have to tell us if you don't want to," I said.

Amaya suddenly snapped her head around toward the backseat. "Did I say something wrong, or that like, offended you?"

"Amaya, let's just—" I whispered before she cut me off.

"No, seriously," she said. "I want to know. Can you just tell me?" Though her voice was clouded with defensiveness, I knew it was a real question demanding a real answer.

I heard Nolan shift in his seat. "Sorry, Amaya, you didn't say anything wrong."

"*Okay*," Amaya said slowly, "so what's up?"

"It's nothing."

Amaya laughed. "Look, you can be real with me. Just tell me."

She was never one to hold a grudge. Amaya's restored good mood must have set Nolan at ease, because he laughed a little and said, "It's kind of stupid."

"I love stupid," Amaya said.

"Okay, well, it made me mad to hear all those people complain about such little things—things that hardly even matter. They were getting worked up about basically nothing and making ridiculous demands. It's like, *really?* Chipped paint on the fire hydrants is the worst of your problems? They don't realize how easy they have it. They sounded so . . . spoiled."

"Oh, *damn!*" Amaya shouted as she banged on the center console. "Tell us how you really feel, Nolan!"

I knew that more joking was not what Nolan needed in this moment. Not after he'd shared something so obviously personal. But Amaya didn't know Nolan like I did.

"I see what you mean, Nolan," I said quickly. "There's definitely a lack of gratitude."

"Can you imagine any of those people saying, 'thank you'?" Amaya said. "Either they don't get what they want, and they go home whining about how evil the city council is, or they *do* get what they want and go home feeling like they saved the world from some terrible evil when all they really did was upgrade the umbrellas at the community pool. We should be thanking *them*."

Her tone was flippant, but her point wasn't bad. "Actually," I said, "that's sort of true. Sometimes it feels like my dad is in a lose-lose situation."

"Right," Nolan said, with obvious relief in his voice. "I don't know how he puts up with it." He continued slowly. "It did make me think how much easier everything must be if you lived somewhere with just one person in charge. I mean, if they were a good ruler, like fair and wise and stuff. But I wasn't serious."

If Amaya had a witty remark for that she didn't get to say it because her phone rang. "Ugh, it's my mom," she said. "She's probably freaking out because I'm about to be one minute late."

She answered the phone with the same irritated tone, which Mrs. Rostami must not have liked, because Amaya grew pricklier. When she switched into Farsi, which she often did when she got emotional, Nolan looked up in surprise. Switching languages again just as smoothly, Amaya promised her mom she'd be home in two minutes and hung up.

"She's *way* too protective," Amaya said. "What's your curfew, Nolan?"

"Um . . . I guess I don't have one. My uncle and I have never talked about it."

"Amazing."

"I didn't know you spoke another language," he said.

"Oh, yeah," said Amaya. "I actually learned Farsi before English."

"Cool."

There was that word again.

I pulled into the Rostamis' driveway and Amaya stepped out of the car. "See you tomorrow," I called after her.

"Hey!" she said, popping her head back inside. "Nolan, you should pretend that you want to live in an autocracy and write about it for the history project. It'd be hilarious!"

"Eh," he said and shrugged. "I don't really want to get a weird reputation at a new school. I'll just write about how it's so great that in a democracy, the people's voices can be heard."

Amaya snorted. "Yeah, and they're so loud, you can hear them from the next town over."

She said goodbye, and I told Nolan he should take her place in the front seat.

"Doing okay?" I asked once we were driving again.

"Yeah," Nolan said. "Sorry; I didn't mean to make things awkward."

"I know. And you have a valid point about people being entitled. We have it really good around here, and sometimes we forget that, or take it for granted."

"I'm not trying to make it sound like I grew up in a dangerous or run-down neighborhood," Nolan said. "I didn't. I've just never heard adults demanding to get their way about stuff that seems so . . . unimportant, I guess."

"It's true; a lot of the stuff they talk about is trivial."

Nolan grew suddenly tense. "Sorry. I'm not trying to say that what your dad does is trivial."

I smiled, appreciating how sensitive he was when it came to talking about things that were important to me. "I know you didn't mean it like that. But I wonder if people from other parts of Morley would ever come to a town hall meeting. Like, you've always been welcome, even though you didn't live in Eastside. Maybe then my dad could do more to fix problems that actually exist."

Nolan started twirling his thumbs, and I was worried he might clam up again. "I mean, the bike lanes could be repainted and the bus stops near my apartment are probably decades old." He shrugged. "I'm trying to think about my old boss and teachers and neighbors and if they would go to a meeting. A lot of them think people in this part of town are out of touch with reality."

I sighed. My dad said all the time that one of the biggest problems in Morley was a lack of empathy. "They're not totally wrong."

"Yeah," Nolan said, "but they are *somewhat* wrong. I definitely used to think that all the people who lived near my uncle were selfish and snobby."

"But you don't think that now?" I said coyly, hoping for anything clarifying.

"No, not anymore," he said. He smiled in a way that made me eager to hear what he would say next. However, Nolan took the conversation in another direction entirely. "I can see why my mom did, though. Her family kicked her out and never took her back. Even when she had me."

We had just parked in front of my house, but I made no move to get out of the car. Neither did Nolan. I suddenly felt guilty for wanting him to tell me that he liked me when he was still dealing with what had happened with his mom. I'd been putting off telling Nolan any more about my own mom partly because I didn't want to make his loss about me, and partly because I really didn't like talking about her. My dad was very honest with me about what had happened between them, but it all seemed like ancient history, and the story made me feel frustrated about things I couldn't control. Then again, I wouldn't change the way things were between me and my dad for anything. That's why it was so tricky. From what I knew about it, Nolan's situation was also tricky. Maybe he'd been avoiding it too.

I tried to think of what Dad might say. "I hope you're taking the time and space you need to process everything."

"I am, I guess." Nolan stuck his hands inside his jacket pockets. "My mom hadn't used since I was a baby, but over the summer she had surgery that gave her a prescription for some strong painkillers. She fell back into old habits really quickly. I didn't know what to do, but I became preoccupied with trying to keep us off the streets. At one point, I thought I should reach out to my grandparents, even though my mom hadn't kept in touch with them after they moved away from Morley. My mom kept saying that she'd gotten clean without them once, and she could do it again. Part of me was hoping she was right, and I pretended things would be okay. She pretty much picked up where she'd left off, though. Her body couldn't handle going from zero to one hundred like that."

"Did you . . . find her?" I asked as delicately as I could.

"Yeah," he breathed. "She was unconscious on the couch. She died the next day at the hospital."

A cold sensation swept across my body. "Oh, Nolan. That's . . ." I trailed off. It was indescribable.

Nolan wiped his eyes and stared at the floor of the car. I found myself wanting to fix an unfixable problem.

"Did your mom ever think about going to rehab?"

"She thought about it, yeah, but she was working odd jobs when she could get them and leaving for several weeks wasn't an option."

"Oh," I said, hoping I didn't sound too ignorant. "I can't imagine how trapped you must have felt."

"Yeah," he said, looking up at me. "That was exactly it—*trapped*. I was *so* angry with my mom. I just kept thinking, why can't she get clean? Why doesn't she try harder?" Nolan sighed. "I know it wasn't as simple as her saying yes or no, but even now, I'm still sort of angry with her. Sometimes when I picture her there on the couch, I'll suddenly remember her teaching me to ride a bike. It's like having memories of two different people. The pictures don't fit together, but I can't tear them apart."

I stayed silent, wondering if the pictures I had of my mom weren't accurate either.

"Sorry," he said. "That was too much information."

"No, not at all," I said. "It's just . . . I also haven't forgiven my mom."

"Oh, uh," he stuttered. "I *have* wondered about your mom, but you don't have to tell me about her if you don't want to. Not that I don't *want* to hear, it's just—"

"I know, but I want to tell you."

"Are you sure?"

"Yes," I said. "It's just, I don't know the best place to start." I thought a bit more and then began. "My parents wanted to have kids, but I was definitely a surprise. My mom had really bad postpartum depression. The first few months were hard on her, and on my dad. I guess that was sort of the beginning of the end. It sucks to think that I was the thing that broke them apart. You know?"

Nolan nodded. I took a deep breath before going on.

"My dad tells me not to think that way, that it wasn't my fault, but it's hard not to blame myself. After I was born, my mom decided she wanted to go to law school and started studying for the LSAT. She got accepted to a law school in California and was dead set on going. My dad didn't want her to, but they were arguing so much that it seemed like some time away from each other may actually be the best thing.

"So, my mom left for law school. She came home for holidays while my dad juggled working full-time with raising me. Obviously, I didn't understand what was going on, but I know that I became pretty sensitive. There was one time during my mom's first year of school that we visited her in California, but the story goes that I was inconsolable for days after we got back to Morley. My parents decided it was best not to disrupt my world like that again, but my mom rarely came home. During her third year, my dad was seriously worried, so he made an impromptu trip out there by himself and—" I paused again. Out of everything my mom had done, this was the worst part to think of. "Well, he discovered that she was cheating on him."

"Oh . . . " Nolan said, shifting around in the car seat.

"Yeah. But he kept things as normal as possible for me. When eventually he told me about the divorce, I didn't understand what it meant. I barely saw my mom as it was, and this new arrangement they'd come up with only gave it a fancy name. The divorce was fairly simple since there was no custody battle . . . " Maybe that was actually the worst part to think of, that my mom hadn't fought for me. I pushed the thought aside and tried to finish.

"She stayed in California after law school and ended up marrying the guy she'd cheated on my dad with. I see her about once a year when she comes to visit. She's invited me to visit California, but I've never wanted to go."

These felt like the wrong words to end on. I searched for some that made the story seem more final. I remembered what had prompted me to tell it in the first place.

"It's just . . . I've been mad at my mom for a long time, but now that I'm older and starting to think about my own future, I can understand her frustrations a bit more. Everything between her and my dad happened so fast, she didn't have enough time to figure things out. She needed more control over her own life."

This ending wasn't much better. I was trying too hard to wrap things up neatly and sound more settled than I really felt.

Nolan didn't say anything immediately after I stopped talking. I was glad, as it gave me a minute to reflect. I stared out the windshield at the quiet neighborhood.

My memories from that period of my life were dull, faded by the passing of years. Sometimes it seemed like they belonged to someone else. Now though, as I blinked back tears, I realized how strong a hold they still had on me.

Finally, Nolan spoke. "That's . . . tough," he said. "Like, *really* tough. I'm sorry." I muttered a "thanks," at the same time Nolan said, "And I know that saying 'I'm sorry' is kind of a lame thing to say because it's all anyone ever says, but . . . what else is there to say?"

"Yeah," I said. "Sometimes I think it's okay to just be quiet."

Nolan looked at me with a small smile. "I do too."

Lights from an oncoming car lit up the dashboard and the garage door opened.

"My dad's home," I said.

Nolan glanced nervously out his window.

"Relax, he's not going to care that we're out here." I grabbed my purse and opened the door. Nolan hurried to follow my lead as my dad approached my side of the car.

"Hey, Dad," I said.

"Hi, sweetheart. You guys just getting home?"

"No, we've been home for a little while. Just talking."

"Well, I for one have had enough talking for today," he laughed. "What about you?" he asked, looking at Nolan. "It's Nolan, right?"

Nolan cleared his throat. "Yes, sir." I couldn't help but feel a bit pleased that meeting my dad was such a big deal to him.

"Ah, no need for the formalities. *Matt* will do just fine. It's nice to officially meet you, Nolan. I've heard nothing but good things."

Nolan's head bounced in a series of little nods. "Yes, it's nice to meet you too, sir, or um, Matt." Furtively, as if he hoped my dad wouldn't notice, his eyes moved to meet mine. "Anyway, goodnight, Harlow."

"'Night, Nolan. I'll see you tomorrow."

He gave another slight nod before turning abruptly and jogging to his uncle's place.

My dad chuckled once Nolan was out of earshot. "What do you think? Did I make a good first impression?"

I felt a twinge of guilt. My dad had no idea how much Nolan already knew about him. Whatever impression Nolan came away with after this brief encounter had been filtered through the story I'd just told him. I didn't want my dad to know the two of us were sharing such personal stories. Not yet.

I matched my dad's relaxed attitude. "Nolan almost made eye contact with you. You're off to a great start."

He gave me a hug and we walked up the path to our front door. It wasn't particularly late, but the evening had been tiring in a way I hadn't expected it to be. I got ready for bed, all the while having a debate with myself over my mom's story, as if it would be possible to finalize my opinion about it tonight. A part of me wished Nolan had chosen a side and told me I should either blame my mom or forgive her. After all, he was stuck between those two choices with his own mom. But even if he hadn't given me an answer, he *had* given me his understanding. Maybe in some ways, that was better.

6

TOPHER

For years, Jojo and I had thought it best for our family to let the past remain unexamined, but within hours of arriving in Morley, I became obsessed with it.

My dad died the morning after I arrived in town. When I cried at his bedside, I found myself picturing my dad in his younger days. He'd been a police officer in Morley, but oddly, I wasn't seeing him in a blue uniform. The uniform I saw was brown. And he wasn't an officer, he was a guard. A member of the Governor's Guard.

Suddenly, I remembered the photo. A man, veins bulging, holding up a crying baby. Every detail was there. I recognized them, I *knew* them. It was Governor Matthias. The baby was his daughter, Lolo.

In that moment, all the memories I hadn't even let myself dip a toe in for sixteen years came flooding back. I remembered my dad giving me a camera for my tenth birthday. I couldn't wait to photograph everything, but he warned me to be careful. "It's a *camera*, Dad, not a weapon," I said. He looked me straight in the eye and told me there wasn't a difference. I hadn't fully understood his meaning until I took the unauthorized photo of Governor Matthias, the one that showed who he really was.

I got up from my dad's bedside and bolted from the room, ignoring my mom's worried calls. Framed family photos passed quickly through my peripheral vision as I ran downstairs. Me riding a skateboard, me graduating, me getting married. But it wasn't me. Those were all photos of Chris. I grabbed a jacket and left the house.

Photographs are what tether me to reality. But the question I couldn't answer right then was *which* reality? The one where I am Christopher "Chris" Collins, a photographer from Morley, Maine, who developed a sudden case of generalized dissociative amnesia? Or, the one where I am Christopher "Topher" Collins, a photographer from the city-state of Morley who rebelled against the Governor, hid in a forest pond, and somehow, resurfaced in another world entirely?

I know which story sounds implausible and which sounds impossible. But, what if I had a way to prove the impossible story? The photo of the Governor had been missing for years, but there might be another piece of evidence, one with my name printed clearly on it. My *real* name, Christopher "Topher" Collins. I used to have an ID card with that name. It had been in my pocket when I went into the pond. I needed to find it.

I was almost to Eastside Park before I realized I was headed for the pond. That's where all of this madness started. I jogged down Mountain Pass Trail, not caring that I was letting myself be controlled by homesickness for a place I wasn't even sure was real.

I had been sure at one point, though. There was a time when I'd believed wholeheartedly that I was Topher Collins, married to Jody, from the city-state of Morley. I broke into a run as more memories swarmed in my head. Sixteen years ago, I'd also believed the pond was a portal. By hurdling myself into the pond to hide from the Governor's Guard, I'd unwittingly traveled to another world and traded places with an alternate version of myself. Chris, my "double." I'd tried to switch us back and get home, but no matter how many times I dunked myself in the murky water, I remained here, in the wrong Morley. That was the rest of the impossible story.

The closer I got to the pond, the more fervently I believed it again.

I reached the end of Mountain Pass Trail and snaked my way through the trees until I found the obscure little pond. Before I stooped down into the muck to begin scavenging for my lost ID, I paused. What if this time, the pond transported me back to the other Morley? Was that what I wanted—to leave Jojo, Cate, and my mom behind? The idea of losing them hurt me. No, I didn't want to leave them. They'd been my family for years, and I loved them. What I *did* want was to find the ID to remind myself that I'd once had another family I'd loved.

I knelt by the pond and began digging. I searched until my hands were numb. I knew I needed to go back to my parents' house. My mom was probably wondering why I was still gone. At least Jojo wasn't in town yet to ask any questions.

I left the pond, but I wasn't even to Mountain Pass Trail when I decided to take a break. Searching for the ID had worn me out, and I sat down in the bushes. As I rested, my mind went back to my first journey through these woods, the day I'd been pursued by Governor Matthias's guards. I was sorry I'd run when I should've faced whatever punishment awaited me. I was sorry for taking the illegal photo of the Governor's family. I was sorry for accepting the job. I was sorry for being a photographer. And I was sorry for any other ill-fated circumstances that had led me to leaving Jody behind. What suffering had I sentenced her to?

And, what suffering had I sentenced Chris to? Maybe the reason I hadn't been able to switch back with him was because he was dead. Governor Matthias had probably arrested and executed him in my place.

All of this was spinning through my head when I met the boy in the woods. It was only after I'd cleaned myself up at my mom's place that I realized how creepy I must have seemed to him. My interaction with the boy had been unlucky, but no harm done. It's not like I'd ever see him again.

7

NOLAN

I rolled out of bed a few minutes before eight on Saturday and hurried to get dressed. I was meeting Harlow for a hike—staying firmly on the trail, in case any more wild-eyed men in windbreakers appeared in the bushes.

I went to the kitchen where I found Uncle Bailey in his stupid monogrammed slippers.

"Well, you certainly bounce back fast," he said, stirring a cup of steaming tea. "I was a bit worried about you there, but you seem to have adjusted well to this new life. I knew you would."

"Mmm hmm," I managed to reply as I picked out a cereal in the pantry. This was typical of my interactions with Bailey. He never seemed to say anything straight. Like now—which was it? Had he been worried about me, or had he always known I'd be okay?

"Sometimes I feel like my girls have forgotten me, too," Bailey said. "You'd think they'd call their own dad at least once a week. You kids move on so quickly."

Rage coursed through me, and I slammed the pantry door shut. "I have *not* forgotten my mom." If anyone was guilty of forgetting about my mom, it was Bailey.

He made a *tsk tsk* sound. "I didn't say you *forgot* her. No, just that—"

I stormed out of the kitchen. Bailey had at least enough sense not to follow me, but it didn't matter. His careless words were already stuck in my head.

When I showed up at Harlow's gate, she was waiting with her hair in a neat ponytail pulled through a blue baseball cap. No doubt her backpack was filled with water and snacks. Futilely, I ran my hands over my wrinkled jacket, feeling suddenly insecure. She greeted me warmly, and I quit fidgeting and returned her smile.

"Did you get a chance to have breakfast?" she said as we started down the hill.

"No," I said. Even though I was hungry, I almost wished I'd lied. Harlow was so put together. It was embarrassing to constantly give her reason to believe I was too helpless to set an alarm or pour cereal into a bowl.

"Here," she said, handing me a protein bar. "Got you covered." There wasn't anything judgmental about the way she said it, and that somehow made me feel even worse.

"I'll um . . . get us some coffee when we get back."

I hated feeling indebted to people. Probably it was something I'd inherited from my mom, who resented being seen as a charity case. But more than that, I wanted to do something nice for Harlow. Not to make things fair, but to make her happy. When I moved to Eastside, I'd been ready to stay angry forever, but things were turning out way different than I'd anticipated. It felt good to have a routine and friends again. As I thought about all the times I'd felt genuinely happy over the last few months, Harlow was always the reason. I wanted her to know that, but every time I tried telling her outright, I got nervous and said something else. I told myself that I was waiting for the right moment, but I didn't have a clue when that moment might be.

"Hey," she said. "Your aunt and uncle are okay with you coming over tonight, right? Amaya will be there too."

"Yeah," I said. "Honestly, as long as they know I'm hanging out with you, the *mayor's daughter*, they won't care where I am."

Harlow made an exaggerated conspiratorial face. "Well then, they'll be thrilled to hear that tonight you'll also being hanging out with the mayor himself."

"What?" I said, almost tripping over my own feet. I'd already made an awkward impression on the mayor, and I wasn't looking forward to possibly doing it again so soon.

Harlow laughed in her easy way. "Relax, Nolan, I'm kidding. My dad will be home, but it's not like he'll be with us the whole time. He said he'd order us pizza."

"Oh, okay, cool," I said, trying not to seem intimidated. "It's nice he wants to do that for us." It was just the sort of thing that Harlow would do, and what mom wished she had been able to do more of for me and my friends. "You guys are a lot alike," I observed.

"Thanks," Harlow said. "I try to be like my dad, and he says he tries to be like the person he should have been all along."

The way Harlow talked about her dad made me more curious about my own than I'd ever been in my life. My mom had hated talking about him, and as a kid, I'd come to accept I'd probably never know much about him. Now though, the mystery of it was starting to bother me. Harlow, who understood what it was like to have a parent leave, seemed like the perfect person to tell.

"It seems like your dad was always a pretty good guy," I said, then took a big breath. "Better than the guy who got my mom pregnant and left Morley two months before I was born."

Harlow's eyes widened, and I immediately felt bad for dropping that on her.

"Sorry, that sounded really bitter."

Harlow shook her head. "No, I'd be bitter too. That sucks. Seriously."

I shrugged, still wishing I hadn't made it sound so dramatic. "Yeah, but I never knew anything different, so it wasn't like I felt the loss when he left. Not like my mom did."

"Still," Harlow said, "is it weird to think how different your life could have been if he'd stayed around?"

It was a scenario I'd thought about a few times. But, having only my mom's descriptions of my dad to go off of—immature, loser, deadbeat—I'd always figured I was better off not knowing him.

"Kind of?" I said. "But maybe it was for the best."

"Yeah," Harlow said, slowing her pace and staring above at the towering trees. "That's actually what I tell myself about my mom. I think it's better to believe that the reality we're living in is the best version possible, like all the other lives we could have led wouldn't make us any happier." Her gaze shifted so that she looked at the ground instead of the sky. "Or maybe that's just me being idealistic and afraid of living with a bunch of regrets."

"I know what you mean," I said, kicking a few twigs off the path as we shuffled along. "But also, it's kind of strange to regret something I couldn't have changed. There's nothing I could've done to make my dad stay. Same with your mom." I didn't mention that there probably *were* things I could have done to help save my mom's life. Those regrets were still too raw.

"Yeah," Harlow said, speeding up again. "I know there's nothing I could have done differently—after all, I was only a baby. But then I start thinking that maybe my *dad* should have done something differently, you know? And I don't want to blame him. Not after everything he went through and all the good he's done since." Her voice wavered a bit, but she went on. "So usually, I end up blaming my mom. It's easier. There's no risk of having the picture I've painted of her in my head turn out to be wrong. I'm used to my mom being a stranger. It's case closed." Her fingers curled tightly around the straps of her backpack. She was close to crying.

The instinct to comfort her took over my hand, and I placed it on her shoulder. When I did, I felt a jolt run all the way up my arm. It startled me, but I didn't move my hand away.

"Harlow," I said, "you don't have to justify it to me. I get it."

She nodded and wiped a tear that was trickling down her face. "I know you do, Nolan. It's nice to talk to someone who does." Then, she looked down at my hand on her shoulder. I promptly snatched it away, afraid I'd misread the moment, but Harlow reached out and grabbed it with her own. If she hadn't pulled me forward on the trail, I might have stayed stuck in that spot forever. Only after walking that way for several minutes did I realize how much I liked the feeling of her hand, so soft and sure of itself, entwined in mine. I became completely oblivious to everything else happening around us until Harlow stopped and asked in a hurried whisper, "Did you hear that?"

"No, what?" I asked, irritated at whatever had interrupted us.

"A voice," Harlow said. "Listen."

I did. A few seconds later, I heard it too, someone crying out, *"Dad! Dad?"*

The voice was coming from the right, somewhere off the path. Harlow began inching forward, but I held her back.

"Wait," I said, squeezing her hand, enjoying that she let me. "Maybe we should turn back. It was only last weekend that I saw that weird man out here."

The voice called out again.

Harlow frowned. "They sound young. Not an old guy." She let go of my hand. "C'mon, they might need help."

I had no choice, really, but to follow her. We listened for the voice, but it was the sound of crunching leaves that told us we were close. Harlow crouched down in the bushes and I followed her lead. Even if it was a kid out there, I wanted to see them before they saw us.

The shaking bushes must have caught the person's attention, because their footsteps stopped abruptly.

"Dad? Dad is that you?" The voice was high pitched.

"Definitely a kid, a girl," Harlow breathed. "I'll stand up first."

I nodded, and she slowly stood up. "Hey," she called out.

The other person gave a short scream.

"Sorry, I'm sorry," Harlow said quickly. "I didn't mean to startle you. My friend and I overheard you calling for your dad." Harlow glanced at me and tilted her head up. I rose to my feet and she calmly continued, "I'm Harlow, and this is Nolan."

Several feet away and half-obscured by foliage, stood a girl who looked a little younger than me and Harlow. She was cute, maybe fourteen or fifteen with light-brown skin. The girl brushed a section of curly hair away from her rectangular glasses.

"Hi," she said shyly, "I'm Cate."

"Do you need help finding your dad, Cate?" Harlow said, taking a few steps closer.

"Yeah, I . . ." Cate scanned the forest, as if hoping her dad might appear and save her from explaining the story to two strangers. I didn't blame her. "I lost track of him out here. I was on my way back to get some help."

"Have you called him? Service can be spotty out here, but it's worth a shot," Harlow said.

"I tried that already."

"Is your dad familiar with the trails?"

"Well . . ." Cate crossed her arms over her stomach. "Maybe? He hasn't been here in over fifteen years, but he . . . well, he took off like he knew where he was going."

"He just left you behind?" Harlow's surprised tone matched my own reaction. My mom never would have left me out in the woods on my own.

"No, no, he didn't ditch me," Cate said. "He told me to stay put. But he's been gone for so long." Her voice got fainter. "I got scared. For me, and for him."

"Anyone would," Harlow said. "Why don't you come back with us? We'll get this all figured out."

Cate turned toward the vast expanse of trees behind her, clearly reluctant to leave without her dad. Eventually, she nodded and joined us. The path was wide enough for the three of us to walk side by side, and even though I wouldn't have left this girl on her own, I was annoyed that she'd cut my time with Harlow short. Like always, Harlow did her best to keep an easy conversation going, but I wondered if she was disappointed too.

"Where are you from?" she asked.

"Scottsdale, Arizona," Cate said. "I'm not used to the cold."

"Oh, try coming back to Maine in January." Harlow laughed. "Then you'll really feel what cold is."

"Autumn is my favorite time of year," I said, trying to be friendly, like Harlow. "So, you came at a good time."

"Yeah, I guess so," Cate said. "But I'm actually here for my grandpa's memorial service."

I felt my face grow warm. Of course, the one thing I said turned out to be wrong somehow. "Oh," I said, "I'm sorry about that."

"It's okay," Cate said. "My dad made it out here just in time to say goodbye to him, and my mom and I flew here for the service. We're staying with my grandma."

I thought about how much I would've liked the chance to say a real goodbye to my mom.

"Where does your grandma live?" Harlow said after a moment.

"Eastside—do you know it?"

"Yeah," Harlow said with a smile, "that's where Nolan and I live."

"It's a nice place. But my dad has been pretty restless. He really wanted to go on a walk today, so I went with him and then . . . well, then he ran off. It's weird. It's like something inside him *snapped* when he got to Morley."

"Well, people react in a lot of different ways when they lose someone close," I said, thinking about how I'd spent hours meticulously cleaning our apartment the day after Mom died.

"Yeah, that's true," Cate said, but half-heartedly, like grief wasn't enough of an explanation. "I just don't want him to get lost out there."

"He won't," Harlow said. "Don't worry, Cate, we'll have decent service pretty soon and then we can call the right people to—"

"I think I'll call my mom first," Cate said. "It's just, I know she'll want to decide what we do next."

Harlow gave Cate an understanding nod. We walked on in silence until Cate got service and called her mom. Harlow and I put a respectful distance between ourselves and Cate as she talked. Even so, we could make out most of her conversation.

"Hey, Mom . . . Yes, I'm fine." Here she looked back to us, rolling her eyes. "Dad is—well, I'm not entirely sure . . . No, Mom! *I* didn't leave him. He sort of—" Cate's mom must have cut her off, because she was quiet for a while, listening.

"Over an hour ago," she said. Then, "No, I'm with some people." Another glance back to us. "Nice people! Some kids. They live in Eastside . . . Yeah, I'll be back soon."

Cate hung up and slipped her phone into her jacket pocket. "Is it always Twenty Questions when you talk to your moms?" she said, rejoining me and Harlow.

Neither of us answered right away. Harlow managed to say, "I get why she's so worried."

<p style="text-align:center">~~~~</p>

The hill that led up to our houses was just coming into view when the sound of someone shouting made us stop and turn around. Cate gasped. "It's my dad!" She bolted back down the path toward the voice, which grew louder and more desperate.

Harlow and I stayed put, neither of us entirely sure what to do.

"Maybe we should make sure everything's all right?' Harlow said.

I agreed. At this point, I was curious to know what was up with Cate's dad.

When we reached Cate, she had her arms wrapped around a man with dark shaggy hair and a dirty jacket. His eyes were squeezed closed as he returned her hug, but I recognized him instantly.

"Harlow!" I whispered, nudging her. "It's him; the man I saw out in the woods."

"What?" she said, dragging her eyes away from what was otherwise a heartwarming scene.

"Remember? The man who seemed kinda off, who asked me about his ID? That's him."

"What?!" Harlow stage-whispered, as Cate and her dad came closer.

I nodded, making my eyes wide for emphasis. "Don't say anything about it, okay? Unless he does." I *really* hoped he wouldn't.

"Thank you for helping Cate," the man said. "I got a bit turned around out there."

"I'm glad she found you," Harlow said, a little too brightly.

"Too bad it was *after* I called Mom," Cate said.

That appeared to worry Cate's dad, and I grew more suspicious of him. "Yeah," he muttered, and he rubbed his hands together to loosen some of the dirt. I tried to catch Harlow's eye, but she was watching the man's movements too.

"In any case," he said, "I'm glad you weren't out there alone." Then, he turned his attention to me for the first time. I swear I saw a flash of recognition pass through his eyes, but he said nothing.

"We should go, Dad," Cate said. "Before you get . . . turned around again."

Cate's dad said goodbye, and I noticed that he avoided looking at me as we parted ways.

Harlow and I walked back to her house, and she opened the gate to her backyard. "That was really weird," she said, pulling off her hat and letting her hair loose. "I mean, right? What's that guy doing out in the woods?"

"I don't know," I said. "But it seems like he's hiding something."

"Yeah, it does." Harlow's eyebrows were pinched together as she thought.

The man's dirty hands suggested that he'd been digging, maybe burying something. I'm sure it was because of my mom that drugs were the first thing that came to my mind.

"What if he's hiding drugs?" I said. "Or money for drugs?"

"That could be," she said, and I was glad she didn't think my idea was too out-there. "Should we tell someone?"

I hesitated. "Maybe not yet. Bailey and Trish might not let me in the woods again if they thought there were drug dealers out there. Plus, if I'm wrong about Cate's dad, it's a pretty serious thing to accuse someone of."

Harlow nodded, but she looked uneasy.

"Actually, what I think we *should* do is talk to Cate again," I said, feeling suddenly protective, like I had a duty to help her. "Maybe we'll see her around. If she's in a bad situation, she might need to talk to somebody about it."

"Yeah, you're right," Harlow said. Then she smiled. "And you know, you're very easy to talk to."

"I am?" I said, a little flustered, but mostly excited, by the unexpected compliment.

"You are."

Harlow made me feel confident, like I could really do something good. I was determined to make sure Cate was okay and talk to her before something serious happened to her dad. A part of me wished someone had been keeping a closer eye on me before it had been too late for my mom.

8

TOPHER

When Jojo and Cate arrived in Morley on Thursday, I overheard my mom informing Jojo in a hushed tone that I'd gone for several long walks that week. I only missed going to the pond to search for my ID on Friday, the day of my dad's memorial service. I composed myself as much as possible around all the people curious to speak with Jojo and me after sixteen years. Chris's friends reminisced about their school days, and I nodded along, pretending like I remembered too.

As I got ready to go to the pond Saturday morning, Jojo suggested that Cate come with me.

"Having her there will remind you of what's important," she said, with worry in her eyes. "We leave tomorrow. Things will be better at home."

"Okay," I said. "Cate can come with me."

At first, it was nice to have Cate's company on the walk, but when we got close to the end of Mountain Pass Trail, I told her to wait for me while I went ahead to look for something.

"Look for what?"

"Just stay there, I'll be back soon!" I called out as I ran. She started to run after me, but gave up quickly. Only after I was done wading around in the pond did I think about how scared she must have been, and what a terrible father I was for leaving her alone in the woods. Finally, when I found her on the path, she wrapped me in a tight hug. I hoped the ordeal was over, that this would just be a weird, singular moment we could move on from.

Then, two more kids appeared. As Cate and I approached them, I recognized one of them. It was him, the boy. He had gone from being a stranger to a witness. I tried not to make eye contact with him, instead talking to the girl who was with him. He kept throwing her anxious glances, but the girl's eyes were fixed on me like she was making an evaluation. Cate was as eager to leave them behind as I was, and we said goodbye.

"Did you find what you were looking for, Dad?" Cate said. I saw the same worry in her eyes that I'd seen in Jojo's.

"No," I said with a sigh. "I didn't."

"You're not going to look for it again, are you?"

"No, I'm not."

I meant the words when I said them to Cate, and we returned to my mom's house. But that evening as I sat on the couch and flipped through old photo albums, I recognized nothing and started to feel more indignant. For the past sixteen years, I'd been living under someone else's identity. The lie was so convincing that I'd often doubted my own sanity and wondered if my memories of Jody and the Governor really were delusions. I had hundreds of photos proving that Chris Collins had existed, and I wanted the one thing that could remind me that Topher Collins had existed too. I wouldn't leave Morley without looking for my ID again.

Jojo walked into the living room as I slammed the photo album shut.

"Chris—" she started.

"What?" I snapped. *My name's not Chris.*

"I need to ask you something. This week, have you been thinking about . . . her?" Jojo said, her voice thin. "About . . . Jody?"

My memories weren't delusions. Jojo remembered too.

She had her arms wrapped tightly around her waist. I didn't want to upset her more, but I also didn't want to tell another lie. "Yes, I have been. But Jojo, don't you ever think about *him*?" I asked. "The real Chris?"

"I . . ." Her face crumpled. "*You're* what's real to me and Cate now. Okay? Don't forget that. Please."

We held each other's gaze for a moment. "I won't," I said. "I could never forget that." Which was absolutely true. But it was also true that I could never forget Jody.

9

HARLOW

On Saturday night, Amaya, Nolan, and I watched a movie together and when it ended, Nolan offered to stay and help clean up. Of course, Amaya noticed. I'd admitted to her the day after the town hall meeting that I had a crush on Nolan. But I'd made it clear I wasn't going to say anything to him about it because I didn't want him to feel uncomfortable. Now Amaya was looking for any sign that he had a crush on me too. I didn't have a chance to tell her we'd held hands this morning, but I knew she'd think that was a big deal. It felt like a big deal to me.

"You just can't bear to say goodbye, huh?" Amaya teased him as he shoved a pizza box into the trash can.

"I'm going in a minute," Nolan said, his red face betraying him. I noted it as one of the signs we were keeping track of.

"Actually, can you stay a little longer?" I asked. "Maybe we could tell Amaya about what happened earlier? On our hike?"

Even though Nolan didn't want to tell an adult about the situation with Cate's dad, the idea that there could be criminal activity happening in the woods where I walked almost every day was bothering me. I wanted to tell *someone* about it, and Amaya was the person I told most everything to. Nolan caught my eye and nodded.

"Good idea," he said.

"Ooh, yes, tell me!" Amaya said, probably hoping I was going to tell her Nolan had asked me out or something.

"No, no," I said. "It's not what you're thinking. C'mon, let's sit down on the couch."

Amaya and I sank into the cushions while Nolan perched a few feet away on a chair.

"Okay, so what's up?" Amaya asked.

"Nolan," I said, "do you want to start? You're the one who saw Cate's dad first."

"Oh, um, sure," he said. He told Amaya about the freaked-out man in the woods who had talked about an ID card. When Nolan was done with that part of the story, he asked if I wanted to tell the rest. "Sure," I said, eager to tell Amaya what we'd seen in greater detail than Nolan had offered. I told her about meeting Cate and her dad, emphasizing how disoriented he'd seemed and how odd it was that his hands and clothes were covered in dirt. Then, finding I wanted Amaya to be impressed by the big reveal, I slowed down. "Nolan *recognized* him. It was the same guy he saw the other day."

"Seriously?" Amaya said, looking at Nolan.

"Yeah, it was him. But he pretended not to remember me."

"Wait," Amaya said, hitting the couch a few times with her fingertips. "You said his hands were dirty, right? What if he was out there burying something?"

"That's exactly what we thought," I said, getting excited. Then, even though my dad was upstairs, I lowered my voice. "We're thinking he might be hiding drugs."

"Oh . . . yeah!" Amaya said, accepting the idea at once. "Do you think his daughter knows what he's up to?"

"She knows *something*," I said. "We want to talk to Cate again before she leaves, but I'm not sure how we'll be able to do that. We didn't actually get her number."

Amaya looked annoyed—she was completely invested in the story now—but, always the quick thinker, she started putting together a plan. "Maybe there's a chance we can 'run into' Cate or her dad tomorrow?"

I glanced at Nolan, wondering if he'd think basically stalking people was a weird idea. I was a little wary of it myself, but he looked interested. I knew it was important to him to make sure things were okay with Cate, so I decided to go along with whatever Amaya was thinking.

"Nolan, you like to bike, right?" she asked. He said that he did. "Okay, good. Biking is way less suspicious than someone circling the neighborhood in a car. Tomorrow morning, you should ride around Eastside and keep your eye out for Cate and her dad."

"And where are we going to be?" I asked.

Amaya already had an answer. "I'll wait at the beginning of the trail, and you'll be at the park gate. That way we'll see them if they're starting or ending another 'nature walk.'"

"Okay," I said. "That should work." I was glad Amaya picked the trail-head for herself. I'd rather wait closer to the neighborhood than the woods. "What do you think, Nolan?"

"Yeah," he said. "That sounds good."

～

After Nolan left, Amaya and I ended up falling asleep on the couch. We awoke the next morning to the gurgling of the coffee pot.

"Morning, girls," my dad said. "How do omelets sound?"

Amaya sat up and stretched before flopping back down onto the cushions. "Yes, please!"

"Two omelets, coming up," my dad said.

"Um, actually," I said, hating that I was blushing a little, "do you think you could make it three? Nolan will be over soon."

"Aw, poor you," Amaya sighed. "You haven't seen him in *ten whole hours*!"

"Oh, shut up," I laughed, tossing a pillow at her.

"Make that three omelets, coming up," Dad said, giving me a quick wink.

I hadn't exactly *told* him about my feelings for Nolan, but he could always read me, and, embarrassingly, it was probably obvious to him. I felt a pang of guilt when I thought about how I wasn't going to tell him what my friends and I would be up to today, like I was betraying the trust he had in me.

Nolan made it over a few minutes later and we ate at the kitchen counter while my dad made breakfast for himself. Sure enough, he asked what we had planned.

"We'll probably go for another hike or something," I said as casually as I could. "It's a nice day." If the situation with Cate's dad turned out to be really serious, I'd tell him more.

~~~

Soon, the three of us were at our respective posts. I brought some homework with me so I wouldn't waste time while waiting for something—anything—to happen. I spread a picnic blanket out on the hill, a few feet away from the park gate. Only a half hour had passed when I heard the gate rattle. It swung open and Cate walked through.

"Hey," I said, and she jumped.

"Oh my god, you scared me!" she said, her hand covering her heart.

"Sorry to startle you. I like coming out here to do my homework," I said, relieved I had a ready excuse.

"That's cool," Cate said. "Well, see you later." With that, she turned toward the woods.

"Wait!" I said, getting to my feet.

Thankfully, she stopped, though when I caught up with her, she looked irritated.

"Are you going for a walk by yourself?" I asked, scrambling to think of what else to say. Our plan had only been to *find* Cate. I didn't know where to go from here, especially without Nolan, who was the one who should be talking to her about her dad. "It's just, if you're not familiar with the paths it can be sort of dangerous." I didn't mention that the black flats and jeans she had on weren't great options for hiking.

"I won't be alone," she said, adjusting her glasses. "My dad is out there."

"Even after he got lost yesterday?" I asked, wishing more each second that Nolan was with me. Cate glanced at her phone, and I sensed her growing impatience. "Sorry, are you in a hurry?"
~~~

She sighed. "Sort of. My family is supposed to be catching a flight out of here in a few hours. My dad's morning hike is taking longer than expected, and he hasn't been answering his phone."

I wanted to grab my own phone so I could tell Nolan and Amaya what was going on, but not in front of Cate. "Can't anyone else from your family help?"

"My mom is busy wrapping things up with my grandma. Besides, she thinks my dad is more likely to cooperate if I go alone."

That was interesting. "Oh, really?" I asked.

"Yeah." She started walking away again and even though I was curious, I didn't stop her. Instead, I texted Nolan and Amaya.

I went back to my picnic blanket to wait. I was nervous about whatever I was getting myself mixed up in and didn't want to venture into the woods if Cate's dad was out there. Soon, Amaya arrived at the park gate.

As I was telling her about my conversation with Cate, Nolan rode up on his bike. He said he'd passed a house with an open garage and SUV in the driveway packed with suitcases. Maybe that was Cate's family, but there was no sign of her dad. He seemed disappointed when he heard that Cate had gone into the woods alone.

"I'm sorry, Nolan," I said. "I probably could've stalled Cate more, but I didn't want to go into the woods without you."

"No, don't be sorry," he said, his blue eyes widening with what I hoped was concern. "I'm glad you didn't go out there alone." Yes, it was definitely concern.

"Maybe we should go now, together, to see if she's okay," I said, feeling more at ease. Nolan and Amaya agreed, and we walked down to Mountain Pass Trail. We hadn't gotten very far when we ran into Cate coming our way. She looked surprised, and then sort of annoyed, to see us, like she knew it wasn't a coincidence we'd found her again.

"Any luck finding your dad?" I asked. We stopped on the path and, reluctantly, Cate did too.

"No," she said. "Maybe I missed him and he's already back at the house. I should hurry; we're leaving soon."

"Can you wait?" Nolan asked. "Just a second?"

"Why?" Cate asked, frowning.

Nolan started fidgeting, but he spoke clearly. "We just want to be sure everything's okay. If there's anything serious going on with your dad, you should think about getting someone to help you."

"No," she said abruptly. "I don't need help."

"Okay," Nolan said, "but maybe you should get your *dad* some help." The way he said it—like he thought Cate's dad was in imminent danger—made me wonder if Nolan wished he'd been able to get help for his mom. What happened to her wasn't at all his fault, but I worried he might blame himself anyway. I knew how heavy that sort of guilt could be.

"What? No," Cate said, her voice defensive. "He's fine, he's just . . . having a difficult week."

Nolan looked at me, a question in his eyes, but I wasn't sure what to say next either. Amaya, however, was done waiting for answers.

"Is he hiding drugs out here?" she asked. Nolan winced, and even though I was used to Amaya's directness, I was a bit startled too.

"*What?*" Cate said, balking. "No! It's *nothing* like that, seriously." She sounded sincere, like the idea of her dad doing drugs was as absurd to her as it would have been to me.

"Okay, well, sorry," Amaya said with a little shrug.

"Yeah," I said, embarrassed. "Really."

Cate nodded. "It's not drugs," she said, "but there is *something* going on with him. I mean, he's acting so . . . I don't even know. Out of touch? Paranoid?" Her voice quivered slightly, and she went quiet.

"Do you want us to walk back with you?" I said, feeling sorrier for her than ever, but also more anxious. If her dad wasn't hiding drugs in the woods, what *was* he doing? Something worse?

"Yeah, okay," Cate said. We started walking and her phone rang. "Mom? Yeah, I'm sorry . . . I'll meet you there soon. Is Dad with—Mom? Hello?" Cate put her phone down and suddenly increased her pace. Amaya, Nolan, and I looked at each other for a brief second before simultaneously deciding to catch up with her.

"Is everything okay?" Amaya asked, jogging behind Cate.

"I just need to hurry," she said. "My family's going to pick me up at the park so we don't miss our flight."

We reached the park gate and Cate looked through the bars. "I see my grandma's car," she said. "Um, see you later, I guess."

Cate took off running and we followed her through the gate. A red SUV was parked about ten feet ahead. My heart thudded when I saw there were only two people inside: Cate's mom, who was waving at her through the open window, and an older woman at the steering wheel. Her dad wasn't there. Cate, her hand now on the car door, noticed too.

"What the heck? Where's Dad?" she shouted, pulling her hand back.

"We'll talk about it later," her mom said. "Get in."

"No. Where is he? Is he lost?" Cate asked.

"He's not lost," her mom said, leaning out the window. "He's just not coming with us right now. But we need to go."

Cate spun around and darted toward us.

"Cate!" her mom yelled. "Now!"

"Hold on!" Cate thrust her phone into my hand. "Put your number in," she said. "I have no idea what's happening, but if my dad is staying in Morley, I want to know about it."

I hurried to do what she asked. With that, she ran back to the car.

"Well, *now* what?" Amaya said as we watched Cate's family drive off.

"I don't know," I said, wondering if it was smart to give my number out like that. "I don't want to go looking for that guy again, so I'm not sure how much we can do to help unless we tell someone."

"You mean, your dad?" Amaya asked. She knew I was pretty much an open book with him.

"Yeah," I said. Then I turned to Nolan, wanting to see if he was okay with that. "What do you think?"

"That's fine with me," he said and gave me a look that felt reassuring.

"What exactly are you going to tell him?" Amaya asked. I didn't know, so we sat down on the picnic blanket by the gate to discuss it. A moment later I got a text. *This is Cate Collins.*

10

TOPHER

On Saturday night, I scanned through a few more photo albums and barely got any sleep. With the way things were turning out, I doubted if Jojo would ever want us to come back to Morley. It would probably be smart not to, but the thought of never being here again, where I felt Jody's presence so strongly, terrified me. I'd let her go once, and I wasn't ready to do it again. If I had my ID card, leaving Morley would be easier because I'd be bringing Jody with me in some small way. Sunday morning, I got up before everyone else and took off for the woods.

When Jojo called me, she didn't have to ask where I was. "We're leaving soon," she said. "Are you almost back to the house?"

No, I wasn't. I was fleeing in the opposite direction. "I'm not ready to go yet," I said.

"Chris, we can't stay longer. The hospital needs me back tomorrow. Besides, you're never going to find an old ID card out there. You'll feel better once we're home."

Perhaps returning to Scottsdale would repair the damage done by being back in Morley, but I didn't want to suppress the past for another sixteen years. I'd been hijacked by long-dormant memories, and I was done fighting them. "I'm staying here, in Morley."

"What?" Jojo said. I could hear the shock in her voice.

"Not forever," I said, wanting to make that much clear. "But I'm not ready to leave."

"What am I supposed to tell Cate?"

"Just tell her I'm helping my mom sort out a few financial things. And that I love her." I was going to tell Jojo that I loved her too, but she'd already hung up. I kept walking and soon I didn't have service. If my family called again, I wouldn't know about it for a while. I reached the pond and searched for my ID. Already, a part of me regretted my choice to stay behind. When I'd left Jody, it hadn't been on purpose. *This* was. Another part of me though was strangely excited, like this was the opportunity I'd been waiting for.

After another unsuccessful search, I texted Cate as I walked up the hill to the park. *Don't worry about me. I'll be home soon. Love you.* I was trying to figure out what I was going to tell my mom when I heard someone say, "Mr. Collins?"

It was the girl who had helped Cate find me. Next to her was the same boy I'd seen before and another girl with wavy black hair. They were sitting on a picnic blanket. Cate must have told them our last name, and I wondered what else these three kids knew, or what they might be speculating about me. Given the way they kept glancing nervously at one another, it probably wasn't anything good.

"Yes?" I said, trying to seem as nonthreatening as possible.

"Um, well," the first girl said, "if you're looking for your family, they left a little while ago."

"Oh," I said, inching toward the gate. "Yes, thank you." I made a mental note never to come this way again.

"Did you lose something out there?" the girl I didn't recognize said as she stood up. Her friends followed her lead.

"Ah, yes. I dropped something," I said.

"What is it?" she asked. "Maybe we can help."

"No, I don't think so." My hand was on the gate, but then the girl said, "Well, if *we* can't help you, maybe her dad can. She's Mayor Matt's daughter, after all."

I heard the other girl shush her friend, but the name had already stopped me in my tracks. *Mayor Matt.* I hadn't kept up with Morley politics since moving, but when I first arrived here, a man named Patrick Stevenson had been the mayor. I'd noted the name because Patrick Stevenson was also the former governor in my Morley, and Matthias's father. Matthias . . . Matt. Each second it was getting harder to distinguish between the two worlds, and curiosity compelled me to ask, "Matthias Stevenson?"

"Yes, well, *Matt,*" the girl with brown hair said.

The daughter. My heart started to thump loudly as I understood who she must be. Or who her double must be. The carefully drawn line that had existed between the two Morleys continued to grow fuzzier as the girl looked up at me, her eyes so much like the Governor's.

"You're . . . you're Lolo," I stammered.

"Lolo?" she said, puzzled. "No one calls me that."

"Oh, no, of course not," I said, but the revelation that I was standing before the girl who, in some way, had started all of this was rapidly eroding my sense of reality. "Maybe that was just a childhood nickname."

"Whoa, whoa, whoa," said her friend, taking a protective step forward. "How do you know Harlow?"

"I took her photo once," I answered automatically.

"What?" all three of them said at more or less the same time. Their alarm pulled me back to the present moment and I realized how awful the thing I'd just said was.

"No, no, sorry, it's just—never mind. It's hard to explain."

"Then start explaining now," Harlow said, looking truly afraid. Both her friends seemed like they were about to pounce on me. Would they chase me if I ran? Probably. I decided to stay and offer the only explanation I could: the truth. Nobody but Jojo knew it, and she didn't seem willing to acknowledge it. Suddenly, I felt desperate to tell someone else, like I might burst if I kept it locked away for another second.

"It's hard to explain," I repeated. "But I'll try. See, I'm not from Morley originally. Well, not *this* Morley."

"What does that even mean?" the girl with black hair said.

"It's a Morley in another . . ." I paused. There would be no going back after this. "World," I finished. The three kids looked at me like I was mad.

"Another *world*?" Harlow said, as if making sure she'd heard me right.

"Yes," I said, before I could lose my nerve. "There's another Morley out there, with the same people who live here, at least as far as I can tell. It's just the circumstances are entirely different."

The frown on the boy's face deepened. "How can the same people live in two places?"

"They're more like doubles, or replicas, of each other. Down to their fingerprints."

Harlow and the boy exchanged confused glances, but the other girl was holding back laughter.

"It's true," I said, before I lost them entirely. "I can tell you the story."

"Um, that's okay," Harlow said, starting to turn away.

"No, wait, please," I said. "I know how ridiculous it sounds, but I promise, the other Morley is real. It's where I'm from."

The kids glanced at one another again and Harlow shrugged, which I took to mean they would listen, but maybe not for long. I launched into my story.

"I was hired to photograph the governor of Morley, Matthias, and his wife and baby at their manor. It was a tense day between the Governor and his wife. They were arguing, and their shouting upset the baby, who was being held by a nanny. I flinched when the Governor grabbed his wife's wrist. Then, the baby's crying got louder. I pretended to adjust my camera, but the way Governor Matthias was treating his family made me furious. He was nothing like the stately, collected man who appeared in public. I knew the portraits I was supposed to take of his private life would only help solidify that image. I'm no risk taker, but when Lolo didn't stop crying and the Governor yanked her out of the nanny's arms, I had to do something. Who knows? Maybe he'd have hurt baby Lolo if I hadn't distracted him by taking the illegal photograph. I'd captured a moment he didn't want the people of Morley to see.

"When the Governor realized what I'd done, he immediately ordered my arrest. I bolted from the nursery and jumped out an open window. Guards chased me into the woods. There was no point in hiding, but I came across a little pond and waded all the way in. When I came up for air not a minute later, I was totally alone."

The girl with black hair shook her head. "This is crazy."

She meant *I* was crazy. But if what I was remembering was true, then it was the situation that was crazy, not me.

"I waited by the pond, but no one came. I decided to turn myself in because otherwise the Governor might punish my wife Jody for my rebellion. I walked away from the pond, but I never reached the Governor's manor. Instead, I found Mountain Pass Trail. It made no sense. Morley doesn't have any trails leading out of the city-state. Eventually, I walked up a hill to Eastside, another place I'd never heard of. That's where the officers found me."

"Morley police?" Harlow asked.

"Yes. And the strangest part was, one of them looked uncannily like my father. He asked me a thousand questions. Why were my clothes damp and dirty? Why wasn't I at work? What had gotten into me? And, had I gotten a haircut since yesterday?"

All the confusion and fear I'd felt that day was surging back. I spoke faster.

"He kept calling me Chris. I wanted to show him my ID card because then he'd see I was really Christopher 'Topher' Collins. But my ID wasn't in my pocket anymore. The officer brought me to his house and a woman who could've been my mom's twin ushered me inside. Then, Jojo arrived."

"Your wife?" Harlow asked. "Is that Jody's nickname?"

"No," I said, taking a deep breath. "Jody and Jojo are doubles."

All three kids looked at me dubiously.

"I knew Jojo wasn't Jody right away. Her skin was the same golden tone, but it was more vibrant somehow. Her black hair seemed glossier too."

"I thought you said the doubles are perfect replicas," the girl with black hair said. "So, why would they look different?"

It was a fair question, but I wished they'd stop interrupting me. The story was jumbled enough already. "I think it's because Jody and Jojo haven't lived identical lives. They've made different choices, lived in different environments. Those things add up over time. I didn't look *exactly* like Chris, and Jojo could tell I wasn't him. But, his parents thought I was. They insisted on taking me to a psychiatrist. I'd never heard of a psychiatrist before, and when I found out it was a kind of doctor, I told them I wasn't sick, only lost. Chris's dad said that was the point of going to the psychiatrist; that she could help find me."

I paused, suddenly weighed down by the idea that I'd remained lost for sixteen years. And so had Chris.

"Then what?" the same girl asked, less argumentative in manner.

"Then I—or Chris—was diagnosed with generalized dissociative amnesia. The only evidence I could offer Jojo of my story was the photo of the Governor and Lolo. My camera had been around my neck when I went into the pond. It was waterlogged, but the film was salvageable. I developed the photo in Chris's studio. Eventually, Jojo accepted my story because she didn't know what else to believe."

"Where's the photo now?" Harlow asked.

"Lost," I said. Like everything else. "It must've gotten thrown away when we moved."

"What about your other wife?" the boy asked. "Did you try to get back to her?"

"Yes. I found my way to the pond, but when I jumped in, I didn't return to my Morley like I thought I would. I kept trying though, and one time they had to call the Sheriff's Department to bring me back to the city." I decided to omit the reason why I suspected my return trip to Morley had failed: Chris Collins was killed in my place. If my double was dead, I'd have no one to switch places with.

"Does Cate know about this?" Harlow asked.

"No, she doesn't."

Her friend scoffed. "You told some strangers in a park a story you've never told your own kid?"

I sighed. "Honestly, I never thought I'd tell anybody again."

The girl grinned. "Yeah, I can see why."

"Besides, Cate was born after all this happened," I said, wanting to justify myself. "Once I accepted I wasn't getting back to my Morley, I had two choices. Either I could stay with Jojo and live as Chris, or else strike out on my own in a strange world. I decided to stay with Jojo when she told me she was a few months pregnant. We thought the baby would be our chance at a new life together; one we could all remember."

"Then why not go back with them now?" the boy asked earnestly.

I stuck my hands in my pockets. The answer I had to offer wouldn't be satisfying. Now that Jojo and Cate had left, it didn't even feel satisfying to me.

"I've been living as Chris for over a decade and a half. I don't want to lose everything that made me Topher."

"So, you're just going to leave your family?" Harlow asked.

I looked away from her accusing gaze. "I'm not leaving them. But I am going to find a piece of the truth to hold on to."

"How?"

"By finding my Morley ID card. It must have dropped from my pocket into the water, or maybe somewhere close by. If I can find it, it will remind me that the other world exists and sort of connect me with my first family. Whenever I start feeling crazy, it'll be proof that I'm not."

"An ID card will prove that another world exists?" Harlow asked.

It *did* sound rather absurd. I tried to think of a response, but she kept talking. "And if you find the ID, then what? You go home to Arizona and return to normal?"

"As normal as will ever be possible for me."

"If finding this ID card won't really change anything, then why bother? Maybe you should just go home now."

"I can't," I said, growing increasingly uncomfortable. The more Harlow pried, the less confident I felt about my own reasoning. "I'll never know for sure what happened to Jody, but I need some kind of closure."

She ignored my attempt at an explanation. "But what if you don't find the ID?" she asked. "You could spend years searching out there and never find a little piece of plastic. You'd give up your family for that?"

"This is my chance to try to find the *one* link that will tie me to my old life. I'm not staying here forever. I'll even give myself a deadline of . . . two weeks." It was arbitrary, but even as I said it, I realized that having a deadline was important. Otherwise, like Harlow suspected, I may never leave.

"Would you let us help you look?" the other girl asked. "We know the area well. I'm up for a doomed treasure hunt."

I considered her proposal, sarcastic as it was. A few extra pairs of eyes couldn't hurt.

"Yes," I said, "as long as we don't get anyone else involved." The last thing I needed was the mayor of Morley looking into me.

"Ooh, a doomed *and* secret treasure hunt. Even better." She turned to Harlow. "What do you think?"

She hesitated. "Well, I *guess* we can help look for the ID sometime."

"Thank you, Harlow, really," I said. "And thank you . . ." I gestured toward the other two.

"It's Amaya."

"Nolan."

"It's nice to officially meet you."

"You too, Mr. Collins," Nolan said.

"Actually," I added impromptu, "you can call me Topher."

11

HARLOW

ate's dad left through the park gate, and we waited until he was out of earshot to start talking. He'd just told us to call him "Topher," but something about the name made me nervous, like if I called him that, I'd be validating his story about the other world. And there was no way his story could be true. Even if what he'd said had been very specific—but no, I wasn't going to let myself consider believing something so impossible.

"Wow," Amaya said, "maybe he really *is* on drugs."

I quickly turned to Nolan, worried about how he'd take that, but he didn't look upset. "I don't think so," he said.

"Guys," I said, rolling up the picnic blanket, "let's go back to my house and talk. Just in case he comes back." Nolan grabbed his bike and we left the park.

The story, and really that whole interaction, had agitated me. It was troubling how fixated this stranger was on me and my dad, even if he insisted he wasn't talking about us, but our "doubles." Mr. Collins had seemed genuinely scared when he'd looked at me and called me that name, Lolo. No one had ever stared at me like that before; like I was a threat.

The three of us sat in the living room.

"Okay," Amaya said, tying her hair up in a messy bun. "What's with that guy? I mean, at first, I thought he was just crazy, but then he kept going on with all those details and . . ." She paused, a thing that doesn't often happen once she gets going. "I don't know," she said, shaking her head. "It can't be true, but it really seemed like Topher thought it was."

"Yeah, exactly," I said, relieved to hear Amaya say something similar to what I'd been thinking. "And, there might be a way to confirm at least one part of his story."

"How?" asked Amaya.

I glanced at Nolan, quiet as ever, but leaning forward like he was interested.

"Remember when he said a sheriff found him out at the pond? Well, the county keeps records of incidents in the forest. If Mr. Collins *was* wandering around out there sixteen years ago, there'll be a report about it. We could probably find it online. I think it's important to find out if that actually happened."

"Yeah, I think so too," Nolan said, giving me a small smile. I smiled back automatically, before remembering what I'd been going to say next.

"It's just, whatever happened to him, and maybe it was something traumatic, it seems like he's been able to hide it from his own daughter pretty well."

"Oh yeah," Amaya said. "I feel bad for Cate. Are you gonna text her about this?"

I sighed and grabbed my phone out of my jacket pocket, turning it around in my hands. I was imagining being in Cate's place, and how I'd want to be told if it was *my* dad having some kind of mental breakdown. There didn't seem to be any great options. "It's kind of an awkward situation to explain," I said. "I'll just tell her we talked to her dad, and he's staying in Morley to find closure."

I sent the text and we were quiet for a moment.

"Well," I said, "should I grab my laptop and we can search for the report?"

"Sure," Amaya said, hopping off the couch. "But first, I'm starving."

~~~

I made us quesadillas and we sat at the kitchen counter, huddled around my laptop. I found the police archives quickly, but reports were available by request only.

"This is pretty official," I said uneasily. "People at the station know my name. They'll wonder why the mayor's daughter is requesting information about something that happened sixteen years ago."

Amaya scooted my laptop closer to her. "Then let's make up an email address and fill the form out like we're Cate. They'll just think it's some girl looking for answers about her long-lost dad."

~~~

The beginning of the week passed as usual, and there was no word from Cate. I was glad about that, since the more I thought about Mr. Collins's story, the more uncomfortable I felt. After all, Mr. Collins had openly admitted to taking an illegal photo of some kind, and that part of the story could very well be true.

We received the police report on Tuesday. Amaya and Nolan came over after school so we could read it together. We sat in the living room in what had become our normal spots, Amaya and I together in the middle of the couch and Nolan on a chair. I noticed he left more space between us when we weren't alone. Maybe Amaya's little comments were bothering him more than I'd thought.

I opened my laptop and read the report out loud. Sure enough, sixteen years ago, a man named Christopher Collins was found by a pond in a disoriented state and rescued by the Sheriff's Department. I knew this didn't verify the rest of his bizarre story, but having one detail confirmed was unnerving nonetheless.

"I don't want to go hiking again until Mr. Collins has left Morley," I said, glancing at Nolan and hoping he wouldn't be disappointed.

"That's fine with me," he said. "But should you let Cate know about the report?"

I sighed. I was seriously reconsidering my involvement with whatever was going on with the Collins family. Still, I didn't want to dismiss Nolan's concern.

"Okay," I said.

Your dad was found by a sheriff out in the woods sixteen years ago. There are police documents about it.

To my surprise, Cate texted back quickly.

Thanks. Do you know what he was doing out there?

There was so much more to her dad's story than a simple text could ever convey, but I figured the basic truth would suffice. *He was looking for an old ID.* She texted back again saying that was weird. She was right, but she had no idea how much worse it got from there.

I read the texts to Amaya and Nolan.

"So, now what?" Amaya asked, like she was annoyed this wasn't another clue on a treasure hunt.

"I don't know," I said. "I think we've done about all we can do."

12

NOLAN

Harlow, Amaya, and I were sitting in Harlow's living room when we heard the front door open. Harlow slammed her laptop closed as Matt walked into the room. He was wearing gym clothes and he kicked off his shoes as he greeted us.

"Oh, hey, Dad," Harlow said, a little unevenly.

Matt seemed amused as he observed the three of us. "What are you all up to?"

"Nothing," Harlow said. "I mean, just working on a . . . project."

"I see," Matt said, nodding, but his easy smile faded. "Harlow, is everything okay?"

"Yep," she said, her tone uncharacteristically clipped.

"It's fine, Matt," Amaya said, standing up. "She's just stressed out about something that's not worth stressing over."

Amaya was probably trying to save Harlow from having to lie to her dad anymore, but Harlow was clearly upset, and I wanted to come to her defense somehow.

"This, um, project, is stressing me out too," I said.

Harlow turned to me. "Really?" she asked. "You don't think I'm . . . overreacting?"

"Not at all," I said, sort of enjoying speaking in code. "But like you said, I think we've done about all we can do."

Harlow gave me what felt like a grateful smile.

"Well, it sounds like you could all use a study break," Matt said. "Why don't you stay for dinner?"

When Amaya's mom picked her up after dinner, I said I should probably head home too. Even though Harlow's dad was very nice, I'd been anxious about making a good impression the whole evening. Harlow walked me out, lingering in the doorway.

"My dad likes you," she said in a low voice. "I can tell."

"Yeah?" I said, glad I'd been able to hide my nerves well enough. "I like him too."

Harlow looked at me expectantly.

"Um, well," I continued, "I know you won't be up for walking or biking in the woods for a while, but maybe we can still hang out?"

"Yeah, of course," Harlow said. But she seemed a little deflated as I said goodnight. It wasn't until I was in my bedroom that I realized what I should have said to her, what she'd probably been waiting to hear. I wouldn't let another chance to tell Harlow how I really felt about her slip by.

The next day Harlow had a debate team meeting, but she said we could hang out in the evening. As the afternoon dragged on, I got bored and decided to take Duke for a walk. Only through the park, though. If Harlow was avoiding the woods until Mr. Collins left, I would too.

Duke and I were passing by the park gate when I heard my name. I peered through the bars to see Mr. Collins running up the hill. He must have been out on the trail again. Seeing no way out of a conversation, I tugged on Duke's leash and waited by the gate.

"Hi, Mr. Collins," I said.

"Topher, remember?" he said.

"Right."

"I haven't seen you in a few days," he said.

Had he been looking for me? "Um, yeah, I've been busy with school."

"Sure, sure," he said. "It's just, I haven't had any luck out at the pond. If you're still up for helping me look for the ID, I'd really appreciate it."

"Maybe," I said, toying with Duke's leash. "I don't know if I can."

"None of you? Harlow or Amaya?"

"Well—"

"Please," he said, taking a step closer to me. "A bit of your time is all I'm asking for."

I knew Harlow wouldn't want to go, but Topher's earnest gaze, and his even more earnest plea for help, made me hesitate.

"What about this weekend?" Topher asked. "Come to the pond with me Saturday morning. It'll only be a few hours, but it could make all the difference."

I doubted an extra pair of eyes would make any difference in Topher's search, but maybe, deep down, that wasn't the difference he meant. I wasn't exactly sure what was wrong with him, but he was definitely lonely. I could help with that, if nothing else.

"Okay," I said. "But just this once."

13

HARLOW

After I got home from my debate meeting, I texted Nolan to let him know I had too much homework to hang out. Midterms were approaching so that was true, but also, I was feeling a bit frustrated after last night. Apparently, Nolan liked my dad, but how did he feel about *me*? I told myself I was being immature, and I should still see him, but in the end, I thought it would be better for us to talk when I wasn't feeling quite so sensitive.

I was reading on my bed when my phone rang. It was Nolan. My heart started to race as I thought about the reasons he might be calling.

"Hey," I said. I could hear the smile through his voice when he said "hey" back.

"So," he went on, "I know you can't hang out tonight, but I really wanted to talk to you about what's going on."

Going on? Between us? "Yeah? Okay," I said. Nervous energy buzzed inside me, and I got up from my bed.

"It's just, today I saw Topher after school."

"What?" I said, surprised, and then quickly disappointed, that he'd called to talk about something I'd been trying to forget about.

Nolan told me about his conversation in the park and how he'd promised to go to the pond on Saturday.

"I know I told Mr. Collins, er *Topher*, that we'd help him," I said, feeling bad that I was about to go back on my word, a thing I tried very hard not to do, "but honestly, his interest in me is kind of creepy. I don't really want to see him again."

"Okay," Nolan said. "I understand that."

"You do?" I asked. It felt like he was only saying this to be nice.

"Yes, really."

Still, I wanted to give him another reason for my decision. "I'm thinking about Cate, too," I said. "I don't want to have to explain to her that her dad's leaving her family because of some ridiculous quest that I helped organize."

"Yeah," Nolan said, "but if we find the ID, then he'll go back home."

That made me pause. I wondered exactly how much of Topher's wild story Nolan actually believed. "Maybe he did lose an ID out there at some point, but you don't think he's telling the truth, do you?"

"No, but it seems like he's telling what he *thinks* is the truth."

"Yeah, okay," I said, relieved that at least he didn't believe in the existence of another world. "But Nolan, Topher probably needs professional help. By playing into his fantasy, we could be making things worse for him and his family. He's coming at things from a very skewed perspective."

Nolan sighed. "You're probably right. But what if we help Topher look for the ID just this once? I don't want to back out of meeting him now."

Like me, it was important to Nolan to remain true to his word.

"Harlow," Nolan said before I had a chance to say anything, "I understand if you don't want to go. I mean, of course, I *want* you to come with me . . ."

I waited for him to say more. It felt like he was close to saying something important. "You do?" I asked, hoping he'd continue.

"Yeah. I always do. No matter where I am or what I'm doing, you being there makes it better. School, homework, hiking, whatever, all of it. And when you're not there, I miss you. A lot."

I grinned, despite the situation. It was exactly the sort of thing I'd been waiting for weeks to hear. I told him that he made everything better for me too.

"Yeah?" Nolan said. "Cool. And you know, we can always do something together later, once I'm back from helping Topher."

"Wait," I said, suddenly forgetting all the reasons that had made me say no to this idea just a minute before. "If it's just this once, then I'll come with you on Saturday." I didn't want anything to come between Nolan and me now, especially not some stranger who would be out of the picture forever in a few weeks. In that moment, the anxiety I'd been feeling all day became irrelevant.

"Really?" he said, his voice getting higher. "That would be great. You're sure?"

"Yes. It sounds like a reasonable compromise." Then, just to be certain we were still on the same page, I added, "Compromises are what you do in relationships, right?"

"Yes," Nolan said, without a hint of hesitation. "Definitely."

14

NOLAN

couldn't keep the grin off my face when my call with Harlow ended. She called what we had a "relationship," and every concern I had about Topher was pushed to the side. Not that she'd said what *kind* of relationship, but . . . still.

The next day at school we decided exactly how we'd handle the "Topher situation." Amaya would come to the pond too, so there'd be three of us. I understood why Topher made Harlow so nervous. The way he'd stared at her, like he'd truly been remembering something bad, *was* pretty creepy. I didn't get the sense that he was dangerous though, and even if what he described was impossible, a part of me wanted to know how things would turn out.

But, I was too busy thinking about how to ask Harlow out to worry much about the existence of another world. With midterms coming up, she was pretty stressed (even though she studied more than anyone I'd ever met), so I wasn't sure if now was the best time. She invited me to come over after school to study. After a few hours, I gave up on homework and started playing games on my phone. The living room where we sat together was quiet, but not in an awkward way. Harlow and I could be quiet together. That was nice. It was getting late, and I thought maybe I should go home, but something told me not to leave yet, not before I'd asked her out. I just needed to do it already.

"Hey, Harlow," I said before I chickened out.

She looked up from the textbook she was reading. "Yeah?"

"Um, I know we're helping Topher on Saturday, but do you have any plans for Sunday?"

She lifted the book up. "Just this," she said, sounding tired.

"Oh, yeah. It's just um, I was wondering if you'd want to maybe go out to dinner or something." I felt my face start to burn, and I talked faster. "Or not even dinner, it could be breakfast, or lunch, or brunch." I clamped my mouth shut before I listed any more meals.

I couldn't read Harlow's expression at first, but then she closed her book and smiled. "Like a date?" she asked.

"Yeah," I said, reminding myself to breathe.

"Yeah, I would."

"Really?"

"I don't know why you're so surprised." She laughed. Harlow untucked her legs and scooted closer to me on the couch. I worried she'd notice the sweat that was starting to line my forehead. "We've seen each other practically every day since you moved in."

"Yeah," I said, "I guess we have." I thought back over the past few months and how much my life had changed. "I meant what I said the other day. I miss you when we're not together."

"I do too."

"You know," I said, the words practically spilling out of me, "when I moved in, I was convinced my life here was going to suck. I almost wanted it to suck. That way, I'd be able to stay angry. But you . . ." I looked into her sea green eyes, inches away from mine. "It's impossible to stay angry when I'm around you."

Her face grew rosy, and she pushed a long lock of hair behind her ear. I saw that her earring matched her eyes. I never noticed stuff like that.

"It's like that for me too," she said. "You make me so happy. I don't have to be 'debate team Harlow' with you, or 'student council Harlow,' or 'mayor's daughter Harlow.' I can just be my plain self."

"There's nothing plain about you," I said.

She blushed again, and before I could hesitate, I leaned forward. Harlow did too. I just hoped she couldn't hear the hammering of my heart. If she could, then she would have heard it skip a beat when our lips met.

But only one beat. After that, my nerves disappeared. Not even I could doubt something that felt so right.

~

The next day, Friday, Harlow and I met up at lunch before going to our table.

"I haven't told Amaya about us yet," Harlow said, her face as rosy as it had been last night. "Can we tell her now?"

"Yeah," I said, taking her hand. "I want everyone to know."

Amaya, beaming, stood up when she saw us. "Finally!" she said. "I saw this coming from a mile away."

~

Saturday morning, Harlow and Amaya knocked on my door at ten.

"Cate texted me some more last night," Harlow said.

"Really?" I said as I zipped up my jacket.

"Yeah, she said she was able to find out a bit more from her mom. I guess her dad suffered some kind of memory loss before she was born. He was seeing a psychiatrist and had to stop working for a while. But things got better when they moved to Arizona. It's weird. Cate said it's like they tried to forget it ever happened and as far as she knows, her dad never got more treatment. They thought he was fine, but being in Morley brought everything back."

"That does sound weird," I said, but I noted that none of it contradicted Topher's story. I found myself feeling bad for him. Trying to forget that a problem, or a person with a problem, existed was just the sort of thing Bailey had done with my mom. It was like the tighter the addiction had wrapped itself around her, the looser he'd held on. None of them, Bailey or my grandparents, wanted the responsibility. To my mom, it always felt like no one wanted her. I wondered if Topher felt the same way.

"We told Cate we're going to spend one day with her dad to see what's up," Amaya said.

"But we can't keep following him around," Harlow said. "Cate gets it."

"Yeah . . . okay, good," I said, remembering my compromise with Harlow. I was going to keep my promise no matter what happened today.

We set off for the park gate. Topher was waiting for us. His windbreaker was smudged with dirt from all the times he'd been out searching for his ID.

"Good morning, guys," he said. "Thanks for coming."

"Sure," Harlow said. "But before we go, I thought I should let you know that I've been in touch with Cate. She knows we're here."

"She does?" Topher said. "She hasn't been answering my calls or texts." He sighed and looked at his feet.

Harlow glanced at me nervously. I reached out for her hand, and she took it at once.

"Well," Topher said, straightening himself up. "Let's go; it's a long walk."

He led the way into the woods and the three of us followed.

Topher kept a quick pace. A few miles in, Amaya groaned, "I'm hungry; are we ever going to take a break?"

"Hey, Topher?" Harlow called out to him. "Mind if we take a short break?"

He stopped and turned around. A look of uneasiness clung to his face.

"Just for a few minutes?" Harlow said.

"Yeah," Amaya said, "maybe you can tell us more about your life in the *other* Morley."

That did the trick. "Okay, a short break."

We sat down at the base of a wide tree and Harlow passed out the snacks she'd brought.

"In my Morley," Topher said, "the pond in question is a lot closer to civilization than it is here. The forest was cleared extensively by Governor Matthias's father in a search for oil. He didn't find any though."

Harlow bristled when Topher said her dad's name. I tried to change the subject. "Do you want something?" I asked Topher, holding out a bag of chips.

"Not now, thanks."

"So," Amaya said with a grin, ripping into a bag of pretzels, "what's the food like in this other Morley?"

"Um . . ." Topher concentrated like he was trying to access some faraway memory. If he'd caught the sarcasm in Amaya's question, he didn't show it. It struck me again how serious this all was for him. "It's different," he said. "I couldn't believe the first time I went to a grocery store here—the amount of choices was overwhelming. Everything was so complicated and . . . colorful. In my Morley, people receive ration cards for a particular amount of food based on their social class, and there isn't a wide selection."

"Who decides how much they get?"

"The Governor and his Advisory Board," Topher said, like it was obvious.

"What if it isn't enough?" Amaya asked. "Or, what if you wanted different stuff?" If her first question was meant as a joke, now she seemed genuinely interested in hearing Topher's answers. So was I, if only because I kept being surprised by all the details he included. Harlow was listening too, but she'd stopped peeling her orange and looked nervous again. I moved a little closer to her.

"No one questions what the Governor has deemed to be 'enough,'" Topher said.

"Weird," said Amaya.

Weird to someone who had never been on food stamps before. For a couple of years when I was in elementary school, my mom received benefits on the tenth of every month. She treated that day like it was special and tried to make going to the grocery store a fun outing for me. But I remember standing in line to check out wishing our cart could be as full as everyone else's.

"What other things does the Governor decide?" Amaya asked.

"Oh, just about everything," said Topher. "You need to obtain permits for the big stuff, like to study for a trade, get married, or rent an apartment. But smaller, more mundane things too, like staying out past curfew."

"*Curfew?*" Amaya said, laughing. "Does the Governor ground you if you come home late? My mom would love this place."

"I don't think she would," Topher said gravely. "People get arrested for missing curfew." This other Morley couldn't be real, and yet, I felt a sudden chill.

"What else is restricted?" I asked. "Can you get a permit to leave Morley?"

"No, definitely not," Topher said. "Everything is carefully orchestrated to keep the Governor in power. He can't control you if you're not in the city-state. That's why he sent his Guard after me."

"What other kinds of things were banned there?" Amaya asked. "Like, were you guys allowed to have smartphones?"

"No, there was no Internet access. The higher-ranking classes could have TVs, but the only shows were about the importance of the Governor and social duty. Then again, I haven't been back in sixteen years. I don't know if they've kept pace with the technological growth in this world."

Harlow, uncharacteristically quiet, was gazing down the path toward the city, maybe wishing we could turn back. I, however, wanted to hear a little more. If everything was so heavily monitored, did that mean things like drugs and alcohol were too? An abstinence-only world didn't sound appealing, but then, maybe my mom could still be alive in a place like that. The rigid class system Topher described would prevent me from ever meeting Harlow, though. In the alternate world, she was next in line for the governorship. Who was I? A nobody.

Not that any of this matters; not that it's real, I reminded myself.

"Okay, is everyone ready to keep moving?" Topher asked as he rose from the forest floor.

"Just a second," I said. I leaned toward Harlow. "Are you okay?"

She nodded and gave me a tiny smile. "I'm fine."

Amaya came closer. "Sorry if I was asking too many questions," she said. "I know it's all fake, but it's kinda interesting."

"Yeah, it is," Harlow said. We stood up, and even though Harlow said again that she was okay, she still seemed distracted.

"You know," I whispered to her, "the worst thing about Topher's Morley is that we never would have met."

She took my hand, and her smile seemed more real this time. "Then it's a good thing we're in our Morley."

The rest of the hike passed uneventfully. When Mountain Pass Trail ended, Topher was practically jogging.

"So, exactly how long are we staying to look for the ID?" Amaya asked as we tried to keep up.

Harlow looked at me. "Maybe an hour?" she said.

"At the most," I said.

Finally, we arrived at a small, swampy pond. We noticed a number of holes where Topher must have been digging earlier in the week. Harlow took a few pictures. "I'll send these to Cate later," she said. "She'll want to know about all of this."

We began searching, but I grew bored quickly. Digging by hand wasn't getting us very far.

"Are we almost done?" Amaya said after a while. "Even if Topher's ID is out here, we'll never find it. Where is he, anyway?"

"I haven't seen him for a few minutes," Harlow said, and I realized I hadn't either. "I hope he hasn't gone too far off."

"We don't have to stay out here with him," I said, again feeling bad that I'd dragged her into this. "We can go back whenever."

"I don't know," she said. "I don't want to just ditch him out here."

"Then let's find him," Amaya said. "Topher?"

Harlow and I joined in shouting his name. At first, we didn't hear anything, but then, faintly, we heard, "I'm coming!" His footsteps grew louder until he barreled through the bushes. "What? What is it? Did you find it?" he asked, a little out of breath.

"Oh, um, no," Harlow said apologetically, "we just wanted to know where you were. And how much longer we might be out here."

Topher didn't try to hide his disappointment. "It could be a while. I'm trying to cover as much ground as possible, but I still need to search the water."

I watched as Topher's gaze shifted from Harlow to the pond behind her. He stared at it intensely, like he was confronting an old enemy. I guess in his mind, he was.

"You . . . you want us to search in the pond?" Harlow asked.

Topher shut his eyes tightly. "No," he said. "It's too dangerous for you."

"It could be, yes," Harlow said, like she wanted to encourage the idea. "We could get pretty sick, depending on what's in there."

"Sickness is the least of your worries if you fall through that pond," Topher said. Fall *through*, not in. He was adamant about that. "You three shouldn't look there. I don't know what would happen. But I don't think it's possible for me to pass through again. I'll search the pond. Just keep digging in the banks."

With that, he let his windbreaker slide off his shoulders and fall to the dirt. Then he took off his long-sleeved t-shirt, shoes, and socks. Seeing him in just his pants and a lightweight undershirt made me shiver, but he waded into the pond seemingly unbothered by the cold. Topher plunged his hands into the water and started searching.

It was awkward just standing there watching him, but something about the scene made it hard to look away. It was sad, and kind of pathetic, to see an adult flailing around in a disgusting woodland pond searching for an object that probably didn't exist or at the very least would be weathered beyond recognition. At the same time, though, I had a certain respect for this guy who was so committed to his cause.

Amaya sighed loudly. "This is going to take forever," she said, walking away from the water.

"It seems that way," Harlow said under her breath. She looked almost miserable, and it was my fault she was out here. I knew I needed to do something to get us home faster. I bent down to untie my sneakers.

"Nolan, what are you doing?" Harlow asked.

"Helping Topher search. It'll go faster if I do," I said, hoping I sounded sure of myself.

"But you might get sick, and the walk back will be freezing."

"Don't worry," I said, "it won't be for long."

"Okay. But be careful."

Amaya walked up right as I was stripping down to my boxers and undershirt.

"Um, did I miss something?" she asked, raising one eyebrow.

"Yes," Harlow said. "Nolan is going into the pond to help Topher."

"Ew, really?"

"I'll be fine," I said, trying not to make a big deal about it, even though the water did look pretty gross. It was too late to back out now, and I set my clothes on the dry ground.

Amaya laughed. "You're a true hero."

"Hey," Harlow said defensively, "it's more than either of us is willing to do." Knowing she appreciated what I was doing made it easier. I walked to the pond, stopping to dip my toes in the water. It was cold, but not unbearable. The splashing as I waded in caught Topher's attention.

"NO!" he shouted, and I stopped so abruptly that I almost lost my balance. "Nolan, get out of the water. I don't know what it'll do to you."

"It's okay," I said. "I'll only be in for a few minutes."

Topher looked stricken. "That's not what I mean."

Right. He was worried I'd be pulled into another world.

"Maybe stay in the shallow part," Harlow said from behind me. "Just to humor him."

"Good idea," I said. "Topher," I called out, "I'm going to stay close to the shore, okay? I won't go out as far as you."

I took a few more strides until the water almost came to my waist.

"Nolan, don't." He was moving toward me, pushing the water aside frantically.

"I can search like this, see?" I reached my hands down into the soft mud and scooped up two fistfuls to show him.

"Fine," he said, studying me. "Just don't go any farther."

"I won't," I said. Topher nodded and resumed his search.

"Are you sure you're okay?" Harlow asked.

I smiled at her again, liking that she was worried. "Totally fine."

I decided I wouldn't take another step farther into the pond, but would search around the perimeter. I moved to the right and sifted through the mud with my hands. Nothing. I took another step and almost slipped on the slimy pond floor. On my third step, something sharp, probably a rock, pierced the sole of my foot.

"Ow!" Instinctively, I pulled my foot away, and in doing so, completely lost my balance. My body twisted and I was submerged in the pond.

"Nolan!" Harlow's voice was muffled by the water clogging my ears. "Nolan!"

I pushed against the thick mud with my feet, but only sank in further. Desperately, I flapped my arms like wings, trying to propel myself upward as the mud sucked me in deeper. Finally, I had to reach down and use my hands to free my feet. When I resurfaced, I coughed up a mouthful of boggy water.

"It's okay, Harlow," I sputtered. "I'm good."

But she wasn't there.

"Harlow?"

Amaya wasn't on the bank either. I turned around. Topher was gone. And then it hit me.

I was gone.

15

HARLOW

"**N**olan!" I cried out, startled as he splashed beneath the surface. "Nolan!"

He should have come up immediately, but I lost sight of him in the dark water. Then, Topher lunged his way across the pond and hoisted Nolan back up. When he emerged, he was breathing loudly, and I realized there was something wrong about him. Something in his eyes, wild as they were. He was shaking, coughing, and then, screaming.

"Where am I?" His voice was loud and panicked.

"Calm down, you're okay," Topher said as he struggled against Nolan's twisting body. He managed to turn Nolan so that they looked each other squarely in the eyes. That's when I noticed Nolan wasn't wearing a white undershirt anymore. His shirt was green now, and he wore black jeans instead of boxers. My breathing quickened and I suddenly felt hot.

"Shh, listen to me," Topher said, surer and steadier than I'd heard him all day. "You're not in Morley anymore."

Amaya dug her fingernails into the sleeve of my jacket. "What the hell is happening?"

I didn't answer. What seemed to be happening wasn't possible.

"But . . . but how did I get here?" the boy said. The longer I stared at him, the less he looked like Nolan. His hair, while still sandy-blond, was too short. And he was paler, like he rarely saw the sun.

"We'll get to that in a minute," Topher said calmly. "What's the last thing you remember?"

"I was . . . at home. Fixing a leg on our kitchen table."

"And then you were here?" Topher said, excitement creeping into his voice. "You had no choice in the matter?"

"Where *is* here?" the boy said. I could hear him choking back tears.

"Let's get you out of the water and I can explain everything," Topher said. "Girls," he continued as if nothing was amiss, "can you please grab those dry clothes?"

I backed away slowly from the pond, hoping I was on the cusp of waking up or snapping out of whatever horrible hallucination this was. And yet, I could feel Amaya clinging to my arm. I was painfully awake.

"Harlow," she whispered. "Seriously, what the hell?"

"I . . . I think Topher might have been right," I said, not ready to fully commit to this answer.

"About the pond being a portal?"

"That boy isn't Nolan." I knew the words were true as I said them.

"What are we gonna do?"

"We should start by getting him these clothes," I said, trying to focus on this simple task. I grabbed Nolan's clothes and went back to the edge of the pond where Topher and the boy stood.

That's when the boy really looked at me for the first time. His jaw dropped. It was the same terrified expression I'd seen on Topher's face when he'd called me Lolo. That had been unsettling, but seeing it on this boy who looked so much like Nolan made me want to cry.

"No," he said, his eyes locking with mine. "No, no, no." Suddenly, he was frantic again. "Where am I? I didn't do anything wrong, please, I promise."

"Shh, hey now," Topher said as he put his hands on the boy's shoulders. "You're not in trouble, okay? I know this is a lot to take in, but trust me, that girl is not Lolo."

The boy glanced nervously at me. The tears streaming down my face probably didn't make him feel any better.

"She's a *lot* like her," he said.

"But not exactly, right?" Topher asked. "Think about all the photos and videos you've seen of Lolo."

The boy looked at me again. His scrutiny made me uncomfortable, and I moved closer to Amaya so that we stood shoulder to shoulder.

"Yeah," he said at last, "not exactly like Lolo."

Topher reached out and took the clothes from me. "Why don't you get dressed, ah, sorry, what's your name?"

"Nole," the boy said.

"Right," Topher nodded. "My name's Topher, and that's Harlow and Amaya. The four of us will have plenty of time to talk on our walk back to the city."

"Morley?" Nole asked.

Topher paused, but I was desperate to start figuring things out. "Yes," I said. There needed to be some piece of reality I could insist upon. Nole looked at me blankly, then he frowned.

"But how can this be Morley if—"

"This *isn't* Morley," Topher said, cutting him off. "At least, not the Morley you and I are from."

"There's *another* Morley?" Nole asked.

"Yes," Topher said. "One without the Governor, or Lolo, or the rules you think you're breaking by being in the woods with no permit."

Suddenly, my arms were covered in goosebumps. "Oh my god," I said, "that's where Nolan is. He's there in the other Morley. *He's* the one who's going to get in trouble." My heart fluttered wildly, and, without another thought, I charged toward the water.

Topher stopped me before I could get farther than ankle deep. "Harlow, Harlow, that won't help," he said, holding me back.

"But I've got to help him!" I cried.

"Going after him will only make things worse."

I paused my struggle and listened. Any bit of information would help right now.

"If you go through the portal, the Governor's daughter will take your place here." I let Topher guide me back to the dirt. Amaya wrapped her arms around me in a hug.

"Wait," I said, "if I can't go to the other Morley to get Nolan, then why don't we just send Nole back through the pond?"

"*No*," Topher said, a little too quickly. "That won't work. I've, um, tried it already. I think it's a one-way passage."

"Then how are we supposed to get Nolan back?" I asked, dreading that an answer to my question may not exist.

"We'll figure it out," Topher said. "For years I haven't been able to solve this mystery because I've basically been on my own. Now that I've got other people who know the truth, maybe I can."

I eyed him suspiciously. My problem wasn't exactly with the words he said, but how he said them. He sounded too eager, like a scientist on the cusp of some great discovery in which Nolan was merely a lab rat. I was going to say as much when Nole spoke up.

"I . . . I just want to go home," he said. "I'll do whatever I can to help." It was such a Nolan thing to say. Hearing the near-identical voice subdued my anger.

"Thank you, Nole," I said. "We're counting on it."

16

TOPHER

When I first arrived in this Morley, I'd been called "erratic" and "confused" and "crazy." Then for sixteen years, I'd lived in a state of resigned silence. Now, suddenly, I felt vindicated.

I hiked back through the woods with Harlow, Amaya, and Nole, all of them somber and tired. I was acutely aware of the tragic situation that had just befallen us, so I hid my inner satisfaction. It wasn't the only thing I was hiding. When Harlow suggested sending Nole back into the water so that the boys would trade places again, I'd panicked and told a flimsy lie. I knew—or was pretty sure—that the only reason I couldn't go back was because Chris Collins was dead. But I hadn't spoken to anyone from my Morley in years, and I had to know what was happening there. I felt bad for Nolan, but I needed to talk to Nole. If Harlow knew the pond probably *would* switch the boys, she might have pushed Nole back in, even if I explained why I wanted to keep him—just for a little bit. And I wouldn't have blamed her if she did. I more than anybody knew the desperation she was feeling. The more I considered what I'd done, the guiltier I felt.

A few days with Nole, then I'll make sure he's returned safely, I promised myself. Unlike Chris, Nolan hadn't arrived in Morley as a fugitive—and he'd quickly figure out what had happened, which would start him on a stronger foot than I had here. He should be okay there for a little while. As we walked though, another niggling question arose in my mind. Why *hadn't* Nolan jumped back into the pond after piecing together what had happened to him? Theoretically, that should have switched him and Nole again. If he wasn't able to jump back in, that could mean there was something, or someone, in his way.

Dammit.

I could have screamed. It was my own selfishness that had gotten these kids mixed up in this nightmare. Cate was probably going to get mixed up in it too. I didn't see how I would be able to keep this from her and Jojo. I glanced at the three teenagers shuffling behind me, each despondent in their own way. Nole's face was so pale he looked almost sickly. I couldn't fathom abandoning this vulnerable kid to whatever awaited him in his Morley, but then, I was abandoning Nolan to whatever that fate was now. Again, I felt a scream clawing its way through my throat.

"Topher?"

Harlow's voice snatched me away from my thoughts.

"Yes?" I managed to say.

"Can we slow down a bit?"

Though I didn't remember speeding up, there were now several feet between us. "Oh, yes, of course. Sorry." I stopped and waited for them.

"We should probably figure out how we're going to pass Nole off as Nolan," Harlow said once we were walking together again.

Amaya sighed. "That's going to be tough. But it's better than explaining what's *really* going on."

"Nole," I said, "all of us are going to be here for you."

If only someone could be there for Nolan.

17

NOLAN

This can't be happening. It's not possible, I thought as I scanned the empty forest, eager for a sign that this was a dream. But it was happening; it was possible.

I stood knee-deep in the pond. A cold breeze rustled through the trees, and I wrapped my arms tightly around my trembling body. Just then I heard a sound I'd only heard in movies: the cocking of a gun.

I whipped my head to the right where the sound had come from. A uniformed guard, a boy probably not much older than me, stood at the edge of the forest. His gloved hands were clutching a gun and his eyes bore into mine.

"Don't move!" he yelled. I wasn't going to. It felt like every bone in my body had been fossilized.

The young guard was dressed in a crisp brown shirt and pants. A radio with a small red light was on his shoulder. He crept closer without breaking eye contact. My feet started to sink into the mud.

I should have listened to Topher, but I hadn't believed his story about the magic pond. I'd just wanted to go home faster, to make Harlow happy. At first, nothing had happened. I had been fine standing in the water. It was only when I'd lost my footing and fell all the way in that things went wrong.

The guard's eyes flickered up to the sky. I followed his gaze but didn't see anything. I stole a glance at the water that had somehow brought me here. If I dunked myself under before the guard could shoot, would I go home? Although, if traveling back and forth was so simple, Topher probably would have done so by now. Hadn't he said he tried going through the pond again, but it didn't take him back? In my shocked state, I honestly couldn't remember.

The guard was staring at me again and I held myself completely still. I wondered with whom exactly I'd been switched. Another version of myself? An alternate Nolan who had taken my place? They'd realize it wasn't me, wouldn't they? *Harlow will notice,* I thought, *she's got to.*

The quiet whistling of the forest breeze morphed into a loud sound with an unmistakable mechanical whir. The trees began to shake as the blaring noise got closer. I looked up and saw a helicopter descending. Before I could even register what was happening, a foldable ladder fell from the open door and another guard started climbing down.

"Do not move," a loud voice boomed.

The guard on the ladder grabbed my arm and yanked me out of the churning water. Fragments of Topher's story flashed through my mind. From them, I was able to piece together a single coherent thought: *the Governor knows I'm here.*

18

NOLE

One second I was at home, and the next, I was underwater. It seemed impossible, and yet, here I was in the woods with three strangers. Before we left the pond, I stepped behind a tree to change into dry clothes, the ones that belonged to the other boy. "Your double," the man, Topher, had called him. I had no idea what that meant. I had no idea what any of this meant. A little white tag in the pants read MADE IN CHINA. I'd never heard of such a place. Was China another city-state like Morley?

When I rejoined them in the China clothes, the girl who looked like Lolo, *Harlow*, I reminded myself, held out her hand and said, "Here, I'll carry those. They'll fit in my backpack."

"Thanks," I muttered, giving her my wet shirt, pants, and shoes, still not entirely certain she *wasn't* Lolo. She put them away while the other girl, Amaya, stared at me. I tried not to stare back, but I'd never seen anyone with shiny purple eyelids before.

We walked through the woods for a long time. I kept thinking, why did this happen to me? I hadn't broken the law, so if this was a punishment, I didn't see why I deserved it. I wondered, too, what had brought Topher here in the first place. But all these questions I kept to myself. I'd been taught from a young age to be very careful with my words.

Everyone was quiet until Harlow asked Topher to slow down. That got a conversation started. When I heard Harlow say, "pass Nole off as Nolan," I grew even more nervous than I already was.

"Nole," Topher said, "all of us are going to be here for you."

I stayed silent, not sure whether I was being led to safety or to my death.

"I don't know," Amaya said uneasily. "He looks really similar to Nolan, but his short hair gives it away. We can tell people at school that he got his hair cut over the weekend, but his aunt and uncle will notice as soon as he gets home."

"No, they won't," Harlow said. "They hardly notice him at all."

"My aunt and uncle?" I asked, too curious to hold back. I was thinking of the people living on the other side of the city-state whom my mom and I weren't permitted to speak with. I hadn't thought about them in years. My mom was enough family for me. "You mean Patricia and Bailey?"

"Yes," Harlow said. "Although, here your aunt goes by 'Trish.' You live with her and your Uncle Bailey."

I frowned. "I've never even met them."

"Nolan hadn't met them either until his mom died."

"*Died*?" I panicked. My mom and I had been home together all day. The last thing I remember before ending up in the woods was her asking me if I was ready for lunch. "What do you mean died? She's not dead; I was just with her!" Despite the cold, beads of sweat formed on my neck. "Does Governor Matthias already know I'm missing? Did he send the Guard after my—"

A strong hand patted me on the back. "Hey, slow down, it's okay," Topher said. "*Your* mom is fine. This is Nolan's mom we're talking about."

I nodded, but my heart pounded furiously in my chest.

"How . . . how did Nolan's mom die?" I asked, hoping the same thing wasn't about to happen to mine.

"An overdose," Harlow said quietly.

"A what?" I asked uncertainly.

"An accidental drug overdose," she said, as if that should clear up any confusion.

I frowned.

"Nole," Topher said, "in this Morley, there are recreational drugs that people use to feel good, or at least feel different."

"There are seriously no drugs in Morley?" Amaya asked.

"Only for medical purposes," said Topher. "And they're strictly monitored."

That was one way of putting it. For someone of my class, the wait-list to get the medicine you needed could take years. Oftentimes, it was too late.

"Nole," Harlow said, "what's important right now is that you understand how you came to live with your aunt and uncle."

"It doesn't make sense," I said. "They aren't allowed to talk to my mom and me."

"Not allowed?"

It was unnerving to talk to someone who looked almost identical to Lolo, especially since this girl was clueless about life in Morley. I decided she couldn't be working for the Governor.

"Yeah," I said. "They haven't talked to my mom since she and my dad failed to get a marriage permit."

"Why couldn't they get one?"

"Because, when the government found out my mom was already pregnant, they were obviously denied."

"*Obviously?*" Amaya said. "How would the government even know that?"

I faltered. This place was so different I didn't know how to explain one thing without needing to explain a hundred others.

"It's part of the normal marriage permitting process," Topher said, saving me. I was growing more curious about how he'd ended up here. "If a couple is found to be pregnant, then the permit is denied. After that, they basically drop to the lowest rung on the social ladder."

"Can they still live together, even as outcasts?" Amaya asked.

"No. They have to apply separately for economy housing units. Contact between the couple is forbidden."

Amaya shook her head. "That's *insane.*"

"That's Morley," Topher said. "Social advancement is possible, if rare, but there's no shortage of ways to become an outcast."

"That's so unfair!" said Amaya.

"Perhaps, but the rules are quite clear. Living with well-defined bound-aries gives people a feeling of safety. At least, it did for me."

He was right about that. I felt the opposite of safe here. With a pang of homesickness, I wondered what my mom was thinking had become of me after I'd vanished from the apartment. I hoped she hadn't put herself in danger by going out to look for me. I worried that Catherine might go out looking too. I was supposed to meet her this evening. Would she think I'd forgotten about her?

"Nole," Harlow said, pulling me from my thoughts, "what kind of opportunities do *you* have back there?"

"Opportunities?" I repeated, uncertain what she meant.

"Yeah, like options for your life?"

"Um, well, I've started training to be a car mechanic," I said, hoping that would answer her question. "I got to choose between that or building wind turbines. I like mechanic work so far. I'm getting better at it."

Harlow nodded. "Nolan is good at mechanical work too. Bikes, though."

"I guess that makes sense," I said, even though it was the first thing my "double" and I seemed to have in common.

We continued in silence for a few minutes. Eventually, the conversation resumed, and I learned a bit more about life in this Morley. I tried my best to follow along, but when they described something called the Internet, I had to slow them down. Harlow pointed to Nolan's pocket, and I reached in and pulled out a small black rectangle. Amaya told me it was a phone, but it didn't have any buttons. This Morley was unbelievably complicated.

Harlow and Amaya kept talking, but I barely heard what they said. I just wanted to go to sleep and wake up in my apartment.

At last, we reached the end of the trail.

"In your Morley, the edge of the forest leads to the Governor's manor," Topher said as we hiked up a small hill. "Here though, it only leads to a nice neighborhood."

"Eastside, remember?" Harlow said.

"Um . . . right," I said. It was probably the first in a long list of things I didn't remember.

At the top of the hill there was a fence that looked nothing like the huge wall that surrounded my Morley. As soon as we stopped moving, I realized how exhausted I was.

"It's okay if you forget some stuff, Nole," Harlow said, sounding tired herself. "Get some rest tonight. Tomorrow, we'll meet up at 10:15 and go to brunch together."

"Brunch?" I said, almost too worn out to ask.

Harlow offered me a smile then, but there was something sad about it. "It's a combination of the words 'breakfast' and 'lunch.' We'll have plenty of time to talk then."

"That was supposed to be you and Nolan, wasn't it?" I heard Amaya ask quietly.

"Yeah," Harlow said, and her clear worry for Nolan—whom I gathered she'd at least been dating—made me think of Catherine. It wasn't my choice to come here, but I still felt guilty for leaving her without a single clue as to where I'd gone.

"Topher," Harlow said, "you'll keep working on how to switch Nolan and Nole, right?"

Topher was poking at his black rectangle. *Phone*, I reminded myself. "Yes," he said, without looking up. "Sorry, I'm just seeing some missed calls from Cate."

"She probably wants to know if we found the ID," Harlow said. "Are you going to tell her what happened?"

I didn't bother trying to make sense of what they were talking about. Every moment I grew more tired.

"I think so," Topher said. "But listen, I'm sorry for everything that happened here today. We'll get it sorted out."

I didn't fully believe him. No one said anything.

"Nole," Topher continued, "I'll put my number in Nolan's phone. We'll talk more soon."

I handed him the phone, but he said I needed to unlock it with my thumbprint first.

"The phone knows my thumbprint?"

"Yes," he said, unimpressed. Once it was unlocked, Topher's thumbs slid easily over its surface. "When you want to call me, go here to contacts and search for my name. I'm in here as Topher Collins."

"Collins?" I said, startled. Catherine's name was Collins, too.

"Yes?" he said, noting my interest. "Nole, is the name Collins familiar to you?"

"Yeah, it is," I said slowly, not sure how much I wanted to say with him staring at me so intently. I didn't see how talking about Catherine here could put her at risk in any way, but I felt protective nonetheless.

"Who do you know with that name?" he asked, agitated.

I glanced at Harlow and Amaya. They both looked curious. For a place that prided itself on the many choices it offered its citizens, these three weren't leaving me with much of one.

"The Collinses are my neighbors," I said. "There's Jody and—" I stopped when Topher stumbled a little and cried out like he was in pain.

"Topher!" Harlow said. He leaned against the fence to steady himself. "Isn't this good news? Isn't it nice to know your wife is alive?"

He started crying and I tried to piece together what was going on. Harlow and Amaya looked like they felt as uncomfortable as I did.

"Topher, someone in the neighborhood is bound to hear you," Harlow said. That actually seemed to help, because his crying grew quieter.

"I'm sorry," he said, barely above a whisper. "It's good to know Jody is alive, but . . . you know that social ladder I was talking about? She *plummeted* down it. She went from living in one of the nicest spots in Morley to one of the worst. And it's all my fault."

So, this was Catherine's father. She'd grown up believing he'd been executed before she was born. At times, Catherine was resentful of her dad because his rebellion is what caused her family to, like he'd said, *plummet* down the social ladder. Mostly though, she wished she could know more about him. That was something I understood well myself. Both Jody and my mom are pretty tight-lipped about the subject of our fathers.

"It can't be one of the *worst* spots if Nole and his mom live there," Harlow said. It was surreal to hear Lolo's double defend me. I only knew Lolo as the cold, distant girl pictured next to her father on signs and screens all around Morley, and I doubted she would care about the plight of my family or Catherine's.

Topher sighed. "I'm sorry; that's not what I meant. I'm sure she's met good people there, but her quality of life decreased suddenly and radically. Fewer ration cards, no car, spotty electricity . . . there was nothing Jody could do." He lifted his gaze from the grass to my face. "But you've never seen someone who looks like me before, have you? Someone who lives with Jody?"

I shook my head. "No. Jody's husband died a long time ago. She barely talks about him. Catherine was always trying to find out more, but she hasn't brought it up in a while."

"Catherine . . . ," Topher said slowly. "I have a . . . she's my . . ."

It was clear he wasn't going to be able to finish a sentence in the state he was in. I thought we'd both had a pretty huge shock today, but I'd never been one to express myself so openly. I watched him start to cry again with a helpless feeling. "I think we'll have to finish this conversation later," Harlow said, taking charge once more.

The four of us went through a small gate that led to a park. From there, Topher went one way, and I followed Harlow and Amaya back to Nolan's house. "That's it right there," Harlow said, pointing to a tall gray house. "Nolan's key should be in your jacket pocket. I'm right next door if you need anything. I'll see you tomorrow."

"10:15," I said, to show her I was keeping up. She handed me my clothes back and we said goodbye.

I crept up to the impressive house feeling like a trespasser. I found the key and opened the door. You could fit my apartment in the living room alone. I wandered around the house, gaping at every appliance and luxury item. It must be what Governor Matthias's home looked like. Did everyone in this Morley live this way?

I found Nolan's bedroom. It was much sparser and simpler than the rest of the house, and I found myself approving of my double. I lay down on the bed. It was softer than any I'd ever known, but even so, I wanted to be falling asleep at home.

~~~

"Nolan? Hey, Nolan?" a voice said.

Nolan? It's Nole, I thought sleepily. Then it all came rushing back. My eyes shot open and I sat up. A middle-aged man wearing a blue collared shirt stood in the doorway. Uncle Bailey. He did sort of look like my mom.

"Um, yeah?" I said, trying to reacclimate to this bizarre Morley.

"Trish and I are going out, but there's some lasagna in the fridge."

"Oh, um, okay," I said. "Thanks."

Bailey left me alone after that. Harlow had been right. If anything about me was off, he hadn't noticed. An engine rumbled and I went to the window to watch a silver car drive off into the night. I didn't know what lasagna was, but I was hungry enough not to care. I headed for the kitchen. When I got downstairs, a noise from a room with a half-opened door startled me. I'd thought I was alone.

"Hello?" I said.

No answer, but I heard it again, a jingling noise. Before I could panic, a small dog in a bright red collar emerged from the room. DUKE, the jingling tag read. He wagged his nub of a tail and sniffed me eagerly. I'd never owned a dog. Only the highest classes in Morley were permitted to have pets. Curious, I crouched down to the floor to pet him. If Duke could tell I wasn't Nolan, he didn't seem to care. He licked my hand and nestled against my leg. A moment later, my arms were wrapped around him and I was sobbing into his fur.
~~~

19

HARLOW

Before Amaya went home, I asked if she'd come to brunch with me and Nole. It wasn't a date anymore, and I needed her help figuring all of this out. We asked Topher to come too. His input was important.

I told my dad I was tired after the long day of hiking and wanted to go to bed early. For a minute, I thought about telling him what had happened to Nolan. But the story was too far-fetched for any person to believe on first hearing, let alone someone as rational as my dad. He'd probably worry, wondering why I suddenly sounded like a conspiracy theorist.

I tried to sleep, but I couldn't stop thinking about Nolan. He was in danger; I knew that much. But was he cold? Hungry? Terrified? I remembered how thoughts of Nolan had kept me up on the first night I met him. I'd been excited, wondering when I would see him again. Now, I wondered *if* I would see him again. Was Nolan this lonely too?

At midnight, my phone rang.

"Cate?" I answered, feeling groggy. "What's going on?"

"Sorry to bother you," she said. "I know it's late there, but my mom and I are at the airport right now. We're coming back to Morley."

I sat up, alert. "Why?"

"I finally talked to my dad, and he said that today another person got 'switched in the pond.' He kept insisting he'd ruined the lives of his *other* wife and kid. It freaked us out."

I was quiet for a moment, unsure of where to start because I realized I was going to sound just as crazy as her dad when I confirmed his story.

Cate grew impatient quickly. "Well? What happened today? Weren't you helping him search for an old ID?"

"Yes, I went into the woods with your dad, Amaya, and . . ." I couldn't say his name.

"What? What's wrong?" Cate asked.

"A lot of things are wrong," I said, straining to hold back tears, "but your dad isn't."

"What do you mean?"

I took a deep breath. "His whole story about having another life somewhere else? It's true, the other Morley exists. He really *did* switch worlds sixteen years ago."

"Look, Harlow," Cate said, "I don't know what kind of stupid joke you think you're telling—"

"I'm not joking," I said, barely believing it myself. "This is serious. Today, *Nolan*," I forced myself to say, "fell into the pond on accident, and now a boy named Nole is here in his place. I know it sounds completely ridiculous, but I swear, it's true."

"What is this?" Cate said. "Some sort of group hallucination? I don't get it."

I knew that if I were in her shoes, I wouldn't get it either. "You need to talk to Nole for yourself. Can you meet up with us tomorrow morning?"

"By then I'll probably be in a waiting room at the psych ward."

"You *can't* let your dad go there," I said. "We need his help."

"With what?" she said loudly. "Finding an imaginary ID card?"

"No!" I said, now as frustrated as Cate. "With getting Nolan back! Your dad is one of two people who knows anything about the place where Nolan's trapped."

From down the hall, I heard my dad's bedroom door squeak open.

"I've got to go," I whispered.

"Why? I'm trying to understand, but—"

"See you tomorrow." I hung up just as my dad's tall figure appeared in the doorway.

"Harlow?" he asked. "What's going on?"

"Nothing. Sorry," I said, clutching my phone under the covers.

"I think it's safe to say that *something* is going on." He turned on the lamp next to my desk. "You look upset. You sounded upset, too."

I couldn't hide that part of the truth from him. "I *am* upset," I said.

My dad sat on the edge of the bed. "Is it about Nolan?"

There was a knot tightening in my throat, so I just nodded. He'd misinterpret what this meant, but now wasn't the time to explain.

"I'm sorry, sweetheart," he said gently. "Was that him on the phone?"

I nodded again, wishing I didn't have to mislead him like this.

"Is everything okay between you?"

"No," I said as I started to cry. "I don't know how to get to him."

Dad sighed. "Sometimes guys aren't the best at communicating," he said. "I would know a lot about that. What do you say the two of us spend the day together tomorrow? I'll cancel my tee time and we can go see a movie or something."

Even though nothing he said was helping the situation, my dad's nonjudgmental support was soothing. I was tempted to leave this mess of a situation behind and escape to the predictability of an afternoon with him. But Nolan needed to be rescued more than I needed a few hours of feeling safe.

"Maybe next weekend," I said, wanting to let my dad down easily. "I think I'm going to hang out with Amaya tomorrow." At least *that* wasn't a lie.

"That sounds like a good idea too," he said, kissing me on the forehead. "Now, see if you can get some sleep in the meantime."

20

NOLAN

I woke up with a splitting headache. I tried to open my eyes, but the blindfold wrapped around my head was tied too tightly for even that. My heart started to pound. I wanted to rub my temples but found that my arms were strapped down on either side. My legs were bound too. I was lying on a hard surface, and it felt like I was wearing a thin dress, the kind people wear in hospitals, over my boxers and shirt. I had no memory of getting there. The cloth wedged in my mouth muffled my scream.

A whack on the side of the head quieted me.

"He's awake," I heard a deep voice say. Heavy boots thudded across the floor. The cloth was removed from my mouth, but quickly replaced by a gloved hand that pinched my face.

"You will speak only when spoken to. Do you understand?"

I nodded feebly and the hand moved away.

"The Governor will be in momentarily."

At the mention of the Governor, I remembered Topher's story. How it was all true, how there was another Morley, and I was trapped in it.

There was some shuffling, and I heard the same voice say, "Good evening, Governor Matthias. The prisoner is ready for questioning."

I breathed as softly as possible, as if somehow that would make me invisible.

"Remove the blindfold," said the Governor and I almost gasped. He sounded like Harlow's dad. Just gruffer, haughtier.

Once my eyes adjusted to the light, I could see that even if he looked a lot like Matt, the man sitting before me was not Harlow's dad. Everything about him was more angular, like he could cut me with the edge of one of the fingers he kept tapping against the chair's armrest.

"What were you doing in the forest, Nole Fredericks?"

Any answer I could think to give would require a long, rambling backstory. So, I said nothing.

"I have my theories," the Governor went on. "My guards found you *very* close to my wind turbine project. You wouldn't be the first saboteur to attempt damages. But I'm getting ahead of myself. I'd like to hear your story. While I'm still asking."

I knew instinctively that there was no limit to the methods this man would use to get information from me, especially if he thought I was trying to sabotage some energy project. The problem was, the information I could offer would be written off as insane. It *was* insane. Even with Matt's double in front of me, it was hard to believe what had happened, and where I was. I tried to say something that would sound plausible.

"I was on a hike," I said, realizing immediately that was the wrong answer. Not that a right answer necessarily existed in this situation.

"In a restricted area without a permit?" the Governor asked.

"I'm sorry."

The Governor jumped to his feet, tipping over his chair. It clattered loudly on the tile floor. "Sixteen years ago, there was another man who thought he could hide from me in that forest swamp."

I was certain he was talking about Topher, but I didn't have time to follow the thought further, because the Governor grabbed the collar of my hospital gown and pulled me forward as far as the straps on my arms would allow. I cried out in pain.

"Why were you at the pond?"

His snarling face was inches from mine. I shut my eyes. "Please, I'm sorry—"

"Begging will get you nowhere. At this point, the truth may not even help you." He shoved me back and I gulped down a sob rising in my throat, ashamed he'd broken me so quickly. The Governor picked up his chair and sat again. "You'll cooperate for your mother's sake, if not your own."

"My *mother?*" I said, momentarily thrown.

"Liza Fredericks, yes. She has a colorful file, doesn't she? Quite a stain this whole ordeal will leave on her already sordid reputation."

"But my mom is—" My mom was Liz, so Liza Fredericks must be her double. More than that—she was alive. For one irrational second, I actually felt excited.

"What? Innocent?" the Governor said with a sneer. "The longer it takes to bring you to justice, Nole, the more people you will condemn. Your neighbors are next."

"My neighbors?" I asked, lost again.

The Governor was back on his feet. This time, he reached for my hair. "Stop playing the fool!" he yelled, his fingernails digging into my scalp.

"Okay! Okay!" I screamed. He let go and began pacing the room.

"Explain *this* to me," he said. "A man commits a crime, cowers for his life in a forest pond, and is executed. His disgraced family is relocated. Some years later, a boy who happens to live *right next door* to that man's family is found snooping about the same pond." He quit pacing and moved closer to me. "What were you doing there?"

Everything the Governor said confirmed Topher's story, but there was no way he was going to believe anything I said about the other Morley.

I was taking too long to answer. The Governor smacked me on the side of the head, the same spot as the other man. Pain throbbed through my skull.

"I was looking for an ID card!" I didn't have enough time, or clarity, to come up with any other story than the one I knew to be the truth.

"Whose ID?"

"Topher Collins."

"Ha!" the Governor shouted. "I knew this had to do with Collins. Did his wife send you to look for it?"

"No!" I said, not wanting to incriminate anyone else. "Topher did."

"Topher? Topher Collins is dead. The Guard built a special pool just for him. I watched as he was drowned."

The cruel smile on his face made me queasy. Topher wasn't dead, though. The Governor must have watched his double die. I was too afraid to correct him.

When I didn't say anything, the Governor took a step closer to me. "I suppose it makes sense that Jody Collins wouldn't risk her daughter to get back a little memento like an ID." He lowered his voice. "But why would *you* agree to such a dangerous feat? What's in it for you, Nole Fredericks?"

"Nothing," I said, avoiding his eyes. His calmness scared me almost as much as his anger had. I just wanted him to go away. I wanted to go home.

"Well then," the Governor said. "I think it's time we let your mother know where you've been." He gave me another cruel smile. "She'll be so worried."

As dazed as I was, the threat was clear. "No, please," I said, instinctively feeling protective of my mom's double. "She hasn't done anything wrong."

"Raising a son this senseless is a crime," he said matter-of-factly. "She'll find out how serious of a crime soon enough."

"No!" I said. I couldn't bear the thought of any harm coming to Nole's mom. The Governor was nearing the door, and this might be my only chance to tell him what I knew. Convincing him would be next to impossible, but no matter how slim my chances were, it was all I had.

"Wait," I said. The Governor turned around, eyes flashing. One of the guards hit me, this time across my cheek. It had been a stupid idea. I expected the Governor to walk out, but he yelled at me to speak.

"I'm . . . I'm not Nole Fredericks."

"Your fingerprints would disagree." His face darkened. "More lies."

"No," I said, "it's not a lie. My name is *Nolan* Fredericks. I'm from Morley, but not this one."

"What?" he said, looking more confused than angry for a second. "There isn't another."

"It's not just another city," I said, surprised to have his attention, but dreading the moment he would inevitably want me to stop talking. "It's another . . . world."

He looked at me like he didn't know what to make of what I was saying.

I talked faster. "The pond where the guards found me is a portal. I fell into it in my world and traded places with Nole Fredericks. I know it sounds crazy, but it's true. We're different versions of each other, like doubles or copies."

The room was silent, then the Governor chuckled a little. The sound was unsettling. "Is this your way of admitting that you tried to leave the city-state?"

"No, the switch was accidental," I said, my voice shaking. I turned my head away from him as he walked toward me.

"Tell me, *Nolan*, why go to the trouble of spinning such a wild tale? What good can it possibly do you now?"

No good at all, I realized. He wrapped his cold fingers around my face and forced me to look at him.

"All liars will be punished," he said, "but those who tell lies about leaving Morley will be made an example of." He let go. "Who else have you spread this lie to?"

"No one!" I said, wishing I could take it back. I'd only made things worse.

"Your mother, certainly," he said. "I think you're due for a family reunion. Does the pond sound like an ideal setting? I want to know why you find it so intriguing."

The Governor left the room while the guards blindfolded and gagged me again.

What had I done? Liza Fredericks was in serious danger because of me. I didn't want to imagine what the Governor would do to her. Or me, for that matter. Unless . . . I thought about Harlow. If it *was* possible for someone to switch back with their double, Nole should already have returned. Harlow would've known that he wasn't me. Why hadn't she insisted that Nole jump back into the pond to bring me home? The notion that I would likely die here, alone in a strange world, gripped me tighter than any shackles ever could.

∼∽∼

There was no way to tell how much time was passing. At some point, when rough hands finally untied me, I was relieved as well as terrified. Two guards dragged me, achy and sore, hands cuffed behind my back, down a long series of hallways.

A door opened and we moved outside. I was picked up off the ground and loaded into a helicopter again. Maybe they were going to throw me to my death. I felt strangely hollow, like my insides had been scooped out. If the guards did push me out, I might not be heavy enough to hit the ground.

They had other ideas though. The helicopter landed and the guards grabbed my arms. They marched me, barefoot, across dirt and pine needles. Finally, we came to a stop. My eyes and mouth were freed.

The water was so still that, at first, it was hard to see the pond in the darkness. People were weaving through the trees in the distance, a few of them carrying lanterns. They got closer, and I saw my mom. Neat blonde hair framed her round face. It was how she'd been before the summer, when she'd started to look ragged. I reminded myself that this woman wasn't really my mom, but it was disturbing to see someone who looked so much like her be roughly handled by two guards.

"Nole!" I heard her familiar voice cry out. One of the guards hit her face and she went quiet.

"You are not permitted to speak," the Governor said in a formal tone. Then, he made a waving motion with his hand. "Lolo, come here."

I gasped when Harlow—no, her double—emerged from behind his back. The guard on my right kicked me in the back of the knee and I fell to the ground.

"Oh, no need to genuflect," the Governor said. "Lolo is your superior, but not yet your governor. If I do my job right, you'll *both* learn a lesson here tonight."

The guards set me back on my feet and I got a good look at Harlow's double. *Lolo.* Their likeness was insane, but even in the dim moonlight, I could see they weren't perfectly identical. Aside from the fact that I had never seen Harlow dressed in all black or wear such a tight braid, this girl seemed frailer somehow. A ghost version of Harlow. She returned my gaze blankly.

"Observe carefully, Lolo," the Governor said. Then, he stepped closer to Nole's mom. "Ms. Fredericks, is this your son, Nole Fredericks?"

She looked at me. "Yes," she said, but I saw a flicker of confusion pass across her face, and I just knew she could tell something was off about me.

"Interesting," the Governor said. "This boy claims that he *isn't* your son. He seems to think your son is in another world entirely."

"Another *world*?"

I regretted ever mentioning the portal. I'd only given the Governor more reason to toy with us before whatever punishment was coming.

"You seem surprised. Has your son been keeping secrets from you?"

She was fighting back tears and didn't answer.

The Governor approached me. "I suppose we'll have to test your theory about the pond's secret powers, won't we?"

For a second, I felt hopeful. If he threw me back into the pond, maybe I'd go home.

"I'm sure," he said with a glint in his eye, "your mother would be happy to help." He tilted his head toward the pond and the two guards dragged Liza to the water.

"No, please!" she screamed. "*Please!*"

My stomach flipped when I realized I might be about to watch her drown, for who was there for Liza to trade places with? "She doesn't know about any of this!" I said, my fear of being hit forgotten momentarily.

"Nole," the Governor said, ignoring me, "according to the information you provided, your mother should disappear into the water and a living copy will take her place. I'll have so many questions for this new person."

The guards pushed Liza underwater. After a few seconds, they let her go and she came up gasping for air, only to be pushed down again.

"Enough," the Governor called out to them. "Bring her back to shore."

The guards obeyed. Liza's breathing was loud and labored as they stood her back on her feet. I was breathing almost as hard.

"Welcome to Morley," the Governor said theatrically. "My name is Governor Matthias. And who have we here?"

"Liza Fredericks," she said, coughing and crying all at once.

"Where do you live?"

"1900 Terence Street, number 23."

"And with whom do you live?"

"My son, Nole Fredericks."

The Governor shook his head, and his voice grew quieter. "It is evident that your son is a liar, Liza Fredericks."

"No," I said frantically. He might be about to kill her. I'd watched my mom die once; I couldn't do it again. "I'm not lying. My mom is dead in the other world. I think that's why she's still here. A person has to have a double who's alive." It was still only a guess, but I was quickly running out of time.

"Convenient, isn't that?" the Governor shot back.

"Test the theory on me," I said. "Throw me into the pond and see what happens." I tried not to think about how horribly guilty I'd feel about condemning Nole to this fate if the switch worked.

"We saw what happens when someone goes into the pond. Would you like your mother to show us again? Perhaps for the final time?"

"No, please!" I said, glancing nervously at Liza. I tried to think of anything that might take the Governor's attention off her. "I know Topher!" I said. "I've met him in my world."

"We've been through this," the Governor said. "Collins was killed years ago."

"You must have killed his double!" I said, desperation making me bold. "Topher came to my world through the pond and has been living there ever since."

The Governor looked exasperated, then he laughed. He turned to Lolo, as if wanting her to share in the joke, but her face remained stony.

"Nole," he said, facing me again, "this is the most elaborate lie I've ever encountered. Just so I understand, I didn't kill Topher sixteen years ago. I killed a man who happened to look *exactly* like him?"

He was only messing with me, and clearly enjoying it, but I answered him seriously. "Yes. And I think that's why Topher wasn't able to get back here. He had no one to switch with because his double was dead."

"But, if I was to send *you* into the pond, you would end up back in your world. Are you in such a hurry to leave?"

I'd never wanted to leave any place more, but I didn't actually know what the other rules of the portal were. I could be trapped regardless of Nole's being alive. "I don't know," I said. "I'm not sure if it would work. It might be that the same person can't be switched more than once."

"Another *fascinating* wrinkle," he said.

"Test it on me," I said. I had nothing to lose.

"Are you telling me what to do?" At once, he was angry again.

"No," I said, but he wasn't listening.

"If you want to see your theory tested, then we'll need to arrange for some new subjects. In fact, I'll send for the Collins family right now. Let's keep the pond experiment going."

"Sir, may I please—"

It was Lolo. She had taken a few cautious steps toward her dad. Suddenly, he was gripping her chin in his hand, as roughly as he'd grabbed me, a prisoner. "Did you just interrupt me?"

"Sir, I'm sorry, I—"

He squeezed tighter. I winced. It was hard to watch him be so harsh with his own daughter, especially because I kept seeing Matt and Harlow. "Quit groveling. What were you going to say?"

Lolo spoke quickly. "Just that, well, it's late and I would like permission to return—"

"You're *tired*? I bring you out here to teach you an invaluable lesson, but you'd rather nap?"

Tonight was the most terrified I'd ever been in my life, and it was strange to think that Lolo could watch everything happen with such disinterest. It made me wonder what else she'd witnessed growing up with Governor Matthias. Maybe nothing fazed her anymore, but the way Lolo was furiously shaking her head made it seem like she was very much afraid of her father's wrath now that it was directed at her.

"I'm sorry, sir," she said. "It was wrong of me."

"You *were* wrong." The Governor was fuming. "And wrongdoings must be punished."

In one fluid motion, he had her at the edge of the pond. Lolo was wriggling in his arms, but with each passing second, she lost some of her fight, like she sensed it was a battle she would lose because she'd lost it before. I started to feel bad for her, but then it dawned on me what could happen if Lolo entered the water. *Harlow. No.*

"Sir, please," she whimpered. "I'm not a strong swimmer."

I watched in dismay as the Governor lifted Lolo's feet out of the mud and sent her flying into the pond. She landed in fairly shallow water, but her entire body disappeared.

My heart leapt into my throat.

In the quiet that followed the splash, the Governor stood at the pond's edge, his shoulders heaving. Then a head popped out of the water. From a distance, it was hard to see its features clearly. I maintained a sliver of hope that it was Lolo.

"All right, you've learned your lesson," the Governor said. "Now get out of the water." When the person didn't move, he charged in and dragged her to the shore. He let go abruptly when more of the girl's body was visible. We all saw that she was wearing flannel pajamas.

"No, no, no," I began whispering. The guards tightened their grip on my arm.

Harlow must have been in bed a moment before, but she understood where she was now. She looked up at the Governor, her mouth opened in terror.

I wanted her to know she wasn't alone. "Harlow!" I yelled.

There was just enough light from the lanterns for our eyes to meet. "Nolan!"

She started to run, but the Governor grabbed her wrist and pulled her back. "You're not going anywhere."

21

HARLOW

I was sleeping fitfully, worrying about Nolan. Then, suddenly, I was underwater. The water was dark and frigid, and there was a high-pitched ringing in my ears. It was far too vivid to be a dream. I knew where I was before I even lifted my head above the surface. I was in the pond, and this was the other world.

I heard a man speaking. His voice, though fierce, sounded like my dad's. Before I could decide what to do, he charged forward and pulled me out of the water. The man—the Governor—was a harsher, older version of my dad. His chestnut-colored hair was thinning, and a vein bulged in his taut forehead. I stared at him, feeling shock and revulsion. Just then, I heard someone call my name. Nolan.

Relieved I wasn't alone, I shouted his name and began running. A hand latched on to my wrist and snatched me back. "You're not going anywhere," the Governor said.

I tried to twist free, but I was instantly surrounded by two men in brown uniforms. "Please let us go," I said, shaking I was so scared. My arms were pinned behind me and next I felt the cold metal of handcuffs. "I haven't done anything! Please, I—"

I was shoved onto my knees. As I steadied myself in the mud, Nolan said, "Please, stop! Let her go!"

One of the guards holding Nolan hit him across the face.

"No!" I screamed, and mine wasn't the only voice to cry out. I noticed a woman being held by another set of guards. "Nole, cooperate with them!" she said. She must be Nole's mother, but she didn't understand what was truly going on here.

"He will, Ms. Fredericks," the Governor said. He stared down at me. "You all will." I looked away, at a loss as to what I should do.

"Wait, sir," Nolan said. "What about your daughter?" I was surprised that Nolan had spoken up. This was the one time when I actually wished he'd stay quiet, for his own good.

"I'm sure this imposter will be quick to tell us what she knows," the Governor said. "Back at the manor, that is. We're leaving."

And then, I did leave. But not in the way he meant.

In a brief flash, I was no longer kneeling in the mud but twisting and turning underwater.

The handcuffs restricted my movement and in small, awkward hops, I made my way out of the water and collapsed onto the shore. I glanced around the woods for Nolan, but, of course, he wasn't there. I had traveled back to my Morley, abandoning him once again. There was only one possible explanation: Lolo.

22

LOLO

learned at a young age not to sympathize with the plight of the lower classes. They were rebels and radicals, or descendants of rebels and radicals, whose lot in life was deserved. Justice must be carried out, and in Morley, justice took whatever form the Governor deemed prudent.

My father ruled his personal household much like he ruled the city-state. There was always a mystery when it came to the consequences I could incur by disobeying him, and this kept me in line. At sixteen, I rarely questioned his authority.

But this technique of his, which he inherited from his father and grandfather before him, carried a risk of its own, one he probably wasn't aware of as an undisputed male heir: the possibility of my solidarity with others who felt unjustly punished. As a child, I often felt like I was in trouble when I shouldn't have been, and I wondered if the powerless citizens of Morley could relate. I fantasized about escaping into the city-state and meeting regular people who would conspire to overthrow the Governor. Not that such a resistance movement has ever existed. I once mentioned this idea to my mother, the one person who was openly disdainful toward my father. She smirked. "You don't need to overthrow him, Lolo. Simply outlive him." I followed her advice and tried to become more patient. Instead, I became more apathetic. Behaving the way my father wanted me to meant I didn't have to be as afraid of him. Life was easy when I played by the rules, so I did.

I wasn't planning on doing anything differently on the night he brought me to the pond.

Lately, my father had been making more of an effort to prepare me for my future duties as governor. Protecting the city-state was the most important. "That you must do above all else," he told me frequently. Sometimes I thought maybe *he* was the biggest threat to the citizens' safety, but I never said so. My father seemed to believe that everything he did was ultimately for their good. Tonight, he wanted to teach me a lesson about interrogations, and thus my presence was required at some little pond behind our house. I really didn't want to go. I had few opportunities to interact with the citizens of Morley, but the interrogations were always the same: The prisoner begged for mercy and my father didn't listen. I usually felt sick after watching an interrogation or execution, but I did my best to hide that from my father. He didn't like it when I went "soft."

When I arrived at the pond in the middle of the night, I could tell right away that this would not be any routine questioning. Though he had a flair for the dramatic, my father was not one to waste time on trivial issues. Whatever this boy and his mother had done, it was bothering him greatly. We were close to my father's wind turbine project, and I wondered if that was somehow connected. Lately, as blackouts lasted longer and became more frequent, he'd grown obsessed with finding a new energy source. He said reducing our dependency on trade with other city-states was a key part of protecting Morley.

As my father taunted the two prisoners by the pond, I listened closely, intrigued by the absurd conversation. I stole several glances at the water that was apparently keeping so many secrets. It was an impressive thing to do in Morley.

I flinched when the woman was dunked in the pond. Her mournful cries scared me, but my father was unaffected. I tried to look just as bored as him.

Most people who were arrested learned quickly that they shouldn't lie to my father. Unless, of course, they were telling a lie he wanted to hear, one that would likely incriminate someone else. The boy's story couldn't be true, but the fact that he held to it so tightly made me wonder if, at least, *he* believed it was. His mother's life, not to mention his own, was in serious jeopardy.

As the night wore on, I began to think of ways I could get out of having to watch any more of the interrogation. Something about it was troubling me more than the others I'd seen. Aside from the strange location, it was unusual for my father to question a citizen who looked like he was about my age. Most kids weren't brave enough, or foolish enough, to do something that would bring them face-to-face with the Governor. As far as I could tell, that fear of my father was about all I shared with the other kids of Morley. If I asked him for permission to leave, I didn't think he would immediately lash out at me. As a general rule, he didn't discipline me in front of citizens, or even guards. It wasn't good for optics, he said. I figured I would get into trouble with my father later, but even that was better than staying at the pond to watch this boy and his mom die. I was toying with the idea of leaving when my father mentioned arresting another family. Watching them all drown in the pond was more than I was prepared to see. I couldn't stop it from happening, but I didn't want to be a witness. I crept toward my father and spoke up.

A few words were all it took to redirect his fury. Immediately I began backtracking, but it was for naught. His hand was so tight on my face that I thought he might break my jaw. I wished I'd had the good sense to keep quiet like my mother always instructed me. When he lifted me up, I thought he was going to push me into the arms of one of his guards to be dealt with later. So, I was surprised to find myself at the edge of the pond. At first, I put up a struggle, but my father was strong, and I knew it was futile.

"Sir, please," I said, hating my puny voice. I would never doubt the extreme measures he'd take to prove a point again. He tossed me forward.

Once under the water, I waited before pushing myself back to the surface because I didn't want to look at my father's face. I didn't want to look at the prisoners' faces, either. More than anything, I felt embarrassed.

Soon, though, I needed air. When I resurfaced, no one was there. I turned around, thinking at first that my father and the prisoners and guards were standing behind me. They weren't there either.

I felt goosebumps run across my arms.

"Hello?" I called out. "Is anyone there?"

I stayed in the pond for a moment, unable to fathom what was happening to me. Then, I remembered the boy's outlandish story. I couldn't bring myself to believe it right away, despite the evidence. As I waded out of the pond and wrung out my braid, I noticed the mud was missing the many fresh footprints that should have been there. *Maybe the "lesson" I'm meant to be learning isn't over*, I thought, desperate for it to be true. *Maybe everyone is hidden behind the trees.* But I was slowly accepting that this was too elaborate to be a setup. I was in the other world.

I peered up at the trees and into the dark sky. From this particular spot, this new world looked more or less the same. I was tempted to explore, but if I didn't figure out how to get back quickly, my father might think I had tried to escape. That would make me the worst of criminals in his eyes.

My only chance to return home was the pond. I stepped back into the cold water, my heart beating faster as the reality of my situation sank in. *Please, please work.* I closed my eyes, held my breath, and plunged underwater.

An instant later, I came back up. I didn't dare open my eyes for fear of what I might see.

"Lolo? Lolo!" My father seized my arms and pulled me out of the pond. I cried because it hurt and because I was so relieved to be back.

"Where were you? What happened?" His tone was demanding and impatient.

"The other world," I said. "It's real. I was there."

"What did it look like?"

"It looked a lot like this," I said, realizing that his concern was only about the other world, and not my well-being. "There was a pond and trees. That's all I saw."

"And you came back through the pond?" he asked.

I was shocked at how readily he believed me, but then I recalled what the boy had said about everyone having a "double." My father must've seen my double, whoever she was.

"Yes," I said. "I got out of the water for just a minute, then I jumped back in." I craned my neck to glimpse the boy. He was still in the grip of the guards, staring ahead at the pond with wide eyes.

"Incredible," my father said, just above a whisper. "It seems you *can* travel both ways." He turned to the prisoners. "You'll be coming back to the manor with us. I've got *special* accommodations prepared." The ice in his voice made me shiver. I didn't want to know what awaited them inside. I would be keeping my head down even more than normal. Most likely, this unfolding situation with the pond would distract my father for a long time, and I would be able to think things through alone, like I usually did.

23

NOLE

I woke up in a strange bed. It took me a minute to remember where I was, and another minute to convince myself that yesterday had actually happened. Somehow, this was all real.

Nolan's phone—which was, oddly, also a clock—told me it was 10:02. Harlow was expecting me at 10:15. I didn't want to worry her by being late, so I forced myself out of bed to get dressed. I found more China clothes in Nolan's closet. They fit perfectly.

When I opened the bedroom door, I could hear voices and the clinking of dishes coming from downstairs. Too bad—I'd been hoping to avoid the aunt and uncle. I found Uncle Bailey and a woman who must be Aunt Trish sitting at a glass table. Even though the sun coming in from the kitchen window was plenty bright, the room was lit by several lamps and a hanging light decorated with crystals. The wastefulness irritated me.

"Just getting up?" Bailey asked.

"Yes, um, I was tired." I almost pulled my hood over my head but stopped myself. That would only draw more attention to my short hair.

"Teenagers are *always* tired," he said, laughing at his own observation. "Anyway, do you want breakfast?"

"No, thank you," I said quickly. "I'm meeting Harlow now."

"See you later, then," Bailey said with a little wave.

"See you." I practically ran out of the house.

When I got to Harlow's door, I knocked a few times and stepped back to wait. She didn't answer, and after a few minutes I tried again. Still nothing. I checked the time. It was 10:20. I wondered if she'd left without me, but that didn't seem likely. She needed me to be there.

I thought about calling Topher for help, but the shiny, flat phone intimidated me too much. When it rang fifteen minutes later, Amaya's name lighting up the screen, it took me some fumbling to figure out how to answer it. When I finally did, her voice on the other end sounded worried.

"Nole? Oh good; I'm glad you answered. Where are you? Where's Harlow?"

"I don't know. I'm at Harlow's house but I don't think she's here."

"What? Are you sure you went to the right house?"

"Yes," I said. I'd done at least that much right. "I've been waiting for twenty minutes or so."

"Okay, that's really weird," Amaya said. "Harlow's not answering her phone either." There was some noise in the background, and I heard a muffled, "She's not with Nole. I don't know what's going on." Then, back to me again: "Okay, stay there. Topher and I will be there soon."

She hung up and I sat down on the front step, suddenly exhausted. I was close to falling asleep when Amaya shook me awake. Her eyelids were blue today.

"Nap time's over," she said. "We've got to find Harlow."

Behind Amaya was Topher and—

"Catherine!" I said, jumping to my feet before I remembered, a second too late.

"Um, it's Cate," the girl said.

"Cate, this is Nole," Topher said. "Remember, I told you? He knows your double, Catherine, from the other Morley."

Cate looked a little dazed. "You've told me a *lot* of things."

Cate had Catherine's warm brown skin and tightly curled hair. The most noticeable difference between them was that Cate wore glasses. Catherine had worn glasses when we were younger, but she grew out of the one pair she had and had been waiting for years for her new prescription. "It's okay; it's not like I'm going blind," she would say, trying to be positive. It was either that, or fret about something she could do nothing to change.

"We need to get inside Harlow's house," Amaya said. "I know the door code."

"You're sure no one's home?" Topher asked. "This is the mayor's house, after all."

"He usually goes golfing on Sunday mornings. Trust me, he's not here."

Amaya unlocked the door and walked into the house calling Harlow's name. Topher, Cate, and I waited outside.

"So," Cate said, turning to me. "You're not . . . from here."

"Um, no, not exactly," I said. "I'm from another Morley. It's very different."

"But you recognize me?" She looked at me skeptically. Even though I knew this wasn't Catherine, it still sort of hurt that her double had no idea who I was.

"Yeah, Catherine and I have lived next door to each other my whole life."

"That means Catherine doesn't live in Scottsdale?"

"No," I said, confused. "I've never heard of that. Is it another city-state?"

"Cate," Topher said, "in Nole's Morley, traveling is highly restricted. Communication outside its borders has to be approved by the Governor. Usually it's for trade, like negotiating oil imports from other city-states. Who's to say if Scottsdale even exists in the other world?"

I noticed he'd said "Nole's Morley" instead of "my Morley," and I wondered how long it took for this Morley to feel as real to him as his first home. I didn't think I could ever get used to this world. Although, based on the way he'd broken down yesterday when he'd learned about his family, it seemed like Topher hadn't *fully* adjusted to life here either. Maybe he didn't want his daughter to know that.

A moment later, Amaya came running back outside. "Harlow's not here," she said, without stopping. "Her phone is upstairs, but there's no sign of her."

"Amaya, wait," Topher said. He chased after her, Cate and I following right behind.

Amaya opened a gate on the side of the house and led us into the back-yard. Her panic was quickly rubbing off on me, even though I didn't know exactly what it was about.

"I think Harlow's gone into the woods," Amaya said. "She's probably going to get Nolan."

She looked at me a little sadly then. If what she said was true, I wished I could have gone with Harlow. Even though Topher seemed to believe I couldn't go home through the pond, I thought I should at least give it a try. I didn't want to steal Nolan's life any more than Harlow wanted me to. I'd only spared a few thoughts for Nolan, but all at once I pictured what might be happening to him in my Morley. Most likely, he'd been arrested. If I traded places with him, *I'd* be the one in trouble. I wasn't sure which was worse, facing the Governor or facing life in this confusing world.

"Maybe we can stop her," Topher said. "Depending on what time she left, we could catch up."

"Then let's go," Amaya said. She led us through another gate and down to the woods. I kept a few paces behind the others, feeling more out of place than ever. I didn't tell them I was thinking about jumping into the pond. Topher might try to talk me out of it, but I was eager to find a way home, despite whatever awaited me there.

<p style="text-align:center">~~~~</p>

About fifteen minutes into the walk, Amaya screamed, "Oh my god, Harlow!"

We weren't anywhere near the pond, and I was considering going on by myself. However, I abandoned the idea when I saw Amaya with her arms around Harlow, who was crying into her shoulder.

"What happened? What's going on?" Amaya asked, stepping back to take a look at her. "What the . . ." Her voice drifted away, and I came closer to see what the matter was.

Harlow was handcuffed.

And that wasn't the only thing strange about her appearance. She was wearing pajamas. If she'd planned to rescue Nolan, pajamas were an odd choice. Her long hair was damp, and her feet were bare. Without thinking, I pulled off my jacket and handed it to Amaya, who draped it around Harlow's quivering shoulders.

"Did the Governor do this?" Topher asked, placing his own jacket around her.

"Yes," she said, "and he's got Nolan. They were at the pond. There were guards everywhere and one of them hit Nolan—" Her voice grew higher and harder to understand with each word. Now that I knew exactly what my fate would be if I returned, the resolve I'd felt earlier began to fade.

"Harlow," said Amaya, "why did you go there by yourself?"

"I didn't. I fell asleep, and the next thing I knew I was in the pond." For the first time, she looked at me. I figured she was thinking about Nolan, but she said, "It's like what happened to you yesterday, right, Nole?"

"Yes," I said, surprised at how good it felt to have someone else understand what traveling through the pond was like. "I've never felt so disoriented in my life."

"*Exactly*," Harlow said, like I'd described it perfectly. "This must have been Lolo's doing. She's the one who initiated the switch both times. The Governor was actually about to take me away when I was suddenly back here."

"How long were you in the other Morley?" Topher asked.

"It was probably only a few minutes, but it *felt* like a long time."

Topher nodded. I did too. It felt like I'd been in this world for much longer than one day. "It was dark when I got back," Harlow said, "and I didn't want to walk through the woods alone until the sun came up." She gasped. "Wait, does my dad know I was gone?"

"No," Amaya said. "He wasn't at your house."

"Okay, good. But we should hurry."

"It might be time to let your dad know what's going on," Topher said.

Harlow looked conflicted. "I do want to tell him, but not while I look like this." She moved her arms. "He'd freak out."

"And he'd be right to," Topher said. "We need to get you home."

Home. The four of them began walking, but I stayed put to think. By traveling to my Morley and back again, Harlow had proven it was possible to cross between the worlds more than once. Since Governor Matthias's own daughter had traveled here, he would *have* to believe my story about being switched. As long as he gave me the chance to talk, there was a possibility I could explain the misunderstanding and go home to my mom.

"Nole?" Harlow asked when she realized I wasn't following. "C'mon, let's go."

"Um, no, I can't," I said. The four of them turned to look at me.

"You *can't*?" Amaya said. "Why not?"

Topher's eyes flared. "No, Nole, you can't go back." He was next to me in an instant, his hand on my shoulder. "It's too dangerous."

Of course it was dangerous, but I wasn't going to let that stop me from at least trying to get home. "Is that the reason you didn't go back to your family?" I asked, shaking him off. "You were too afraid?"

"Listen," he said. "I did try to get back to my family. But I—" He threw a nervous glance at Cate. "I must have been too late. I think the Governor had already killed my double."

I saw Cate's eyebrows go up, but she didn't say anything.

"Okay," I said, trying to remember the point I'd been about to make, "but if Nolan is alive, then it's possible for me to switch with him. I'll be fine. I can tell Governor Matthias what happened to me. He'll appreciate my honesty."

Even I knew this sounded idealistic, and Topher certainly wasn't buying it. "He is *not* an understanding person, Nole. Trust me. We shouldn't send you back."

"Well, why not?" Harlow asked, approaching us. "If Nole is willing to go, then Nolan would be free." She looked at me, and her face softened. "Sorry, Nole, I don't mean to sound insensitive. Really, I hate to think that you might return to a bad situation."

"I know," I said quietly. I didn't blame her for wanting Nolan back. I had people I wanted to be reunited with just as badly. "I have nothing to hide from the Governor."

"*That's* where you're wrong," Topher said. "Nole, why do you think travel is prohibited for Morley citizens?"

"For safety and security," I said, reciting the words I'd known since early childhood.

"For the *Governor's* safety and security," Topher said. "Not yours. He doesn't want people leaving and finding out there are other, better ways to live. If you go back and admit you've seen the world beyond Morley, that will make you a serious threat. I don't see Governor Matthias ever letting you go free."

Topher was probably right, but I'm not sure how truly free I'd ever feel in this world either. Especially since I had no way of knowing what was happening to my mom.

"So, we let Nolan remain stuck there instead?" Harlow asked. "How is that fair?"

Topher put his hands on his hips and stared at the ground. "If Nolan comes back here, there's no doubt that the Governor would treat him as an escaped criminal and do anything to find him. The Governor's got no short-age of loyal men, *lethal* men, who would volunteer for the task of switching worlds and tracking Nolan down."

"But couldn't he do the same thing with Nole?" Harlow asked. "Send guards here after him?"

"Well . . . yes, actually," Topher said. "And our timeline could be rather short."

I felt breathless, like that timeline was coiling itself around my neck. I hadn't even considered that possibility.

"But what if we have something the Governor wants?" The sudden sound of Cate's voice, so much like Catherine's, startled me.

"What do you think the Governor wants, Cate?" Topher said with curiosity.

She hesitated for a second. "A photo of himself, maybe? Holding a very unhappy baby."

I didn't understand what a photo had to do with any of this, but Topher sucked in his breath so fast he almost started choking. "The photo of the Governor?" he managed to say. "You found it?"

I wanted to know what he was talking about, but I was also annoyed that we'd gotten off topic. If I couldn't convince them that my going through the pond was a good idea, I might have to go out on my own after all. Maybe I'd regret it the second I landed back in Morley and was at the mercy of the Governor, but that was a chance I'd have to take. It was better than waiting to be hunted by the Guard.

"Yeah, Mom and I found it in Grandma's basement this morning," Cate said. "We were going through some old stuff that she said was yours before you moved. There was an envelope that said, 'Governor Matthias and Lolo,' and the photo was inside."

"Why didn't you tell me?"

Cate shrugged. "Mom said not to. Does it change anything?"

Topher thought for a minute. "It might."

"How?" Harlow asked.

"C'mon," he said. "We can talk on the way." He started down the path in a hurry. I sighed and followed along. If Cate had stumbled upon something that could help me, it might be worth finding out about it before leaving this Morley.

"Nole," Topher said, "you'd have to swear to the Governor that you won't tell anyone else about the existence of the portal. If you return with my illegal photo—"

"Wait," I said, trying to keep up. "You have an *illegal* photo of the Governor?" Maybe Topher was braver than I'd thought

"Yes," he said. "It's what got me into trouble sixteen years ago."

"Then how would it help me now?"

"You could show it to the Governor and tell him that even though I tried to convince you to stay here, you came back because you didn't *want* to live anywhere but his Morley. Yes, your journey began as an accident, but if you play it right, it could end up sounding like you took the opportunity to retrieve some long-lost contraband."

I felt overwhelmed listening to Topher, but it made me realize how naive my plan of just showing up and asking for forgiveness had been. I needed to have my story ready, and if an old photo could provide me and my mom with a least some small assurance of safety, I wanted to have it with me.

"I'll do it," I said.

"You really think Nole would be safe?" Harlow asked.

"Yes," Topher said. Then added, "Possibly."

"When do we go back to the pond?" Harlow asked. "Maybe this afternoon?" That sounded good to me. The sooner the better.

"No," Amaya said. "I can't this afternoon. I have to babysit my sister, and my mom will never let me get out of it. *Please* don't go without me."

"Cate and I need to be getting back to our family too," Topher said. "I owe it to Jojo to explain what's going on, and that's not going to be a quick conversation."

"Fine," Harlow said, "then what about tomorrow morning?"

"Don't you have school?" asked Topher.

"I can miss one day." Harlow shrugged.

"That's a big deal, coming from her," said Amaya. "You know this is important."

One more night here; I could manage that. And I was curious to see Topher's photo. The only ones I'd seen of the Governor and Lolo made them look serious and imposing. It was easy to forget they were real people.

We formed a plan. Harlow told me I should meet her at her house at 7:45. "And this time when you knock on my door," she said, "I'll be there."

We would drive to her school to pick up Amaya, then meet up with Topher and Cate at the park gate at nine. After a few hours of walking, they'd have Nolan back and I'd be home.

24

TOPHER

Once Cate and I said goodbye to the others, I couldn't get us back to my mom's house fast enough. I needed to lay eyes on the photo.

I had the car running before Cate even opened her door. As she got settled, I asked her what Jojo had done with the photo.

"I think it's still in the basement," she said. "But what about all those other old photos down there? They're not really you? Mom was married to someone else? My . . . dad?"

"*I'm* your dad," I said, a little hurt. This was exactly what Jojo and I had been trying to avoid. Last night on the phone, I'd caved and told Cate the story we'd promised never to tell. Jojo tried to pass it off as my faulty memory acting up. But I'd been determined to convince Cate, which is why I'd brought her with me this morning. Now that she believed me about the other Morley, I'd probably be answering her questions for years to make up for lost time.

"Yeah, Dad, I know you are," she said.

I nodded, relieved she wasn't following that thought any further.

"But you were never going to tell me?"

"No," I said. "Your mom and I wanted your life to be as normal as possible, so we decided to keep everything about Morley in the past. Besides, would you have believed me if I'd told you I'm from another world? And, that a forest pond is the portal?"

"I guess not," she said.

The car was quiet for a moment, and I imagined a life in which I didn't have to hide the truth from my daughter. "I understand how hard this is to accept," I said, "but I'm glad you know. And there's so much more I can tell you—"

"Dad," Cate interrupted, "what if we just let it go? Maybe that would be best."

"What?" I said, a bit surprised.

"Yeah. I mean, what difference does it make? You're not going back to the other Morley."

"That's true," I said, but now that we were talking about it, I didn't want to stop. "This isn't just about me anymore, though. Don't you want to help Harlow and Nole?"

Cate exhaled sharply. "Yeah, I guess, but is that really what this is about for you? Helping some random kids?"

"I wouldn't say they are *random* kids at this point, but—"

"Am I a random kid to you, then? You'd rather have my double as your daughter?" Her voice wavered as she spoke, and my heart broke a little. The photo could wait. I pulled the car over.

"No," I said, taking her hands in mine. "You're my daughter and I love *you*."

She closed her eyes and tears trickled down her scrunched-up face.

"Cate, I'm sorry for anything I said to make you doubt that. You aren't interchangeable with anybody."

"Maybe you love me like your own daughter," Cate said, "but can you honestly say the same for Mom? How much do you think about your other wife?"

When Jojo and I left Morley, she'd told me I needed to focus on living in the present. Now, sixteen years later, my daughter was asking me to do the same thing. It felt like a challenge I might never live up to, a lesson I'd never learn. "I do think about her, sometimes," I said, not wanting to lie. "But I love your mom."

Cate wiped the fog from her glasses. "Okay," she said. "But Dad, what if when Nole gives your photo to the Governor, he decides to come after you?"

"What?" I said, worried that Cate's thoughts were taking her to such dark places. Then I remembered I'd been the one to suggest the Governor might send someone into our world to kill Nolan because he takes escaped criminals so seriously. I tried to find some way to reassure Cate. "We'll be safe as can be in Scottsdale. *If* the Governor sends a guard through the portal, he'd be utterly lost."

She nodded slowly and I restarted the car.

"What will we say to Mom?" Cate asked.

I liked that she said *we*. This was our shared story now, and both of us had a say in how it was told.

"Let me check in with her first," I said, "but then all three of us will talk. There shouldn't be secrets between us. Does that sound okay?"

"Yeah, it does," Cate said.

When Cate and I got back to my mom's house, Jojo was still in the basement sorting through old documents.

"Jojo," I said from halfway down the stairs, "we need to talk."

She reshelved a couple of folders and sighed. "I was going to say the same to you. It's about the . . . photo."

"I know," I said, stepping all the way into the room. "Cate told me you found it."

"And how did you explain it?" Jojo asked.

"Please," I said, gesturing to the faded yellow couch. "Let's sit."

Jojo closed her eyes for a few seconds, then stooped to pick up an envelope. I recognized it immediately.

"Did you know that photo was here the whole time?" I asked. "Did you hide it from me on purpose?"

She carefully brushed away a bit of dust from the envelope. "Yes," she said. "I hid it down here before we moved. I thought about throwing it away, but I couldn't bring myself to." Her brown eyes were brimming with tears. "It was all the proof we had that your world existed. The world where Chris went."

Slowly, Jojo walked to the couch, and we sat together.

"It's okay," I said, draping my arm around her. "I understand." It was a relief to remember just how much Jojo and I had in common.

After a few minutes, she said, "I want to hear exactly what's been happening over the past few weeks. Will you tell me?"

"Yes," I said. "But Cate should be here too."

Once Cate joined us on the couch, I started with my arrival in Morley and how watching my dad pass away triggered a memory of my other father. "The longer I was here," I said, "the more scrambled my memories became. And yet, the more vivid they became, too." I told Jojo about my searches at the pond, and how Cate and I had met a few local kids who were now mixed up in this madness.

"Chris," Jojo said seriously, "you *have* to help them get home."

"Yeah," Cate said. "I still want to help Harlow and Nole tomorrow."

"We will," I said. "We'll take the photo with us to the pond. "

"Do you think you'll be okay at the pond?" Cate asked. "You *really* won't want to stay and keep looking for your ID?"

"No, I'll be fine," I said, even though I wasn't sure that was true.

Cate must have sensed my hesitation. "Dad, maybe we shouldn't go with them."

I relented quickly. "Okay. We'll pass on the photo in the morning, but we won't go to the pond." I wanted to make sure Nole got back to his Morley and be there to help Nolan, but I wanted to leave with my family intact even more. We booked a flight home for Tuesday night.

25

NOLAN

When I was blindfolded and loaded back into the helicopter, I didn't put up a fight. Harlow had gotten away, but it wasn't any thanks to me. I hated feeling so helpless.

Now that she knew I was a prisoner, I wondered if Harlow was going to make sure Nole and I were switched. Maybe, I thought, as doubt snuck in, Nole was the better version of me. The idea that Harlow might not try to bring me home stung, even though I told myself it was stupid.

The guards chained me to a metal chair. I was offered a few sips of water, but no food. I waited a long time before someone tore the blindfold from my eyes. Governor Matthias again.

"Good morning, Nolan," he said, his tone strangely relaxed. He sat down across from me. I think more than anything, it was this guy's unpredictability that made me so afraid of him. Right now, he seemed at ease, but I'd watched him throw his own daughter into the pond without flinching. Even if he hadn't understood that he was going to switch her with someone else, it was still a shockingly cruel act.

"Tell me about the girl who appeared here when Lolo went into the pond," the Governor said.

"What?" I asked. I didn't like that he was thinking about Harlow.

His face hardened into a frown. "You heard me!" he shouted. "You two clearly knew each other."

"Yes," I said, his sudden anger making me nervous.

"But how *well* do you know each other?"

I didn't see why that mattered, and I really didn't want to tell him anything about Harlow. "Pretty well," I said.

"Enough for her to care about what happens to you here? Are you important to her?"

Discovering that I was important to Harlow had been one of the happiest moments of my life. As I remembered that happiness, my doubts fell away. I knew then that whatever might be standing in her way, Harlow was fighting for me. I didn't want to share that with the Governor though. His interest in our relationship was both confusing and uncomfortable. But when he began to stand up, I said, "Yes! I'm important to her."

He froze where he was, halfway to standing, and stared at me. "She'll want to protect you? She'll be motivated to keep you alive?"

"Yes," I said, then grew uneasy again. The Governor clearly had a plan.

He sat back down and pressed a button on the radio that was clipped to his belt. "This has already been very helpful. Perhaps there's a bit of sense in you yet."

A moment later, the door opened and Lolo appeared. With a notebook in hand, she reminded me more of Harlow than she had at the pond. Quietly, she took a seat on the remaining chair.

"Listen carefully," said the Governor. "There are to be *no* misunderstandings." He remained perfectly still except for his eyes, which flickered back and forth between me and Lolo. She had the same sort of bored look she'd had at the pond. I'd thought Lolo was bored because she was used to watching interrogations, but that was before she'd traveled to my world and back. I didn't see how she could be bored after *that*. Now I wondered if she was protecting herself in some way, detaching from reality like I had done over the summer. Sometimes that was easier. I wished there was a way for me to talk to her, but the Governor went on.

"We find ourselves in a strange predicament. The question of *why* that portal exists will be discovered in due time, but the most pressing issue is what to do about our friend, Nole Fredericks."

I squirmed in my seat.

"Oh, not *you*, Nolan," the Governor said. "I mean the Nole Fredericks you seemed to have switched places with."

"Are you going to switch us back?" I asked. To me, it still seemed like the most obvious solution.

The Governor frowned again. "Should you return to your world and tell others about what you've seen here, more strangers may want to see my Morley for themselves and come snooping about. After all, isn't that why you're here? Because that bumbling photographer couldn't keep his mouth shut?"

"It was an accident," I said, but I'm not sure he heard me.

"If people from your world decide to travel here, that will result in *my* citizens being transported to a strange land. For their sakes, I cannot tolerate the possibility of such a threat. It would be devastating for the entire city-state. Therefore, you are not going back."

I could feel myself shrinking under his hard gaze.

"Do you understand?" the Governor yelled.

"Yes," I said. I *wanted* to say that I wouldn't tell anybody back home about what I'd seen here, and even if I did, they wouldn't believe me. I didn't see why people in a parallel world mattered to him so much. But then again, I wasn't a power-hungry maniac.

"No, Nolan, you won't be going anywhere near the pond, but *Nole* might get it into his head to return here, thus setting you free. Or, he might decide to stay in the other world and follow in the footsteps of the photographer by luring others to the pond. We're going to ensure he doesn't have the opportunity."

The Governor spoke as if he expected one of us to challenge him, but I, at least, didn't dare. "The answer is obvious: Nole Fredericks must die."

My whole body went rigid. If Nole died, I would be trapped here for the rest of my life. However long that was.

"That's where you come in, Lolo," the Governor said. "You will switch places with the other girl again in order to impersonate her. Your task is to ensure that Nole consumes the arsenic I provide. Afterward, you'll return to the pond and come home."

Lolo's fingers curled around the sides of the chair. "You want me to . . . kill him?" She sounded afraid, and I found myself feeling bad for her again.

"The arsenic will kill him; you'll merely be the one administering it."

Lolo kept fidgeting, clearly uncertain. "What happens when the girl is returned to her world? Won't we have the same problem? She could tell others about our Morley. Maybe she already has."

Yes! I cheered her on in my head. *Say whatever will keep Harlow safe.*

"Then you'll agree we can't tolerate any delays," the Governor said. "You see, it will be made *very* clear to the girl during her second trip here that she is never to speak of our Morley. The several hours you are gone will be plenty long for her to fully comprehend what is at stake for her dear friend here. She'll travel home knowing that if anyone from her world is found in the pond again, *he'll* be the first to answer."

He pointed at me while keeping his eyes on Lolo. She nodded, her expression unreadable.

"Please, sir," I said, before I lost my nerve, "you don't have to bring Harlow here. You've already made it clear to *me* that I should never talk about this Morley. You can send me through the portal. I promise, I'll keep it a secret."

He slammed his fist on the table. "You have seen too much! And why should I trust you to stay silent? There would be no one here for your silence to protect."

"Nole's mom," I said, my voice almost squeaky. "I would stay silent to keep her safe."

"Why should you care about her? You don't know her. But Harlow knows *you*, and we're about to find out how well you know her."

The Governor told Lolo to open her notebook. Even if his plan ended with Harlow getting away, I didn't want to picture what might happen to her here. I suppressed an urge to scream.

"Nolan," he said. "You are going to tell Lolo everything you know about her double. She must have as much information as possible."

And if I don't? I almost asked. But there wasn't any use. I already knew this man had no shortage of techniques to get answers out of me.

The questions began. I tried to be as vague as possible, but the Governor pushed for specificity. Although I'd only met Harlow a few months ago, we'd spent enough time together that, unfortunately, I was able to answer most of his questions. I hated myself more with every word I uttered, yet I had no choice but to tell him what he wanted to hear. Lolo took notes and asked a clarifying question every now and then, but at least without any of her dad's creepy enthusiasm.

The Governor got frustrated when I told him that Harlow usually drives us to school. Lolo had never driven a car before.

"She could pretend to be sick," I said. "Lolo will just have to text Nole to meet her at the house once Harlow's dad leaves."

"*Text* Nole?"

As I explained how smartphones worked, I began to feel jealous of all the time Nole was getting to spend with Harlow while I was stuck here. At least on this particular morning, he'd be with Lolo.

And getting himself killed.

That made me forget my jealousy and I went back to being afraid. I stayed that way for the rest of the long, tedious interview.

Finally, the Governor stood up and announced I had fulfilled my obligation and would be transferred to "suitable accommodations," whatever that meant. "If everything proceeds as it should, you will be reeducated and allowed to assume Nole Fredericks's identity, living out the rest of your days with his—your—mother in Morley. Where I can keep an eye on you."

I didn't want to impersonate Nole, but I wanted to die even less. Living in Nole's place was the one chance I had to leave this prison alive. Not that there was any reason to believe the Governor would actually let me go. Most likely, he wouldn't hold up his end of the deal, and I'd find out too late that he'd said it just to keep me cooperative.

Governor Matthias and Lolo left the room, and a guard unchained me. I was blindfolded once again and led through what felt like a winding series of hallways. Eventually, we stopped and the blindfold was removed. I was in a cinderblock cell. There was a cot with a brittle-looking blanket, a sink, a toilet, and a cracked concrete floor. There was no food or water. On the cot lay a stack of books. I'd never been much of a reader, but the sight of books was a relief. It would be something to do. I picked them up and read their titles in the faint light.

The Governor's Legacy

The City-State Citizen's Duty

Morley Society, a Brief History

I dropped them onto the floor. I didn't want to read any of that garbage.

Although I was tired, sleep seemed impossible. I was too worried. Had Harlow made it home safely after the switch? Did her dad know what was going on? Had she told the others what she'd seen here? I knew I would lose my mind thinking about it all. I stared angrily at the books splayed out on the ground. Garbage or not, they were the only things to distract me from thoughts of home.

26

NOLE

Harlow's dad was still gone when we arrived at her house. I suggested some gardening shears to take the handcuffs off, but Amaya was able to do it, pretty ingeniously, with a paperclip. We were sitting in the living room when Amaya's phone rang.

"Yeah, hi, Mom," she said when she answered. "Brunch was . . . good." She shrugged at us. But then, several sentences of completely unintelligible words left her mouth. I tried not to gawk, but I was unable to make sense of the strange sounds. Harlow, meanwhile, didn't look at all concerned. I wondered if there was something wrong with my ears.

"How soon until you have to leave?" Harlow asked when Amaya put her phone away.

"A few minutes. My dad's gonna pick me up."

Now I could understand her again. It wasn't like me to pry, but I had no idea what to make of what I'd just heard, and I was tired of feeling so lost.

"Um, Amaya," I said, my voice higher than usual, "sorry, but what exactly were you . . . saying?"

She looked at me curiously. "You mean when I was speaking Farsi?"

I didn't know if that was what I meant. "Maybe? It sounded like you were talking but you weren't saying words."

Amaya balked. "What? So, everything other than English is nonsense?"

"What's 'English?'" I asked, even more confused, and alarmed, by her anger.

"Wait, do you not know about . . . languages?"

In Morley, we had words everyone understood, nothing more or less. "I don't know," I said, suddenly feeling self-conscious.

"I bet it's about control," Harlow said, relieving me of having to say more. She was sitting curled up with a blanket on the couch next to Amaya, but nothing about her seemed relaxed. "If there's only one language with which to communicate, it will be obvious to the leader if it's being used against them."

"Yeah, I guess so," Amaya said. "But Nole, does that mean everyone in Morley is the same race, too?"

"The same what?"

"You've *got* to be kidding me," she said, turning to Harlow with a look of exasperation.

"No, that can't be," Harlow said. "Cate's mom is Black, and we know she has a double there."

"True," Amaya said. She turned to me, an excited look on her face. "This is so weird, Nole. I didn't even think about how different your history must be from ours."

I'd been too busy trying to keep up with the present to think about this world's past, and if I was going home tomorrow, I'm not sure I wanted to know about it. I'd like to be able to tell Governor Matthias truthfully that I didn't seek out any dangerous information. Still, it couldn't hurt to tell Amaya and Harlow about Morley's history, if they were interested.

"Well, there's a lot of history in my Morley," I said. "About a hundred years' worth."

"What?" Amaya said. "That's it? That's not even that long."

"Yeah, how does it not go back farther?" Harlow asked.

I was annoyed that they were challenging everything I said, and that made me want to explain it better. So, I told them about the time before

Morley's history, The Chaos, when violence and fear were all anyone knew. Harlow stopped me when I mentioned the name David Stevenson.

"That's my great-grandfather's name," she said, looking sort of embarrassed. "He *founded* your Morley?"

"Yes," I said. "He was the first of the three governors we've had. Morley has always been under the Stevenson family."

"Hasn't anyone ever tried changing things?" Harlow asked.

"Change them to what?" I asked, not understanding. How could we change the way things simply were?

"I don't know," Amaya said. "To something that doesn't *suck*?"

"It's not all bad," I said, feeling defensive again. "Everyone has a job to do and as long as you follow the rules, you can get by peacefully."

"But Nole," Harlow said, "you said you aren't allowed to talk to your own aunt and uncle. Doesn't that bother you?"

It hadn't, really, until these people started making such a big deal about it. "No," I said.

"So, you're okay with people living divided up like that?" Amaya asked.

It was starting to feel like I was being blamed for the way things were in my world, things I had no part in creating. "What?" I said impatiently. "Are people not divided at all in this world?"

I half expected one of them to say, "Of course there are no divisions in our perfect world," but Amaya and Harlow actually paused and gave each other meaningful looks.

"Well, no," Harlow said. "We have a lot of divisions here too."

"Yeah," Amaya said, sighing.

"Well, okay then," I said, feeling I'd proved my point.

"It just seems like your divisions are more enforced, like, legally," Harlow said, "and are based primarily on wealth—is that right?"

"Yes," I said, glad she was finally getting something. "But the divisions are also based on who has broken a law and who hasn't."

Harlow nodded. "So, Governor Matthias doesn't care if everybody looks different, but he insists they all share one culture and language and allegiance?"

I realized I'd never thought about it that way before. "I guess so."

"I'm sorry, Nole," Harlow said. "We're not mad at you. We're just trying to understand better."

"No, it's okay," I said, sorry I'd let my irritation show.

"Yeah," Amaya said, smiling. "I'm actually paying more attention to you than I do to my real history teacher."

I smiled too, relieved we weren't arguing anymore.

"Do you go to school in your Morley?" Amaya asked.

"Of course," I said, a bit offended again. I'd barely been here twenty-four hours. Just because I wasn't an expert in the ways of their world didn't mean I was uneducated.

"Okay, sorry," she said. "You're smart, I can tell, but I bet our school is a lot different."

"Yeah, probably."

Amaya's phone buzzed. "I gotta go, but I'll see you tomorrow." She hugged Harlow and stood up from the couch. She was leaving the room when she turned and said, "Nole, my parents didn't move to this country until they were in their twenties. Since no one speaks Farsi in your Morley, do you think that means my family isn't there?"

I thought about this for a moment. No one in Morley spoke anything but "English." The government conducted trade deals with other city-states, but otherwise, no one went in or out of Morley.

"Yes," I said slowly. "I think that's what it means. If you have a double out there somewhere, she wouldn't be living in Morley."

Amaya tilted her chin up. "Good for her."

27

HARLOW

Soon after Amaya left, I told Nole he should go too. "My dad thinks I'm upset with Nolan," I said. "It would just bring up a bunch of questions if you're here when he gets home."

"Okay," he said, but there was a troubled look on his face.

"I'll see you tomorrow. Everything will work out."

Nole gave me a weak smile. He knew as well as I did that everything might *not* work out. We said goodbye and I was alone.

I sat twirling the ends of my hair, picturing over and over again the moment the guard had hit Nolan. As I worried about what else might be happening to him in the other Morley, I started to feel light-headed. Only when I heard Dad's car roll into the garage did I get up and rush to my room.

I wasn't exactly trying to avoid my dad, but I had no idea how to tell him about the situation I was in, and the story was only growing more complicated. I decided that since Nolan was (hopefully) coming back tomorrow, there wasn't any reason to involve him. This would all be over soon, and I could forget this nightmare.

I took a shower, rinsing off the residue of pond water, and got straight into a clean set of pajamas. Though I was sleepy, I had barely studied over the weekend. I sat down at my desk to do homework.

I was absorbed in my reading when there was a tap at the door.

"Hey, sweetie, how was your day?" my dad asked.

I pried my eyes away from the book and tried to give him a normal smile. "Good, I guess," I said.

"You and Amaya hung out?"

"Yeah, she left a while ago. How did golfing go?"

He laughed. "I've had better days."

Me too, I thought, but instead I said, "You'll get 'em next time."

Then he gave me a look, one that told me I wasn't doing a great job of acting normal. "Harlow," he said, coming in to sit on the edge of my bed. I swiveled around in my chair, nervous for what might come next. "Are you really feeling all right? Whatever's going on between you and Nolan can't be easy."

You have no idea. "Oh, it'll be okay," I said as lightly as I could. "Just a misunderstanding. I'll see him tomorrow. I'm giving him a ride like normal."

"And that's okay with you? I'm sure his uncle can take him."

"No, I don't mind. It'll be good to talk things through. I just needed some space."

Dad nodded. "If you're okay with it, I am too." He stood up, a good-natured smile back on his face. "I'm hungry. What do you say we order in?"

"Yeah, sounds good."

I felt somewhat better after having dinner with my dad, but he knew me too well not to notice my edginess that evening. As he said goodnight, he checked in one more time.

"You *sure* there's nothing you want to tell me?" he asked.

I realized then that I wanted to tell him about the other Morley. I wanted his advice and his comfort. Clearly, whatever my friends and I had stumbled upon in the woods was too big for us to manage alone. My dad was the smartest person I knew, and once he understood the truth, his help in getting Nolan and Nole home safely would be invaluable.

But the story was long and convoluted. It could take hours to convince Dad that something so mind-bending could be true. I didn't have the strength to tell it now as I lay in bed, already drifting to sleep.

"There is something," I said. "There's a lot. It's complicated. Can I tell you tomorrow?"

"Of course," he said. "We can talk tomorrow night. I love you, Harlow."

"Love you too."

28

LOLO

I've always been a dutiful student, and I'm sure any of my tutors from over the years would attest to that. When I was younger, I used to cry at the end of the school year, knowing I would never be allowed to see that particular tutor again. I learned not to get too attached. Keeping my distance was how I protected myself, but I think the system is really meant to protect my father. If I'm indifferent about my tutors, then he doesn't have to compete with them for my loyalty. It's a lesson on who is and who isn't replaceable in Morley.

Studious as I am though, learning how to be another person in a matter of hours was simply impossible. I was studying for a test I couldn't afford to fail, and yet, I wasn't entirely sure I wanted to pass. I'd never killed anyone before.

Of all the tasks before me, jumping between worlds was the least intimidating. I would have enjoyed the absurdity had I not been so afraid of what my father might do if I didn't follow his instructions perfectly.

Once the interview with Nolan was over, I was locked in the library and told to study the notes I'd taken. Later that night, I was escorted to the helicopter.

"Sir," I said to my father as we climbed aboard, "can I say goodbye to Mother?" It wasn't so much that I wanted to see her, as she likely wouldn't have anything encouraging to say, but I was looking for any way to delay my departure, if only for a few minutes.

"It's midnight; she's sleeping," he said curtly.

"What will you tell her?"

"I'll tell her that you're on an important assignment."

At least that much was true.

My father and I, along with two members of his Advisory Board, landed in the clearing and began the short walk to the pond. In the distance, a pair of guards waited for us. I could have asked my father a thousand questions, but knowing that time and his patience were limited, I chose just one.

"Will Nolan really be released to live with Nole's mother when I return?"

"Would *you* release him?" he asked, leaning down to look me in the eye.

"If . . . if I could trust him to stay quiet about the pond and simply live as Nole."

"Do you suppose Nolan is that trustworthy?"

"No, sir," I said, faintly, even though I wasn't sure I believed that. I'd given my father the answer he wanted to hear, but I thought *I* could trust Nolan. Everything about him seemed pretty earnest.

"Correct. However, Nole's mother will be released. She'll be grateful for the act of mercy and understand why her rebellious son couldn't be treated the same."

"Yes, sir."

"This bag has been packed with essentials for you," he said, changing the subject. He handed me a waterproof backpack. "It's got food, water, a towel, dry clothes and shoes, a flashlight, a compass, your notes, a knife, and the vial of arsenic." I nodded. The closer we got, the dizzier I felt. I was practically shaking when I put the backpack on.

"Remember," my father said as we approached the pond, "this shouldn't take you more than two days. Aside from administering the arsenic to Nole, your main goal is not to arouse suspicion."

"Yes, sir."

We stood together at the water's edge.

"Ready," he said.

It was a statement, not a question, and it was directed toward the guards. They picked me up by the arms and dragged me into the pond.

"Goodbye, Lolo," my father called out as I was pushed underwater.

I kicked frantically until I was able to get my head above the surface. The woods were quiet, but I wondered what might be hiding in the trees.

Quickly, I exited the pond and dropped my backpack in the dirt. The first thing I grabbed was the flashlight. Then I wrung out my hair and found the towel. It was in a plastic bag along with a watch and dry clothes. Everything was black, per usual. I put my wet clothes in the bag and took out the compass. Nolan said the pond was about a mile north of something called Mountain Pass Trail. I should head south, find the path, and follow it all the way back to Morley. I'd never had to navigate anywhere by myself before, but now wasn't the time for doubts. I took a few tentative steps in what I thought was the right direction, pushing branches and bushes out of my way. Each time I snapped a twig my heart jumped. Twice I almost dropped the flashlight. I kept going anyhow.

Soon, I saw a break in the trees and I started to run, hoping I'd found Mountain Pass Trail. I could see faint, dusty footprints on the dirt path. I bent over, my hands on my knees, and breathed heavily. This was the trail. I told myself the hardest part was over.

Nolan said the hike would take approximately two hours if I kept a good pace. That would get me to Harlow's sometime after two a.m. For the first time, I wondered what was happening to Harlow back in my Morley. Knowing it wasn't good, I didn't allow myself to dwell on that thought. Instead, I set my mind to recalling as many details as I could about Harlow's life. *My* life, for the next few days.

Aside from stopping to sip water, I didn't take any breaks. Even though at this hour I would usually be sleeping, I didn't feel tired. My nerves were doing a solid job of keeping me alert.

Eventually, I reached the edge of the forest and saw the hill Nolan had mentioned. Replaying his instructions in my mind, I trudged upward until I reached a gate. I turned off my flashlight and peered through the bars. This was the park, illuminated at this hour by only a few lampposts. I turned right and counted five more gates until I reached Harlow's. Judging by the darkness and quiet, the entire neighborhood was asleep, but even so, I was hesitant to shine my flashlight on the keypad for the few seconds it would take me to punch in 3-7-4-1.

There was a muffled *click*. I gripped the handle and opened the gate slowly, its faint creaking too soft to attract attention.

I tiptoed across the lawn and located the side door. A light came on above me, revealing a small security camera. There was nothing I could do but move faster. I punched in the code. If the soft beeping of the keypad didn't give me away, I was sure my pounding heart would. Thus far, everything had gone smoothly, but I was only a sneeze or a fumble away from waking Harlow's father.

Without wasting a second, I stepped inside, closed the door, and went searching for the staircase. My boots squeaked softly as I tread up the wooden stairs, but the carpet on the second floor masked my footsteps. I turned right and went down a hallway until I reached the door I believed was Harlow's. It was slightly ajar, and I pushed it opened further to see if I had the correct room. An empty, unmade bed confirmed that I did.

I slipped inside and immediately tucked my backpack under the bed. I rummaged through a few drawers in a dresser and found a set of red flannel pajamas. Once I stuffed the clothes I'd been wearing next to my backpack, I practically collapsed onto the bed.

Then, I began to cry.

My tears were tears of relief more than anything. I lay there with them streaming silently down my face, no doubt mixing with the dried sweat that had accumulated during my long walk. It would have been nice to take a shower before getting in bed, but I couldn't entertain that idea now. I didn't really want to entertain *any* ideas now.

~~~

I must have fallen asleep, because the next thing I knew, I was being woken by an obnoxious ringing. I reached under the pillow, where the noise seemed
~~~

to be coming from. I grabbed a small device and tapped all around the screen until it stopped. This must be Harlow's phone. Nolan had said it would read my thumbprint and unlock so I could type messages, make calls, and do a thousand other things. Hopefully, I wouldn't be in this world long enough to have to understand what any of those things were. Anything I did wrong could "arouse suspicion," my father's stern voice kept reminding me in my head. Carefully, I tapped the phone again, and the screen lit up to reveal it was 6:46 a.m. This was when Harlow typically got up for school, but since I wasn't going, I replaced the phone under my pillow and fell back to sleep almost instantly.

The next time I woke up it wasn't because of the phone.

"Hey, Harlow?" The voice was similar to my father's, only I'd never heard him speak with such gentle concern before. "Harlow, your alarm must not have gone off."

My eyes shot open. Thankfully, I was laying on my side and facing away from Harlow's father, who was now lightly shaking my shoulder.

Sick, I'm supposed to be sick, I reminded myself.

I coughed a few times before saying, "I don't feel well."

"Oh, sweetheart," he said, sitting down next to me. "What's wrong?"

"My throat hurts, and I have a headache," I said, burrowing deeper under the covers. "I don't think I can go to school."

"I think you're right," he said. "But Harlow, if you're willing to miss a day of school, it must be pretty serious. Maybe I should take you to the doctor."

"No!" I said, probably a little too forcefully. "I mean, um, I just need to rest."

"Are you sure this doesn't have anything to do with the problem you were going to share with me? It's okay if it does. I wouldn't blame you for needing a mental health day."

I didn't know what problem he was talking about, but I decided to play along, since it sounded like no matter what, he was going to let me stay home.

"Yes," I said. "I think so."

"In that case, you take the day to relax, and we'll talk about whatever it is that's going on this evening." He leaned over and kissed me on the forehead.

I bristled slightly from the unfamiliar sensation. "Check in with me soon, okay?" He got up from the bed and left the room.

I remained still for a moment and then rolled onto my back, staring at the ceiling. It had been strange, almost eerie, to hear my father's voice speaking so kindly and sympathetically. Did Harlow always get treated like this? I began to feel self-pity. That feeling grew worse as I propped myself onto my elbows and looked around the room. The walls were decorated with pictures and posters, books lined the shelves, and the open closet door revealed several dresses hanging in a row. Harlow seemed to have everything. I hadn't been allowed to decorate my own bedroom. My father furnished it with uncomfortable couches that I didn't use, and the walls were bare except for three austere portraits of him, my grandfather, and great-grandfather.

Sometimes I made self-pitying comments to my mother, but she always reminded me that as much as I resent my father, the people of Morley resent him more.

"Then why don't they do something about it?" I'd asked once.

"Why don't you?"

I'd considered her question for a minute. "I'm too afraid."

"And they are more afraid."

But my mother wasn't in Harlow's room with me, and so I kept on feeling sorry for myself. *Maybe I don't have to leave,* I thought suddenly. *I could just assume Harlow's perfect life forever.*

My enthusiasm lasted only a few seconds before I realized that my father would never let that happen. He'd toss Harlow back into the pond sooner than he'd let me escape his authority. My best chance was to complete the mission, go home, and continue to stay in his favor until it was my turn to be governor. Maybe I'd change how things were in Morley. *That* would be my revenge. The thought was comforting, but my father was healthy and still relatively young. He still had plenty of time—decades, probably—before I would succeed him. I shuddered to think he might start trying harder to make me just like him.

I kicked the covers off and paced around the room. All of those concerns would have to wait. Right now, I needed to focus on getting the arsenic to

Nole. If Nole didn't come over on his own, Nolan had advised I text him. I picked up Harlow's phone and unlocked it. But after that it was a mystery. Even with the notes I'd taken, I wasn't sure exactly how to send a text. And I didn't want to do anything that would draw unnecessary attention to myself. "Try not to interact with too many people," Nolan had said. "Amaya—that's Harlow's best friend—will definitely be on to you. There'll be no fooling her." As far as I could tell, no one had texted or called yet.

I waited until eight to poke my head out of the bedroom door. It was quiet, so I decided it was safe to venture downstairs and get something to eat.

The kitchen was well stocked, but with foods I didn't recognize. I had never cooked before, and thankfully, I didn't have to. In the refrigerator was a plate with small muffins and blueberries. A note said, "Take it easy today, Harlow. I love you. —Dad."

I sat down at the kitchen counter and ate the breakfast that wasn't really mine, trying not to think about the person whom it was for.

29

NOLE

On Monday morning, I knocked on Harlow's door just before 7:45. When the door opened, it wasn't Harlow who greeted me. Instinctively, I took a few steps back from Governor Matthias in the doorway.

He isn't the Governor, I reminded myself. I tried to smile at him.

The man who was not Governor Matthias said, "Good morning, Nolan."

"Good morning," I said.

"Listen, I've got some bad news. Harlow isn't feeling well. She's going to stay home."

"Oh," I said. "I'm sorry to hear that."

"I am too. It takes quite a bit to keep Harlow from getting to school." He paused and looked at me thoughtfully. I worried something about me was making him suspicious. "Are *you* feeling okay today?" he asked.

I wasn't quite sure what to make of his question. "Yes," I answered as evenly as I could. "I hope Harlow feels better." I wondered what was wrong. Was she sick, or was it the stress of traveling to my Morley that was getting to her? Whatever the case, if Harlow wasn't going to school, then the plan might have to wait. I began to turn away when Harlow's dad stopped me.

"Nolan, since Harlow was your ride to school, do you need any help getting there?"

"Oh, no, that's okay," I said quickly.

"Are you sure?"

"Yes." I hoped that he'd leave me alone and I could go back to Nolan's house and hide until Topher or Amaya reached out.

"Well, it's too late to figure out an alternative now," he said. "I'll take you. I'm about to leave anyway."

"Oh no, sir, that's okay."

"Hey, it's 'Matt,' remember? And it's no trouble. Let me just grab a few things."

He ran back inside. I thought about texting Amaya to let her know what was happening, but the phone in my pocket was still too much of a mystery.

Matt appeared a minute later with a briefcase and a jacket draped over his arm. "Ready to go?"

"Okay." It seemed my only option was to play along, so I followed Matt to the garage. He opened the door to reveal a black car. It was connected to a blinking box on the wall by a thin tube and nozzle. It looked sort of like a gas pump, but Matt unhooked the nozzle with ease, no sign of dripping gasoline. A car powered by electricity? It took all my self-control not to ask if cars in this world really used electric power. I don't think the electrical grid in my Morley could handle that kind of demand for even a single day.

Not knowing where I should sit, I opened the door directly behind Matt's.

"You can ride up front," he said. I would have preferred the backseat, but I wasn't going to argue. I walked around the car and got inside, carefully tucking Nolan's backpack, ready with dry clothes, in front of my feet.

"Seat belt?" he said.

"What?"

He frowned slightly. "Don't tell me you forget to wear a seat belt when Harlow's driving."

"Oh, no," I said. I'd never actually worn a seat belt before. I worked on cars in the mechanic shop; I didn't ride in them. Matt pulled a strap from the top corner of his seat. I followed his example, but it took me a few tries to secure the buckle properly. I could feel Matt's eyes watching my clumsy movements, but he didn't comment.

"How do you like Cardiff Hall?" Matt asked once we were driving.

"It's been good so far," I said, trying to keep things vague.

"Who's your favorite teacher?"

"Um . . . I don't have one yet."

"Well, that's okay, so long as you don't have a *least* favorite," he said with a laugh.

"Oh, yeah, I don't."

He changed the subject. "So, Harlow tells me you used to work at a bike shop before you moved. What was that like?"

"It was very interesting. I liked the problem solving," I said, which was true.

"Problem solving, now *that's* a great skill," Matt said.

I smiled. For some reason, it felt nice to have his approval.

"I do a fair amount of problem solving in my jobs," he continued, "but I have to say, there's something satisfying about having a tangible product that proves how hard you worked. Most days, all I have to show for myself is a stack of paper." He laughed again.

"Yeah," I said, finding I agreed with what he'd said. "I really like that sense of accomplishment and working with my hands."

"Do you want to continue working on bikes?"

"I think so."

"That's great," he said.

I'd never met the Governor in person of course, but the more I talked with Matt, the less he reminded me of Governor Matthias.

"Hey, is classic rock okay?"

"Um, sure," I said. I knew what those two words meant separately, but put together, they didn't make much sense.

Matt hit a few buttons and music started playing. In my Morley, music was only played to celebrate the Governor or remind us of the importance of civic duty. It was loud and slow, like it was written to be heavy and pin us down. Whatever was playing now made me feel like I was rising up. I didn't recognize the instruments or understand some of the lyrics, but I was mesmerized all the same. I'd almost forgotten where we were going when we arrived at the school.

"Have a good one, Nolan," he said as I tried to unbuckle the seat belt. I got it on the second try and stepped out of the car.

"You too, Matt. Thank you."

He waved as he drove off. The music was gone, replaced by the sounds of shoes shuffling on pavement and people talking. I looked up at the imposing brick building and tried to figure out my next move. To my relief, I heard Amaya's voice from across the lawn.

"Nole! Hey, Nole!" She jogged toward me with a smile. "You made it. Where's Harlow?"

"At home. Sick."

"Sick?"

"Yes, I'm not sure with what."

"That can't be right. Harlow's never sick."

"That's what her dad said, too."

"You talked to Matt?"

"He gave me a ride here."

"Oh my god," Amaya said. "This is bad."

I suddenly felt awful, like I'd made a mistake. Amaya called Harlow, but there was no answer.

"Okay," Amaya said. "I'm going to see what's up with her."

"How are we going to get back to Eastside?"

Her eyes lit up. "We'll call Topher." She grabbed my arm and led me across the lawn.

"Where are we going?" I whispered.

"Away from here," she said as we slipped behind a line of parked cars.

Amaya called Topher, but I didn't hear much of their conversation. I was too distracted by the dozens of store windows we walked past. Some of the stores only sold a few products like patterned socks and bars of soap. A candle store bothered me in particular. At home, rolling blackouts made candles a necessity, and my mom and I burned them down to the wick. They certainly didn't smell like warm vanilla or calming lavender. The people here were so picky about everything.

"Okay, Nole," Amaya said, pulling my attention away from the stores. "Since Topher and Cate were planning to meet us at the park at nine, they can't pick us up quite yet. They'll come get us at Terry's Diner in about an hour."

"What's that?"

"It's a restaurant."

"A restaurant?" I repeated. I was tired of all these new vocabulary words.

"You don't have *restaurants* in your Morley?"

"No?" I didn't know what the word meant, at least.

"Wow, um, okay. A restaurant is a place where they serve food and you can hang out. Did you have breakfast?"

"No, but I don't have any ration cards with me."

"Me either," she said. "But I have a debit card, and that should do just fine."

<p style="text-align:center">~~~~</p>

We sat across from each other at a red table in Terry's Diner. It was a brisk autumn day, and I was glad to be someplace warm.

Amaya texted Harlow a few times while I read the food options.

"Order stuffed French toast," she said. "Trust me, you'll like it."

I took her advice and did not regret it. That was, until I realized I was leaving this Morley in just a few hours. Though I was anxious to get home, sitting there at the "restaurant," I admitted to myself that this world wasn't all bad. I liked the food and the music, and it was exciting to think I might be able to own my own car here. Or a dog. I tried not to think about what I'd be leaving behind. Sometimes it's better not to know what you're missing. Instead, I pictured how happy Mom and Catherine would be when they saw me again.

"Harlow always texts me back." Amaya's fidgeting leg bumped against the table. "This is really weird."

"Don't people in this Morley get sick?"

"*Nole!*" she practically shouted, then glanced around the mostly empty restaurant and lowered her voice. "What if Harlow isn't sick? What if she's . . . gone?"

I paused, my fork halfway to my mouth. "You mean, what if Lolo is here?" I asked.

"Yes. I'm starting to think that makes the most sense."

Lolo had already been through the pond once, and if Harlow's behavior this morning really was out of the ordinary, then Amaya might be right. I suddenly felt a little nauseous. "It does make sense," I said.

~~~

Topher and Cate picked us up at the restaurant, and I climbed into the back-seat of their car with Amaya.

"Thanks for the ride," she said as she slammed the door. "You're lifesavers."

As soon as we got to Harlow's, Amaya bolted from the car. I waited behind with Cate and Topher, who was tucking a plastic bag under his arm.

"Is the photo in there?" I asked.

"Yes," he said.

I didn't know if the photo would do me any good with Governor Matthias, but it was my ticket home.

We approached the house. Amaya was pounding on the front door and calling Harlow's name, but most of the curtains were closed, and it was impossible to tell if anyone was inside.

"Harlow's not answering," Amaya said when we joined her at the door. "The real Harlow would let me in."

"Try calling her one more time," Topher said. Amaya did, but no answer. The palms of my hands were starting to feel clammy, and I wiped them on my jacket. I was *so* close to making it back to my world, but if it really was Lolo inside, everything about our plan would have to change.

"Maybe her dad took her to the doctor?" Cate said, but even she didn't sound like she believed that was the case.
~~~

"Should I just open the door?" Amaya asked.

"No," Topher said quickly. "We shouldn't do that again."

"*Okay,*" Amaya said, "then what are we going to do? We can't just stand here."

"Nole," Topher said, turning to me. "Why don't you try now?"

"Me?" I said, suddenly on edge. "Why?"

"Let's say for argument's sake that Lolo is here. She hasn't met Amaya, but since you're from her world, she might be willing to talk to you."

"Talk about what?"

"I'm not sure," Topher said. "But there's only one way to find out."

Again, these people were leaving me with little choice. Topher was from Lolo's world too, why shouldn't *he* talk to her?

"You don't have to do this, Nole," Cate said.

When I looked at her, I saw Catherine. I felt determined to get home. "Yes, I do." Cate, Topher, and Amaya stepped to the side so that if someone answered the door, they wouldn't be seen right away.

I raised my fist and knocked. "Hello? It's Nole," I said tentatively. There was no response, so I tried again, a little louder. "Is anyone there? It's Nole."

I heard the lock turn, and the door opened a few inches. For a second, I felt relieved. This couldn't be Lolo. But as I stared at the pale, wide-eyed girl, I felt less sure.

"Harlow?" I tried.

"Hi," she said.

"I'm sorry you're not feeling well."

"Yes, thank you. I was just going to have some hot chocolate. Would you like some?"

"Um . . ." I'd never had hot chocolate before, and the careful way she'd asked me made it sound like she was reciting the words. I glanced over at Amaya, Topher, and Cate. The girl—Harlow or Lolo, I couldn't say for certain—leaned forward to see where I was looking and gasped.

"What's wrong?" I asked, immediately more suspicious.

"I . . . I don't think I have enough hot chocolate for everyone," she stammered.

What was she talking about? I couldn't imagine Harlow, who was so intent on getting Nolan back, would waste time like this. This girl had to be Lolo.

I thought Lolo might shut us out, but she just stood in the doorway like she was stuck to the spot. After seeing images of Lolo my entire life, it was odd to be standing next to her. She seemed so ordinary now that she wasn't behind a lens.

"Oh my god," Amaya breathed, looking the girl up and down. "You're not Harlow."

She didn't confirm or deny. She simply wrapped her arms around herself and gazed at the floor.

"I mean, you look *so* much like her, but . . ." Amaya turned to me. "She's more fragile looking, or something." I nodded. *Fragile* was the last word I'd ever thought I'd use to describe the Governor's daughter, and yet, Amaya wasn't wrong.

"Topher," Amaya said. "This isn't Harlow. This is the Governor's daughter."

Lolo's head snapped up. "No," was all she said.

"*Yes*," Amaya said, "and you're going to tell us why you're here."

Her head fell forward again. We waited for her reply, but her breathing became shaky, and she started to sniffle. I couldn't believe I was watching the future governor start to cry. Of all the things that had happened to me over the past few days, this might be the strangest.

"*Well?*" Amaya said.

"Lolo," Topher said gently, "it's all right. You can tell us what's going on."

"No, I can't," she said, her voice breaking.

"Why? Because of Governor Matthias?"

"Yes," she whispered. I'd never considered that Lolo might be scared of her father like everyone else in Morley. In some ways, it could be worse for her. She actually had to *live* with him. "Lolo," I said, taking advantage of this rare chance to talk to her, "are you afraid o' him?"

She looked at me, and I saw the truth in her green eyes. Yes, she was afraid. Still, she answered no. I guess she was like every Morley kid in that way: You say what will protect you, not what is true.

Amaya, who had been bouncing on her toes, couldn't hold back any longer. "If you're here, that means Governor Matthias has Harlow. You've *got* to tell us what's going on right now."

"Shh, Amaya, don't—" Topher started to say, but Lolo cut him off.

"Amaya," she said, like she recognized the name. "You're Harlow's best friend."

Amaya was surprised. "Yeah," she said, raising an eyebrow. "I am."

Lolo looked thoughtfully at Topher and Cate. "You must be Topher and Cate Collins." That made me nervous. If she knew who Cate was, then she might have seen Catherine before.

"How do you know that?" Topher asked.

"Yeah," I said. "Have you met their doubles?"

"No, I haven't," said Lolo, and I relaxed a bit. "Nolan told me about the Collins family."

"Nolan?" Amaya said. "Nolan talked to you?"

"Yes, a good deal," Lolo said, no longer on the brink of crying.

"About what?"

"About a lot of things, anything that would help me learn how to be Harlow."

"Learn to be Harlow?" Amaya said angrily. "Like, take her place forever?"

"No, not forever," Lolo said, shrinking back again.

"Then for how long?"

"Well, um . . ." her voice trailed away. I thought maybe I'd misjudged Lolo all these years, but that wasn't quite right. After all, I only knew what the Governor wanted me to know about Lolo—that she was a pillar of strength and someone to fear. Maybe *he* was the one who had misjudged her. But then, Lolo's sunken eyes traveled to meet mine. "I'm only supposed to stay until I give Nole the arsenic. Until he's dead."

30

HARLOW

The shock of cold water wrenched me out of a dream. Strong hands wrapped themselves around my arms and hoisted me upward. My eyes were immediately covered by a cloth, but I didn't need my vision to understand where I was. *Not again.*

Handcuffs clasped around my wrists, then earplugs were shoved into both of my ears. They were depriving me of my senses one by one, and I'd only been in this Morley a few seconds.

I was carried from the banks of the pond, dripping wet. The noises around me were muffled, but I was too lost in my panicky thoughts to try to guess what they might be. The speed at which I'd been arrested told me the guards had been waiting for me. There was clearly a plan at work, one I had a role in. I was picked up and strapped to a thinly padded seat, a guard on either side. I could make out the sound of whirling blades and I guessed this was a helicopter. My stomach lurched as we lifted up. I was trapped.

I remembered Nolan saying that "trapped" is how he'd felt all summer, and now I understood him better. It wasn't just that he'd been stuck, but he must have felt what I was feeling right now: the sense of moving toward some inevitable unknown event. I felt short of breath as I realized that no one in my world would notice I was missing for at least a few hours. I wished I'd told Dad what was going on. I'd never felt so utterly alone.

Once we landed, I was pulled roughly out of my seat. My feet barely grazed the floor as I was steered inside and led down a series of halls and staircases. Suddenly, we stopped. There was a loud rumbling sound that my earplugs were no match for, and I was pushed forward

In a few swift movements, the guards removed the blindfold, earplugs, and handcuffs. A glaring white light pierced my eyes. Then the guards sat me on a white wooden beam, my feet dangling just a few inches above the floor.

"Don't move," one of them said. They both left, and a heavy white door rolled shut. A camera watched me from the corner of the room.

What the hell? I wondered if this was some kind of sick torture, and if so, why was I being subjected to it? Nerves flooded my already tense body, and I began swinging my feet back and forth.

"I said, *don't move*," an angry voice called out over a speaker.

I froze, and the argument in my head grew fiercer.

I was pretty sure I needed to be alive in order for Lolo to switch back with me, and I didn't think the Governor would risk losing her to my world forever. Then again, maybe he knew something more about the rules of the portal than I did. The longer I sat on the beam, the less I could reassure myself. I stared at a fixed spot on the floor and tried to figure out what the Governor wanted from me. It must be something, for why else would he bother sticking me in this horrible room? If the Governor was going to interrogate me, I'd probably have no choice but to tell him what he wanted to hear.

My feet prickled slightly. They were turning red from the chill.

In the stillness, I began to feel how cold my wet pajamas really were. The room seemed to drop a few degrees every couple of minutes. I shivered.

"Stop moving," the voice commanded.

I wondered in horror if Nolan was being kept in a similar room. Soon, I could see my breath in the frigid air. I shivered again, more violently this time. No voice told me to stop moving and I thought whoever was watching hadn't noticed.

A few minutes later, the door rumbled open. The Governor stood in the doorway.

"Cold?" he asked. His taunting voice sounded like some nightmare version of my dad. This felt like a trick, so I remained quiet.

He looked over his shoulder and nodded. The two guards appeared, and one of them held a big metal pot in his gloved hands. Steam rose steadily from its open top.

No.

"Cold?" the Governor asked again.

"No!" I said as the guard with the pot inched closer. "No, I'm not cold!"

"Don't *lie*."

The pot was held above my legs and tipped forward. A cascade of searing hot water splashed onto my lap and a pain unlike anything I'd ever known shot through my legs. I let out a hysterical scream. The first guard held me in place as the water continued to pour. I wriggled wildly until he let me fall forward off the beam. I screamed louder, dizzy from pain. The guard stood me back up while the other dumped the rest of the scalding water onto my shins and bare feet. My toes curled inward, and I lost my balance. The guard caught me before I fell all the way to my knees, and I dangled helplessly in his arms. Then, he and his partner sat me back on the beam. I howled when their rough hands dug into my burning flesh.

Once I was back in place, they left the room and the door rolled closed. I sat there, crying heavily and calling for my dad.

My pajamas clung to my stinging legs. With shaking hands, I wiped my tear-stained face and snotty nose. Maybe I'd been wrong about the Governor's plan. I wasn't in this room to be interrogated. I was here to be broken.

31

TOPHER

When Amaya leapt forward, I thought she was going to attack Lolo, but instead, she placed herself firmly in front of Nole. That gave me an opportunity to step in before anyone made a rash move.

"We need to take this conversation inside," I said, holding up my hands between the teenagers.

"What we *need* is to take this to the pond so we can throw her back in it," Amaya said.

Lolo inched backward. If I didn't know who her father was, I never would have guessed that this cowering girl was next in line for the governorship. She may have been sent here to kill, but to me, Lolo simply looked like a vulnerable kid trapped in an impossible situation. I was surprised by how much I wanted to protect her, but maybe I shouldn't have been. Wanting to protect Lolo is what started all of this in the first place.

"We'll discuss it when we're inside," I said, pointing to the house. The last thing we needed was for some neighbor to complain about a grown man fighting with a group of kids. "Now let's go."

Lolo bowed her head and went in. The rest of us followed, Cate sticking closely to my side.

"This is a waste of time," Amaya said once we were standing in the foyer with the door shut. "There's nothing to discuss. Harlow comes home. Now."

While her care for her friend was admirable, she didn't understand how delicate the situation was. "Amaya," I said, "we've got to do this right. The Governor could keep switching them back and forth until Lolo's assignment is complete." I glanced at Nole who stared unblinking at some point on the wall.

"Then what's your plan?" Amaya asked.

A fair question. I had no plan yet. "Well," I said, "whatever we do, it will require Lolo's cooperation." I looked down at Lolo, who stood next to me. I tried to come across as calm as I could, since any sort of confrontation seemed to shut her down. "You understand you won't be doing what you came here to do?"

She frowned, then closed her eyes like she was trying to block out the world around her. Or maybe she was imagining what would await her at home if she returned a failure. The Governor had no tolerance for errors, and that probably included his daughter's.

"Hey, Lolo," I said, "it's going to be okay. We'll figure this out."

"Yeah, you keep saying that," Amaya snapped, "but what does it mean?"

"Lolo," I said, keeping my focus on her, "will you agree to work with us?"

Her eyes fluttered open. "Yes," she said. She sounded tired, resigned, even. "Good. Thank you."

I was about to suggest that we sit down in the living room when the front door opened and a man walked in. It took me a second to remember he *wasn't* a more mature, more muscled Governor Matthias.

"What's going on here?" the mayor asked, looking right at me. "Who are *you*?"

I stepped forward. "Christopher Collins. I can explain."

"You better," he said, dropping his briefcase. "Let's start with why you're in my house."

"It's a long story," I said quickly, "but our daughters became acquainted recently on a hike."

"So why are you here *now*?" Suddenly, he looked at Lolo. "Did you *invite* him?"

"No, sir, she didn't," I said, trying to get his attention back on me.

"So, you all decided to pay her a visit at the same time while she's sick?" he asked, growing more agitated. "Harlow, I've been worried; you didn't respond to any of my texts this morning, and now—"

"That's not Harlow," Amaya blurted.

A part of me was glad she said it. I understood why the mayor didn't trust me, but he might be more willing to listen to Amaya. With his daughter missing, not telling him about the other Morley didn't seem like an option.

"What?" he said, like he hadn't heard her right.

"And this isn't Nolan," Amaya continued before more questions could be asked. She placed her hand on Nole's shoulder. "His name is Nole; he's sort of a 'double' of Nolan."

"Amaya, *what* are you talking about?"

"Matt, listen," she said, "I know this is going to sound completely insane, but you've *got* to hear me out. Nole is from another world where there's a different version of Morley."

"I'm sorry—a different *world*?"

"Yes." She said it with the same conviction I'd had when I'd first explained things to Jojo. "He's here by accident. But *she*," Amaya said, pointing to Lolo, "is an imposter here on purpose."

The mayor's mouth hung open like he was about to speak, but he remained still, an incredulous look on his face. It was so close to the look the Governor had given me when he'd realized I'd taken his photo that I had to glance away for a second and remind myself, again, this was Mayor Matt, not Governor Matthias.

"It's true," Nole said. "I'm not Nolan."

Matt frowned. "What's gotten into all of you? Nolan, I took you to school this morning. How did you get back here?" Quickly, he turned to me. "Are you helping them all ditch school? Were you going to take them somewhere?"

"No," I said, even though I was doing both. I decided that Matt needed to hear the full story. "They're telling the truth."

"What?" Matt said, his eyes flashing. "You believe this?"

"I do," I said, bracing myself for his response. "I'm from the other world."

He threw his hands up. "You've *got* to be kidding me. That's it—"

"Matt, we can prove it!" Amaya said. "Ask that girl a question only Harlow would know. She won't be able to answer."

"This is ridiculous," he said. "I'm not—"

"Matt, please," Amaya begged. "You've got to trust me. Ask her something." Maybe it was his own curiosity or maybe it was Amaya's watery brown eyes, but Matt sighed and said, "I'll humor you for *one minute*, that's it." He faced Lolo. "On our trip to London last year, what was the name of our favorite pub?"

I thought that was a good question. No matter how much she'd learned about Harlow's life from Nolan, Lolo wouldn't know what London or pubs were. She averted her eyes. When she didn't answer, Matt tried again.

"What did we dress up as on Halloween when you were in kindergarten?"

More words she wouldn't recognize. It made me think back to all the words and concepts I'd had to learn in this world. Thankfully, Jojo had been there to patiently explain things like voting, going to college, and most baffling of all, the Internet. Again, I felt sorry for Lolo, having all this thrown at her in a rigged contest. She stayed silent.

"See?" Amaya said. "Harlow would know that stuff. Even *I* know that stuff."

"She's not feeling well," Matt said defensively. "I'm sure that when—"

"Her ears!" Amaya shouted. "Harlow has her ears pierced. I bet this girl doesn't. Check, please just check."

Matt took a step toward Lolo. He put his hand under her chin and carefully tilted it so that her hair fell behind her ears.

"Oh my god," he whispered.

~~~

We moved to the living room where Matt heard the rest of the story. I began with a shortened account of my escape to this world and failed attempt to
~~~

get back. Matt listened attentively and asked several questions about the other Morley. Amaya, Nole, and I traded off answering.

Matt said, "My 'double' isn't a mayor, but a governor?"

"*The* Governor. Leadership is hereditary."

And: "There's no contact with the outside world?"

"No, only the Governor and his Advisory Board can communicate with other city-states."

And: "How did the portal get there?"

"We don't know."

Matt looked at Cate. "How long have you known your dad is from the other Morley?"

"Only a few days," she said.

"You're glad you know, right?" I said, suddenly afraid that she might not forgive me for getting her tangled in this situation.

Cate, clearly a little rattled by my question, thought for a moment. "I'm glad I know the truth, Dad," she said. "Really."

I felt relieved, but her response made Matt groan.

"I should have *insisted* that Harlow tell me what was going on," he said. "She wanted to tell me something important last night, but we kept putting it off."

"Don't feel guilty, Matt," Amaya said. "That wouldn't have stopped *Loco* here from jumping into the pond."

"In any case, Harlow's coming home today," Matt said. "All we have to do is put her back in the pond, right?" He pointed to Lolo who nestled deeper into the cushions of her chair.

"Actually," I said, "it's not quite that simple."

"What do you mean?"

"I mean that we need Lolo to work with us," I said. "If she tells the Governor that Nole is still alive, he'll keep sending her back here until the job is done. Or maybe he'll send a guard instead, and that will mean whoever the guard's double is would be switched." I couldn't stand the thought of trapping even more innocent people in this mess.

"Then why don't we just send them *both* back?" Matt reasoned. "Harlow and Nolan would be returned to us, and he'd have Nole . . ." He looked at Nole as he said his name and his voice tapered off. It was one thing to talk about people theoretically, another to openly condemn a teenage kid to his death while he sat, panic-stricken, in front of you.

"If Nole returns with Lolo," I said, "I don't think any story, or any old photograph of mine, would be enough to convince the Governor to spare him."

"You didn't ask for any of this, did you?" Matt asked Nole.

"No, sir."

Matt nodded.

"And neither did I."

All of us turned to Lolo, surprised to hear her voice. "I want to go home," she said. "When I said I'd help you before, I meant it."

32

LOLO

The moment my true identity was revealed, I knew I wouldn't be returning to Morley with my father's mission accomplished. That was a relief. I didn't actually want to kill the boy, and if these other Morley people could figure out a way to get me home without my father finding out I'd failed him, then I'd play along.

I listened closely as they rattled off questions and talked over each other. It was both fascinating and a little scary. I'd always been taught that an open discussion such as this was dangerous and would inevitably lead to violence. That was how The Chaos got started, after all. These people didn't agree on everything and sometimes they raised their voices, but so far, no one had gotten hurt.

Everyone's deep concern for Harlow made me wonder if anyone at home was missing me. My mother would certainly notice I wasn't there, but "miss" seemed like too strong a word. I remembered Nolan saying that Harlow's mother had left her a long time ago. Maybe mine would have done the same, if given the chance. Our mothers might be similar in their aloofness, but our fathers, it seemed, were opposites. It was when Matt expressed genuine sympathy for the boy on his couch who was practically a stranger that I couldn't keep silent anymore. I wanted my side of the story told too.

The moment I spoke up, five pairs of curious eyes stared at me. I sat straighter in the pillowy chair. "I want to go home. When I said I'd help you before, I meant it."

Everyone looked nervous. I'd seen that same uneasy, untrusting look on people's faces a thousand times before. Usually it was from a distance, like from the back of a car when I was driven through the city-state. Finally, Topher smiled. "Thank you," he said. "Your help is going to be invaluable."

So far, Topher was the only person willing to give me half a chance. It was certainly more than my father had given *him* after the photography incident. Encouraged by his show of appreciation, I continued. "I can return to Morley and tell my father that Nole took the arsenic. You'll have Harlow back and no reason to fear her being switched again."

Instead of more gratitude, I was met with murmuring and skeptical looks.

"What about Nolan?" Amaya asked.

"I can only help with getting Harlow home safely," I said, irritated that she was complicating things.

"Trust me," Amaya said, "once Harlow's back, she won't stop until Nolan is here too."

You don't know that, I thought wryly. My father was determined to make Harlow understand there was nothing she could do to bring Nolan back to this world. I didn't doubt that whatever methods he chose would be extremely effective.

"I want to go home too," Nole said faintly. "I have people waiting for me." It stung to think this low-class boy was more missed by his family than I was by mine. No matter how badly he wanted to get home though, I couldn't let that happen. It would get me into too much trouble with my father.

"Actually," I said, "you can't go back. Ever. If you return to our Morley, it will be obvious to my father that I didn't follow his instructions."

"What would he do if he knew that you'd disobeyed him?" Matt asked.

I didn't know exactly what he would do, and that was part of what made me so afraid. "When it comes to my father," I said, "a more appropriate question is what *wouldn't* he do?" Then, hoping they'd forget about Nolan, I added, "Harlow is likely finding that out right now."

Matt was on his feet in an instant. "What is he doing to her?"

In his sudden anger, he reminded me of my father, and I instinctively put my hands in front of my face. "I don't know, really! But it would be better for her to come home sooner rather than later."

"Then let's go," Matt said. "We're bringing Harlow home now."

Amaya jumped up. "He's right, getting her back comes first."

Topher and Cate rose from their seats, followed by Nole, who looked a little sick. Topher patted him on the back. "It's going to be okay," I heard him say. That comment made me nervous. Did Topher mean it was okay, Nole could go home as soon as I was out of the way? I couldn't risk that. If Nole showed up in the pond, my father would know I'd lied about killing him.

"Wait," I said as everyone moved toward the front door. "I need you all to *promise* me that Nole won't switch with Nolan. That's the only way this plan works. Harlow will return home to you, and I'll tell my father that Nole is dead. He can continue his life here as Nolan."

Matt had stopped putting on his jacket mid-sleeve to listen. "And the real Nolan?"

"He'll be free to live as Nole, with his mother," I said quickly. "Now please, promise me."

They exchanged somber looks, no one appearing especially convinced even though it was probably the best job of lying I'd done all day.

"Okay," Matt said.

It wasn't much of a promise, but I decided it didn't matter. Nolan was to be killed soon after my return. Then they could toss Nole into the pond all they wanted. There would be no one for him to trade places with. I would be safe.

33

NOLAN

After flipping through the pages of the books in my cell, I fell asleep on the cot. My sense of time was all messed up, but I must have slept for several hours. I woke up, still tired, to the sound of the slot in the door being opened. A single piece of bread was pushed through, and it fell to the floor. I rushed over to grab the cup of water before it too could be dropped.

As I ate the sorry excuse for a meal, I wondered how Harlow was doing, hoping the Governor was treating her better than he was treating me. I decided to try again with the books. If I was lucky, they would put me back to sleep and keep me from stressing out about a situation I could do nothing to change. All three were equally tedious, but I went with *Morley Society, a Brief History*. Even a few paragraphs in it felt like I was reading a propaganda piece instead of an actual history book. I read:

> *The Chaos began long ago, before Morley was a sovereign city-state. We were only one of several cities under the jurisdiction of a large and unwieldy government entity. The cities were occupied by masses of unruly and stubborn people. They were vehemently opposed to order and peace. It was inevitable that widespread death and destruction would be unleashed.*

The weak and simpering government officials proved themselves unworthy of their authority, while the masses displayed their great need for consistent leadership and well-defined boundaries. What was once unified, however loosely, could not be reunified. For decades, the land was ruled only by violence, fear, and turmoil.

From out of this splintered wasteland arose a man with a vision for a strong and inextinguishable new society. Our esteemed founder, Governor David Stevenson, established a city-state that continues to thrive on its commitment to stability in the government and accountability for its citizenry. Among his triumphs was the establishment of the Governor's Guard, a group which continues to play an indispensable role in Morley by reminding the population of the importance of unity and discipline. Within the walls of the city-state, people lead lives of purpose, unburdened by danger and free to enjoy security of the highest caliber.

I slammed the book down, already annoyed. I wanted to know what "The Chaos" was, but this book definitely wasn't going to tell me anything more. That knowledge was probably deemed "too risky" for the citizens of Morley. They might get ideas, like, what if living in a police-state isn't as great as the Governor claims it is?

I laid back down on the cot. If this was the reality I was going to have to survive in, I might not survive for long. I was pretty nonconfrontational, but judging by the standards in Morley, I'd be the most opinionated person here. And apparently, opinions didn't belong to the masses.

I suddenly felt short of air, like there wasn't enough of it in the tiny cell I was trapped in. Taking a deep breath, I escaped in the only way I could, by closing my eyes and trying to go someplace else in my head. I imagined what Harlow might think of the nonsense I'd just read. No doubt she'd come up with a bunch of theories right away. Her voice was so clear I almost thought I was hearing her out loud. How long before I forgot what she sounded like?

Never, I decided. I'd never forget.

Just then, the cell door opened. A guard ordered me to stand, and I did so immediately. He blindfolded and handcuffed me, and soon I was being led through the maze of hallways again. I told myself this was a good thing. Maybe Lolo was back and the Governor wanted to talk to me about my new life here. That would mean Harlow had gone home safely and I would leave with my mom's double. I knew she wasn't *my* mom, but I was curious to talk with her. Anything even slightly familiar in this world was going to be welcome.

We entered a room where I was pushed into a chair and told to keep still. I waited there until the Governor's voice broke the silence.

"Hello, Nolan."

"Hello, sir," I said. Even though I couldn't see, I sensed he was only a few feet away.

"I trust you're enjoying the reading materials I provided?"

"Yes, sir," I said, playing along with whatever game this was.

"Good. I won't keep you from them for long. I thought you might be interested in helping your friend, Harlow."

"She's here?" I asked, sitting up straighter.

"She's close by," the Governor said, "and I believe you can help her understand something."

"Okay," I said, starting to feel wary of where this was going.

"Once you have completed your education here, you will be released into Morley as Nole Fredericks, under the condition that your previous life is never spoken of. However, it is not only *your* cooperation that is required, but Harlow's too. If she, or anyone else from your world, is found in the pond in the future, *you* will answer for it. Is that clear? No one will ever travel between our two worlds again."

As isolated as the pond was, I didn't see how I'd be able to ensure no one *ever* stumbled into it again. I wasn't about to tell the Governor he was being unreasonable though. "I agree," I said. "I think Harlow will too."

"Yes, she certainly will agree to these terms. And you will be the one telling her."

"I get to see her?" I asked, probably too eagerly.

"See her? No. And she won't see you. But she will hear you."

There was some shuffling, and I sensed an object being moved toward my face.

"You will speak into this microphone, repeating clearly only the words I tell you to."

So that's what this was about. I was to be his mouthpiece. If this was the last time I ever spoke to Harlow, I didn't want to be spewing some dictated speech. I thought for a fleeting second about saying what I really wanted to say to her. The blindfold and handcuffs quickly reminded me how stupid that would be. Maybe, hopefully, just hearing my voice would be a comfort to Harlow. I know hearing hers would have comforted me.

"Begin by saying her name," the Governor commanded, and I did so, the word "Harlow," filling me with warmth. From there, I did as the Governor asked, repeating line by line the instructions that would keep Harlow safe. The microphone was pulled away as soon as I said the last word.

The Governor dismissed me. I was seized by the guards and led back to my cell. All the while, I thought of what I would have said to Harlow if we weren't having a one-sided conversation under constant surveillance. I pictured her soft pink lips and dimpled smile.

Harlow, I wouldn't trade a single moment we had together for anything. Even if it means I end up in this same exact spot, it was worth it. You are the best thing that ever happened to me or will ever happen. When we met, I was at my ultimate low, and I might have stayed in that low place forever if it hadn't been for you. I'll replay the memories I have of you every day. I'll think about you every day. I'll miss you every day.

Tears dampened my blindfold as I felt the full weight of my loss. *It's true,* I continued saying to the Harlow in my head, *no one will ever replace you.*

34

HARLOW

I sat on the beam for hours, my burnt legs and feet throbbing with pain. The harsh white light never dimmed, and icicles formed in my hair. I was too afraid to ask for a drink of water. Whenever I came close to passing out, the guards jostled me back to full consciousness. The Governor wanted me to experience every second. Remember every moment.

Soon, I noticed that some places on my legs were numb. I worried what that might mean. I told myself the Governor would have to let me go home to my dad, that this couldn't last forever. But it had lasted long enough. I didn't know how much more pain I could endure.

When I heard Nolan's voice call out to me, I thought I was hallucinating.

"Harlow," it said. I stared at the unchanging white floor, not believing my ears. This was just my overwrought nerves at work.

"I am doing well. They are treating me fairly."

When I heard his voice again, I looked up, half expecting him to be standing in front of the door.

"Soon, I will leave this place as Nole Fredericks with my mother."

Nolan wasn't in the room with me. Of course. But he kept talking all the same.

"I can live in peace and safety. But I need your help."

I'll do anything to help you, I thought, listening more closely now.

"You can never speak of this Morley again. If you return here," his voice cautioned, and for a wild moment, I thought I was going home, "or if anyone from our world travels through the pond, they will be tortured, and I will be killed."

No. I gripped the beam tightly so I wouldn't fall.

"Don't let that happen."

I won't.

"From now on, we must live separate lives," he said, a fate that sounded terrible.

"But we will live."

How, Nolan? I wanted to call his name, but the room went quiet. I longed for Nolan to come back. My brain was tired and foggy and the stinging in my flesh intensified. I tried to recall some of what he'd said to me. He would stay alive here as long as there was no contact between the two worlds. Why would Nolan want that? Why did he want to live apart from me?

He wouldn't, I thought. In the heavy silence, I wondered if it had all been a trick of my senses after all.

Just then, the door opened. In a panic, I tensed all my muscles, which only aggravated the burns. As two guards entered the room, I decided that I really had heard Nolan's voice. His speaking to me wasn't a trick of my senses, but a trick of the Governor. It was another way to bend me to his will.

The guards went behind me and in a swift, synchronized motion, pushed me off the beam. I landed on my feet, heavy with blood from sitting the same way for so many hours. Immediately I collapsed onto the floor, making the burns on my legs scream. I screamed along with them.

The guards lifted me up and placed me back on the beam. From somewhere, from everywhere, I heard the Governor's voice say, "Do you understand, Harlow?"

I was crying and shaking. I couldn't answer.

"I knew you would."

35

LOLO

After I retrieved my backpack from upstairs, Harlow's father practically shoved me out of the house. Topher said he and Cate wouldn't be going to the pond, so it was me, Matt, Amaya, and Nole trekking through the woods. I didn't like that Nole was with us since he shouldn't be getting anywhere near the pond, but they insisted he come. It felt like whichever world I was in, what *I* wanted didn't seem to matter.

"Hey," Amaya said once we reached the tree line at the bottom of the hill, "you're wearing Harlow's pajamas. Shouldn't you change into your own clothes?"

"No," I said. I'd already thought of this. "From my father's perspective, the thing that makes the most sense is me poisoning Nole and then wasting no time getting back."

"Fine," Amaya said. "Just be sure to take that blue jacket off before you jump in. Harlow likes that one."

I nodded. It's not like I'd be allowed to wear it back in my Morley anyway.

"Hey," Amaya said, looking at me thoughtfully. "I've been wondering something. If your dad is the third generation to be governor—the third man—will you still be allowed to take over, even though you're a girl?"

I looked at her in surprise. It was the first thing she'd said to me that didn't sound like it was meant to start an argument. "Yes . . . why do you ask?"

"Because," she said tersely, "from everything I've heard, he seems like he'd be really misogynistic."

"What does that—"

"And there's no one else *qualified* to be the next governor?"

"No," I said, giving up on my own question. "My father wanted a son, but even though they tried, he and my mother never had another child after me. I was ten when he started to insist that maintaining our direct bloodline was the truly important thing, even if I was a girl."

Amaya just shook her head, which made me feel like I'd said something wrong, so I added, "He even has two women serving on the Advisory Board now."

"How progressive," she said, but it sounded snide. I normally wouldn't come to my father's defense or care if people were judging him, but the condescending way all these strangers kept talking about my world was tiresome. My father wasn't just a mindless murderer. I think he truly *did* want to keep Morley safe for the citizens.

After that, there was little conversation on the long walk. I practiced what I would say to my father when asked for my report. *Everything went according to plan. The mission was accomplished.* But there was no telling what he might say after I gave him my opening remarks. The arsenic for Nole had been disposed of at Harlow's house and I was carrying the empty vial. Aside from my word, it was the only evidence my father would have.

I imagined how I might be feeling and acting if I *had* killed Nole. I knew I would feel guilty. Scared, too. Nervous, confused, sick. All of that would be too much. I'd probably just be numb. I could let myself go numb; I did it all the time.

I started wondering what would happen once my father was satisfied with my story, once Nolan was gone, and once I could forget that any of this ever took place. I'd decided not to bring back the photo that Topher had taken of me all those years ago. I didn't care to see it, but the main thing was,

I didn't want my father to see it. A clear reminder of a past threat like that could make him clutch his power even tighter.

And what would I do when *I* had that power? My visit to this Morley had been brief, and though Harlow's friends and family were overbearing, they did make me reconsider whether the way my father ran our city-state was really the best way. If anything, now I knew that his wasn't the *only* way.

We approached the end of Mountain Pass Trail.

"Are we almost there?" Matt asked.

"Yeah," Amaya said. "Maybe fifteen more minutes."

She guided us through the trees. Nothing looked familiar until the pond came into view. It was so unassuming that it was hard to believe there was a whole other world, my world, lurking beneath its dark surface.

"How exactly does this work?" Matt asked. "Lolo jumps in, and Harlow reappears?"

"Pretty much," Amaya said. "But remember, if we fall in, we could get sent to the other world ourselves. So don't run all the way into the water when she gets here."

"Especially not Nole," I said, glancing at him.

"I *know*," he said. He sounded angry, but this was the way things had to be.

I walked to the pond's edge. Hopefully, there would be a towel and change of clothes awaiting me. I felt a pang of jealousy when I realized Harlow would be greeted by people who would be happy to see her again.

"Well, bye, Lolo," Amaya said, reminding me further that there was no one like her waiting for me. I had subordinates in Morley, not friends. It was probably for the better that I didn't make a friend here. I'd rather not know what I was missing and could never have.

"Goodbye," I said. I slipped out of the blue jacket, stepped into the water with my backpack, and dove into the center of the pond.

When I resurfaced, I looked right to the place where Amaya had been standing. She wasn't there. Instead, two guards rushed toward the pond, stopping when they got to the waterline. One of them said something into his radio while the other extended his hand to pull me up the slippery shore.

No greeting, nothing. I was merely a job to be completed. The guards took my wet backpack and handed me a towel. The short helicopter flight to the manor was silent. As we landed, I saw my father striding over to meet us. He didn't wait for the blades of the helicopter to stop rotating to begin our conversation.

"Were you successful?" my father asked, his eyes searching mine as if the answer could be found there. I needed to be careful that no part of me betrayed the truth.

I nodded. "Yes, sir."

"What happened?"

I clasped the towel tightly, realizing he wasn't going to wait for me to dry off before hearing the story.

"Everything went according to plan. The mission was accomplished."

"Nole consumed the arsenic?"

"Yes."

"When?"

My body trembled. I hoped my father attributed this to chills, not to my being nervous about telling a lie. "This morning. I pretended to be sick, and Harlow's father left for work. Nole came over for a ride to school. I told him I wasn't going because I didn't feel well and invited him inside. He didn't want to go to school without Harlow so he agreed. I prepared the hot chocolate, and he drank his unsuspectingly." I paused to take a breath.

"Then?" he said.

"Then I left the house and walked back to the pond."

My father's eyes narrowed. "If you left for the pond this morning, why did it take you so long to jump back? The walk is only two hours."

"Oh, um . . . I walked rather slowly." I said. "And," I added to cover up my clumsy answer, "I took a wrong turn in the woods, but I realized the mistake and changed directions."

"You're sure no other mistakes were made?" he asked, bending down so that his eyes were right at my level.

"Yes, sir," I said, my heart pounding.

"Very well," he said, after a minute of silence. "You were successful."

It was as close to a compliment as I ever got from him, and all because he thought I'd just killed someone. I hoped that my supposed success today didn't mean he would start sending me on similar assignments. If I was ordered to kill someone in our world, there'd be no way for me to get out of it.

Finally, I was allowed to shower and change. I stuffed Harlow's pajamas into a bag to be discarded so I'd never have to see them again. I wanted to sleep for the rest of the day. Maybe when I woke up, they'd tell me that Nolan, having served his purpose, was no more. Then I could truly live without fear of Nole changing his mind about staying in the other world.

Before I could lie down, my father summoned me to his office to receive instructions for one more task. This surprised me. When I entered the room, he was sitting behind his spotless desk, hands folded in his lap. My first thought was that Nole had come back, but my father said, "You will have a final conversation with Nolan."

I shut my eyes for a moment. This day was endless. "Can I ask the purpose of this conversation, sir?"

"You didn't find your last exchange with him interesting?"

"Yes, sir, I did," I said through gritted teeth, "but since I don't need to know anything more about Nolan's world, what are we to discuss?" If my father wanted to pry further information from Nolan about life in the other Morley, he certainly didn't need my help. Obtaining intelligence was one of his specialties.

"*What* you two discuss I leave to your discretion. Although, I recommend something that will put Nolan at ease, something to make him less suspicious of the drink he will be offered."

"The drink?" I said, then my heart dropped into my stomach. I understood what he meant.

"Of course," he continued, "having done this once already you'll know that in such circumstances, it is easier when the criminal is unaware of your intentions. It's less *messy*, don't you agree?"

"Yes, sir," I said, my throat dry. He wanted me to kill Nolan, to lure him to his own death under the pretense of a peace offering. By the time he realized what was happening to him, it would be too late. His final moments would be spent knowing he'd walked right into the trap of my false friendship. Nolan needed to die for my secret to be completely safe; it wasn't the logic I objected to, but the idea that I would be personally responsible.

My father, observing me closely as I stared at the floor, picked up on my discomfort.

"What is your hesitation about? Tell me."

I curled my fingers so that my nails dug into my thumbs. "I have no hesitation," I said.

"Yes, you do." Slowly, he rose from his chair and leaned forward with his hands on his desk. "Whatever doubts you have, they are distracting you from the one thing that matters: protecting the city-state."

"Yes, sir. I will protect the city-state." That's what everything circled back to with him, and maybe it was exactly what I needed to focus on now. If Nolan lived among the people of Morley, he might spread confusion and start a panic about the existence of the other world.

My father stood up to his full height. "Lolo," he said, "*who* do you think I mean when I say, 'the city-state?'"

The pointed way he phrased the question caught my attention. There were two possible answers. The first, that the citizens were the city-state, was the one my father proclaimed to the public, and whenever he was explaining one of his decisions to the Advisory Board. The second answer, the one I'd never heard him state explicitly, was that he, as the governor, was the very embodiment of Morley. I maintained a naive hope that it was the first one.

When I didn't answer, he slapped both hands on the desk. "*I* am the city-state!" he yelled. "And you must fully understand what that means before *you* become the city-state."

"I will, sir!" I said, hating that he'd confirmed what I'd been afraid to hear. The longer this situation dragged on, the harder it was going to be to step back into my normal life. I didn't want to think of my father as *completely* self-serving, or that our lives here were as backward as Amaya and all the rest seemed to believe. Not when there was nothing I could do about it, at least not for a long time. My father scowled at me, but he stayed hunched over, taking long, deep breaths.

In that moment, I saw him not as the domineering authority figure I was used to obeying without question, but as a paranoid man on the brink of collapse. All of this anger and alarm over what—a single boy? Either Nolan was a greater threat than I knew, or my father—the city-state—was actually quite vulnerable. This was about preserving the way of life in Morley only so far as it preserved *him*. For the first time in my life, I wondered: Did he care about the citizens of Morley at all?

"Go," he said, pointing to the door.

I turned from him immediately. Years' worth of unpleasant memories surfaced, each one increasing my resentment as I remembered how selfish and controlling he'd always been. Usually, I would tell myself to forget it, as unchangeable circumstances weren't worth fretting about. Maybe, though, my circumstances weren't as unchangeable as I'd been taught to believe.

As I left the office, a tray with two cups was placed in my hands. "The green one is for the criminal," a guard explained. "The black is for you."

I nodded, but as I followed him to the interrogation room where Nolan was waiting, I felt my old childhood sympathies rising. I'd wanted to talk to the people of Morley and ask what they thought of their governor, but there'd been no way to communicate with them. I'd tried not to think about nameless and faceless people whom I wasn't allowed to meet. That was, until I traveled to the other world. I pictured Amaya, Matt, Nole, Topher, and Cate. Would any of them do what I was on my way to do now? Sacrifice a life for the sake of appeasing one selfish person?

No, *two* selfish people. I was acting out of self-interest just as much as my father was. I wanted Nolan dead not because I was really worried about him spreading panic among the citizens of Morley, but to protect my own self, my own lies.

When we reached the room where Nolan was being held and swung the door open, Nolan jumped in his seat. Initially, his eyes brightened a little like he was excited, but only for a second. I was not Harlow, he realized. Two guards entered the room and stood at opposite walls. No one said anything as I stared at the table where I was meant to place the tray.

If I were to refuse this task, the consequences would be severe, but *how* severe was unknown. It was important to my father that he have a direct descendant as an heir because he believed it was a key part of maintaining stability in Morley. It seemed unlikely that he would have me killed.

But not impossible.

The tray started to shake in my hands, and I quickly sat down.

"Hello, Nolan," I said.

"Hi, Lolo." His eyes found the two cups and stayed there.

A criminal's rations were heavily restricted, so he must be thirsty. Nolan's handcuffs meant he couldn't reach for a cup himself. If I was going to do this, I'd have to pour the arsenic down his throat while he thanked me for the drink.

Again, I doubted my ability to commit murder. To stall, I took a sip from the black cup.

"Did . . . the plan work?" he asked when I didn't say anything.

"Yes," I said, staring down at my water.

Nolan breathed a sigh of relief. "So that means Harlow is home for good."

"Yes," I said again. She was home with her father who loved her, and her friends, and her life full of possibilities.

I looked up from the cup and into Nolan's eyes. He averted his gaze right away. *He's scared of me*, I thought. Just like everyone else. And I knew then that by killing him, I'd only be validating their fear as perfectly reasonable. This fear is what protected my father's power, but I felt that I didn't want it to protect mine. Still, what could I do?

"Are you thirsty?" I asked, my voice suddenly hoarse.

"What?" Nolan said. He looked warily at the cups.

"You must be thirsty," I said, picking up the green cup.

"Oh, um, that's okay."

I stood up unsteadily and kept my eyes fixed on the cup, not on Nolan.

My hand was shaking as I brought it toward his closed mouth. It must have been obvious to him by then that this was no ordinary drink of water. His eyes, like mine, were quickly filling with tears.

"Please," he whispered. "Lolo, please don't."

"I have to," I said.

"Why?" he asked.

Because I always did what I was told. Because otherwise *I* might be the one in handcuffs. Because my father believed I'd already done this once. Because I had to. But was that reason enough?

"I'm sorry," I said. "I don't want to, but—" And I realized that not only did I not *want* to kill Nolan, but I *couldn't* kill him. I didn't have it in me.

I dropped the cup, and it was like I'd been cut loose from a chain. When I'd defied my father's will in the other world, it hadn't been my choice. This was. However, the strange exhilaration lasted only a few seconds.

I heard a familiar voice escape from the guards' radios and I knew I was trapped.

"Nolan," I said suddenly, "I didn't do it. I didn't kill Nole. He's alive in the other Morley." I didn't know why I was telling him this; it couldn't help him, but I didn't want to keep it bottled up any longer.

"What?" he said.

Then the door opened, and I saw my father. His face was twisted with rage. He leapt forward and grabbed me by the shoulders.

"Guards! Take her to a cell!"

36

HARLOW

I was sitting on the beam, expecting to be pushed off again at any second. I dreaded the pain that would consume me whole. Sitting, waiting. They were the only things I could do.

Then, I was underwater. I thought at first they were drowning me, that somehow they'd pushed me into a pool. My legs were deadweights that might drown me even if the guards didn't.

I reached for the surface anyhow. Several voices screamed my name and I heard my dad. If he was here, I was safe. I started paddling, but my legs wouldn't budge. I floundered in the water.

"Harlow! Hold on!" It was Amaya.

My fumbling hands caught onto a large stick, and I held on as it was dragged forward. The water got shallower, and my legs rubbed against the pond floor. The pain was agonizing. I screamed, letting go of the stick.

"Harlow!"

"Dad!" I cried as he rushed knee-high into the water.

"Careful, Matt!" I heard Amaya call out.

My dad attempted to pull me up, and I let out another shrill cry.

"What is it? What's wrong?" he asked.

"It hurts . . ." I said, feeling lightheaded.

Amaya marched into the water and together with my dad, lifted me from either side so that my arms were draped across their shoulders. They brought me to dry land and gently laid me down on my back atop a clean towel. Once I was settled, they crouched beside me, each holding a hand. My dad repeated my name over and over while Amaya brushed a clump of wet hair from my eyes. That's when I saw Nole standing in the background, looking at me in shock.

"Her *feet*," he said.

"What?" Amaya said. Then she looked for herself.

"Oh my god!" she said, clambering toward my feet. My dad was next to her in a second. They stared in horror at the damaged flesh. I looked, too, but only briefly. *Feeling* it was enough.

"They did this to you?" my dad asked in a low, gravelly voice. "We help that girl get home safely, and this is how they—"

"Wait, Matt," Amaya said, examining my ankles. "I think there's more." Gingerly, she rolled up the bottom of my left pant leg. I exhaled sharply as the fabric scrunched up around my knee. Amaya pulled her hands away when I screamed again. "Sorry! I'm sorry!" she said.

Only part of my mutilated shin was visible, but it was enough for her and my dad to understand that the damage was extensive. My pajamas had been fused to my legs for hours. Even soggy from the pond water, removing them might mean peeling my skin off.

"Amaya," my dad said, sounding more collected now, more like himself, "start running back. Stop as soon as you get service and call 911."

"But—" she said, then thought better of it. She stood up. "Okay."

"Tell the operator it's a burn victim. We'll need a helicopter."

"Don't worry, Harlow; you're going to be all right," Amaya said as she darted from the pond. I wanted to watch her go, but my eyelids were heavy. I began to slip away.

"You hear that?" My dad's voice warbled in my ears as if it came from a great distance. "Amaya's right. You're going to be just fine."

I tried to stay awake, but the pain and shock were beckoning me into unconsciousness.

I heard Nole say, "How are we going to explain the injury?"

My dad said, "Let's save Harlow first. We'll craft a story later."

The last words I caught were: "What about telling the truth?"

No! I thought desperately as my mind sank into darkness. Telling the truth wasn't an option. The other Morley had to remain a secret. To save Nolan.

37

NOLAN

I couldn't believe how close I'd come to dying. Lolo was only seconds away from pouring whatever poison was in the cup down my throat when I pleaded with her, and I hadn't expected her to listen. I watched in shock as she dropped the cup.

Then, the room erupted into chaos as the Governor came charging in and the guards handcuffed their newest prisoner. Lolo let herself be pushed out the door without a fight. I thought I might be left alone when the Governor turned around and seized me by the collar of the hospital gown I'd been wearing for days.

"Was this your idea?" he hissed in my ear.

"No, it wasn't, I swear!"

He shoved me back into the chair. "My daughter's loyalty to the city-state was compromised in barely a *day* beyond our borders. Sixteen years undone in a matter of hours?"

It seemed like he was talking to himself more than me. He paced across the room with quick, sharp steps.

"Clearly, everything I've been doing to educate her hasn't been effective. That problem will be remedied immediately." The Governor stopped and stared at me like he was making some assessment. I was already con-demned to die, and I'd rather do it before I was used for another terrible scheme. Knowing there was nothing I could do to save myself made me bolder.

"I won't help you," I said.

The Governor smacked me across the face. I fell from the chair.

"You will do whatever is required of you," he said calmly, like he wasn't the reason I was on the floor. The handcuffs made it difficult for me to get up, but I struggled to anyway. I might have been successful if the Governor hadn't placed his heavy boot over one of my ankles.

"What do you want from me?" I asked, panting as I adjusted myself on the floor.

"Only what I want from all citizens of Morley," he said. "Your cooperation."

"Well, you don't have it."

The Governor put more weight on my ankle so that I thought my bone might snap.

"Okay!" I yelled. "Okay!"

"Ah, you see," he said, slightly lifting up his boot. "Your mind is only as strong as your body is weak. Persuading you with words could take ages. But I've just recruited you to my cause in a few simple movements."

He reapplied pressure to my ankle to keep me from arguing. It made me furious how quickly he'd stomped out my rebellion.

"I have no doubt that Lolo will be similarly persuaded. Soon, we will return to this room so that she may carry out today's original purpose."

He gave me a meaningful look. Killing me wasn't enough—Lolo had to be the one to do it. I could think of nothing worse than dying by the hand of a girl who looked like Harlow. But at least Harlow was safe. That's what mattered now. Then I remembered the other person whom I wanted to keep safe.

"What will happen to Nole's mother?" I asked.

"She was released this morning. The great magnanimity shown to her will only increase her devotion to Morley. She understands why Nole couldn't join her. Some crimes, like trying to abandon the city-state, are unforgivable."

So, she was alive. Traumatized and probably brainwashed, but alive. It was more than I could say for my own mom.

The Governor radioed his guards and almost instantly, two of them appeared.

"Take him back to his cell," he ordered. I was scooped off the floor, blindfolded, and hurried through the twisting hallways. When I got to my cell and was freed from the handcuffs and blindfold, I stood gazing at the white wall for a long time. There was no point in reading the books about this Morley or making plans for my future here. I didn't even want to think about what I would say to Harlow if she were in the cell with me now. That would hurt too much, far more than my bruised ankle did. Instead, I flopped onto the rickety cot and just sat there. Sitting, waiting.

38

NOLE

After Amaya left, Matt and I tried to keep Harlow warm while we waited for help to arrive. Finally, a helicopter appeared in the sky overhead. There was only room for Harlow and Matt, so I had to walk back to Morley.

It was lonely walking through the woods by myself. If I got lost out here, how long would it be before someone came looking? Thankfully, I met up with Amaya on the path. She looked as relieved to see me as I was to see her. She asked me all about the rescue operation, and I told her that as far as I could tell, Harlow was safely on her way to the hospital.

"Nole," Amaya said, her voice shaking a little, "what do you think the Governor did to Harlow?"

"I think he burned her, somehow." It was a disturbing thought.

"Yeah," she said, grimacing. "Is that kind of thing normal in your Morley?"

"Being arrested and imprisoned is normal," I said, "but what they actually do to you once you're inside is sort of a mystery." That's what made it so terrifying—the not knowing what might await you. "I want to know if the Governor has hurt my mom, and I hate that *that* will remain a mystery too."

Amaya nodded. "I'm really sorry, Nole. I wish there was something more we could do."

We were close to the city when Amaya groaned. "I can't put off calling my mom any longer. She's left me four messages in the past hour."

"What will you tell her? Maybe we should ask Matt about it first."

"Matt's a little busy right now," she said. "And besides, my mom won't like *any* explanation I give her."

She switched between English and the other language, Farsi, so I didn't understand everything. I got the general idea though, since Amaya pulled the phone away from her ear whenever her mom's voice got too loud. They talked for several minutes before Amaya said goodbye.

"Well, that was pretty much the disaster I was expecting," she said.

"She sounded angry."

"Yeah, but she was worried, too. I've never actually skipped school before, so getting a call from Cardiff kind of freaked her out. Nolan's aunt and uncle probably got a call too."

"Oh," I said. I'd all but forgotten about them. "What am I supposed to tell them?"

"I just told my mom that there was an emergency and Harlow's at the hospital. But I honestly don't know what we should do. I mean, Matt is the mayor of Morley. This is going to be news."

"Okay," I said, "but if Matt is the leader here, can't he just tell the newspeople what to write?"

Amaya gave me a look that told me I'd said something wrong again. I suddenly felt defensive. "Okay, *sorry*; I guess not."

"Yeah, unfortunately, that's not going to be an option. We can't just cover it up."

"Well," I said, not wanting to offer up any more ideas for her to shoot down, "maybe you should call Topher. He might know what to do."

"Yes!" Amaya said. "Why didn't I think of that?"

She called him immediately and the story gushed out of her. As I listened, I was struck again by the feeling that I'd lived an entire lifetime in the span of a few days. I wondered if Nolan was feeling the same way. Even though life in my Morley was simpler, Nolan had a lot to learn in a place with little room for errors. Would my mom help him to adjust? Would Catherine? Jealousy flared up within me. But maybe Nolan was jealous of me too. No doubt he wanted to be home as much as I did.

"Okay," Amaya said, sticking her phone in her pocket. "Topher and Cate are going to meet us at the hospital. He thinks we should tell people the three of us skipped school to go camping and had an accident while boiling water over the campfire. He'll suggest it as a cover story to Matt."

Amaya was clearly worried about crafting the right fake story, but I was tired of keeping track of so many lies. I didn't want to live the rest of my life under someone else's identity. And how could I learn to be Nolan when I couldn't stop thinking about the people I'd left behind?

～～

Amaya's mom was waiting for us at Eastside Park. She threw her arms around Amaya and hugged her, eyes closed, for a long time. Amaya made no move to pull away. Seeing the two of them together made me miss my own mom even more. On the way to the hospital, Mrs. Rostami, as Amaya told me I should call her mom, asked for details about what had happened. Amaya said she couldn't explain yet.

We met Matt, Topher, and Cate in the waiting room at six. Harlow was in surgery, getting a procedure for second- and third-degree burns. Mrs. Rostami gave Matt a hug. He then guided her into a corner of the room where they had a whispered conversation. She looked back at us several times, her eyebrows knitted together. From what snippets I could hear, it sounded like Matt was telling her the camping story.

"Do you think you'll ever tell your mom about my Morley?" I asked Amaya.

"I don't know," she said. "I'm going to be in enough trouble as it is. I don't need her thinking I'm crazy on top of it all."

Topher sighed when she said that. I could only guess how many times he'd heard the word "crazy" used to describe him.

"Nole," Amaya said, "you should probably check your phone to see if Bailey has called." She helped me unlock the screen and open the notifications. She was right: Uncle Bailey had texted and called Nolan a number of times during the day. Amaya read a few messages out loud.

"Why did your school just inform me that you're not there?"

"Where are you?"

"Nolan, what's going on?"

She placed the phone in my hand. "You've got to call him. I bet he'll call the police if you don't."

"But what should I say?" I asked, at once feeling overwhelmed.

"It'll take a long time to convince your uncle of the truth," Topher said, "and you're never going to be able to do it over the phone. For now, just tell him you're safe."

"Okay, but I'm not sure he'll *ever* believe the truth. He and Nolan's aunt haven't seemed to notice that I'm not actually their nephew." As I said it, I felt bad for Nolan. Did he feel invisible living in that big house? I was sure I was going to.

"Maybe not yet," Topher said, "but it's still best that your family knows."

"They're not my family," I said, aware of how stubborn I sounded. "And they'll never understand."

"But *we* know who you really are, Nole," Cate said. "You can always talk to us about what's going on." Behind her glasses, Cate had the same brown eyes as Catherine. The longer I looked at her, the more homesick I felt.

"Maybe I can still go home," I said.

"Nole," Topher said firmly, "that's not an option. If you go back, not only will you be arrested and killed, but the Governor will know that Lolo lied to him."

"She's his only heir; he wouldn't hurt her. Not seriously, anyway."

"You might be right," Topher said, "but Governor Matthias could retaliate in ways that hurt a lot of innocent people, your mother included. And later, down the line, who knows what such a betrayal of trust would do to Lolo. Her paranoia might turn out to be even worse than her father's."

"I know, I know," I said. If I went back to Morley, there could be a lot of unforeseen consequences. Right then though, I wasn't looking for permission so much as sympathy. "But Topher, *you've* got to understand what it's like to want to go home."

"I do, Nole," he said. "But with time, this world really can feel like home." Cate, who had been eyeing him nervously, smiled when he said that.

"*Sure*," I said, slumping into my seat. I wasn't satisfied with his answer, but I didn't see a point in talking about it further. I could either persevere like he'd done until my homesickness went away, or I could go against his advice and my promise to Lolo and travel back through the pond, consequences be damned. I hated both choices.

Matt and Mrs. Rostami finished their private conversation and joined the rest of us.

"You've all got to be hungry," Mrs. Rostami said. "Why don't we go to dinner? We won't be able to see Harlow tonight anyway."

"But we can see her tomorrow, right?" Amaya asked.

"Most likely," Mrs. Rostami said. "Matt will let us know."

"Oh, Nole," Amaya said to me, "you never did call your uncle."

I made no movement to take out Nolan's phone again. This day already had its fair share of difficult conversations, and I was running on empty. I must have looked pretty upset because Matt volunteered to tell Bailey about our "camping trip" for me. He said he didn't mind, and it would give him something to do while he waited for Harlow's surgery to finish.

Topher and Cate left, and Mrs. Rostami took Amaya and me to another restaurant. I only picked at my food. I was still weighing my two options: stay here or go home. Everyone in this world was insisting that I didn't actually have a choice, that I would remain in this Morley forever. Everyone, I realized, except for Harlow. I wondered if she might be the *one* person who wouldn't try and talk me into staying.

39

LOLO

'd only been inside a cell once before. For my twelfth birthday, my father took me on a tour of the criminal facilities. He'd wanted to show me the hard, depressing life that awaited Morley's worst offenders, those citizens who spurned the security that the city-state so graciously provided. I remember being rather unimpressed. The cells were small, bare, and cold, but they weren't as scary or sensational as I'd been expecting. Now, having been locked in one, I was beginning to understand that the cell itself wasn't the worst part, but the fact I could never leave it. My world shrunk so that nothing existed but plain walls, garish lights, and an alarm that sounded whenever I began to nod off to sleep. My father wasn't stingy about using energy if it meant proving a point.

The longer I was forced to stay awake, the more frantic my thoughts became. To distract myself, I started counting the passing seconds aloud. It was no use. My mind kept drifting back to what was happening on the other side of the heavy door.

I wondered what my father had told my mother, and what she made of this entire situation. Most likely, she'd think me foolish for siding with low-class criminals like Nole and Nolan. Then there were the guards. Although

I couldn't see them, I heard their muffled footsteps going up and down the hall. Would my defiance make them question their own loyalty to my father, or would they hate me for being a traitor? I also wanted to know how Nolan was doing. *If* he was still alive. In my attempt to save his life, I might have gotten him killed in a more painful way than poison. The idea was quickly pushing me to my edge.

I'd feel better if I could get some sleep. If I could only nap for a few . . .

The alarm rang out, shocking me back awake.

"Please!" I called out to the empty room. "Please, I'm so tired!"

"*You're* tired?" It was my father's voice, crackling over the speaker. "Then you can only imagine how tired *I* am, having to clean up this mess you've made."

"I'm sorry, Father, please—"

"But I suppose you didn't start this mess," he continued, speaking over me. "*That* honor belongs to your grandfather."

I was so exhausted, to the point of being delusional, that I wasn't sure I'd heard him right.

"Yes," he said. "There's a connection between the pond and Morley's energy project. However, it started long before my wind turbines. I just came across an old file detailing a dangerous experiment funded by my father. He was working on creating a new energy source of his own. But the operation was a failure, and the scientists were . . . dismissed."

I stared at the white wall, trying to figure out why he was telling me this. He sounded angry, but then, he'd just discovered both his father and daughter had been keeping secrets from him.

"When the project was abandoned, all that remained was a pond with tainted water, and your grandfather deemed it too obscure to be of any great concern. He was wrong. And it was that idiot photographer who proved just how irresponsibly he acted."

Topher! Suddenly, I felt wide awake and my heart banged against my chest.

"I know him!" The words burst out of me before I could think twice. "He still has the photo."

"What?" my father said sharply. "You met him?"

"Yes," I said. There wasn't any point in holding back now. "Topher convinced me to spare Nole's life."

"If that's the case, then the next person I send through the portal will see to it that *both* of them are dead." My father's voice boomed over the speakers so that it seemed to fill up every inch of the stark room.

"But why kill them?" I asked, jumping off the cot. "Topher's been living in the other world for years. He hasn't done *anything* to compromise our way of life here. So that means you can let him go, along with Nole and Nolan."

"Oh, is that what it means?"

His tone was mocking, but I answered him anyway. "Yes. Then all of us can move on from this—"

"Ah, so *that's* what you're after," he said. "You just want to move on and save your own skin. That's an instinct we can work with."

"But I'm not just trying to save myself!" I cried, pounding on the door. "I want you to let them all go! After everything I'm sure you did to Harlow—"

The lights shut off. The sudden change made me dizzy, and I blinked several times, hoping my eyes would adjust. But they didn't. The room was utterly dark. And quiet. I waited to hear what my father would say, but a moment later I realized that this darkness was his reply. I crawled back to the cot and curled up into a tiny ball. At least now I could sleep, and if I were to have nightmares, they would be in color.

40

HARLOW

My eyes fluttered open and the first thing I saw was a bright light.

No! I panicked, terrified that I was back in that room.

"Harlow, hey, it's okay." That's when I noticed my dad. He got up from his chair and stood beside my bed.

"Dad . . ." I said, still not fully believing I was safe.

"I'm right here; everything's okay."

I glanced around the room. "I'm at the hospital?"

"Yes, you were helicoptered here yesterday afternoon."

"Helicoptered?"

"And it was a good thing, too. You underwent extensive debridement and skin-grafting for the burns."

At the mention of burns, I stared down at my bandaged legs and feet. I couldn't move them. I felt trapped, almost as trapped as I'd felt in my cell. I started to cry.

"You're going to be okay," Dad said in a soothing voice. "Given time and an ongoing treatment plan, you'll—"

"How long will that be?" I asked, antsy to leave. "What about school? I have midterms."

"Harlow, your health is more important than a few weeks out of school."

"*Weeks?*" I felt more exasperated with everything he said.

"I'll talk to your teachers; we'll figure things out."

I gave a sigh of resignation and leaned against the pillows. My dad sighed too. Suddenly, I felt guilty for not telling him the truth about the other Morley. "I'm so sorry, Dad," I said. "I should've told you what was going on; I just didn't know how."

"Shh," he crouched next to me. "There's nothing to apologize for. Okay?"

It wasn't surprising that he said this, but it was a relief to hear all the same. "Okay."

"How do you feel?" he asked.

Gently, I touched the white wrappings on my legs. "It's sore," I said, then gasped from a blazing pain on my arms and back. I told my dad, and he nodded.

"Those were the donor sites. The doctor said that's to be expected. He also—"

"Dad," I said, cutting him off at another panicked thought. "What will my legs look like?"

For the first time, he looked a little scared. His answer was evasive. "The thing to focus on is regaining movement. You'll be in physical and occupational therapy."

"But the scars will never go away," I said, "will they?"

He tried to smile. "What are a few scars? I've got you back, and that's what matters."

I was back home, but Nolan wasn't, and there was nothing I could do to change that. Even the little scar I'd gotten on my knee during our bike ride was gone, replaced by these scars from the Governor. More tears gathered in my eyes.

"Okay," Dad said, standing back up. "I'm calling a nurse now."

"No, wait," I said. "What if Governor Matthias is hurting Nolan like this?"

"I . . . I don't think . . ." But he didn't have anything reassuring to offer.

I decided then to believe what Nolan had told me; that he would be freed by the Governor to live as Nole. I didn't think I could handle believing anything else.

"I heard Nolan's voice there, when I was in my cell." At the mention of the word "cell," I saw something like hatred pass through my dad's eyes. "Nolan said we would never see each other again, and if anyone from our Morley ever goes through the pond, they'll be tortured, and he'll be killed."

"Then we'll make sure no one goes through the portal," my dad said simply. "I can work with the county to make it a restricted area."

"But that means Nolan will really be trapped there forever," I said, my throat closing on my words.

He took my hand in his. "I'm so sorry, Harlow."

That afternoon, Amaya came to see me, along with Topher and Cate. They were full of nice things to say and wore big smiles, but I found I couldn't match their lighthearted mood, even when Amaya handed me a stack of cards from her family and the whole debate team. I'd already told my dad about the room with the beam, and I figured he asked them not to mention it because no one did. Instead, we got to talking about the story that was being told to the public. In this version, my dad took me, Amaya, and Nolan on an impromptu camping trip. We had a bad accident while boiling water, which required me to be air-lifted to the hospital.

Noticing his absence, I said, "By the way, where's Nole?"

Amaya's face drooped. "He's at his aunt and uncle's house. They're mad at him for ditching school, and now he's pretending to be sick."

"Oh," I said. "But he can't do that forever."

"Yes," Topher said, "that's what I keep telling him. He'll need to adjust at some point."

I wondered then how Nolan was adjusting to his new life in the other Morley, and what it was like for him to meet his mom's double. Maybe being with her would be comforting in some way, but it could just as easily make him miss his real mom even more. I knew there was no way I'd ever be able to see Nole without missing Nolan.

I heard next about the Governor's thwarted plan to poison Nole.

Apparently, Lolo had agreed fairly quickly to spare Nole's life, but she was adamant that he could never reenter the pond. It seemed she was as afraid of the Governor as everyone else, and I couldn't blame her for wanting to keep her lie a secret. If Nole went home, then not only would he be tortured, but Lolo might be too. It felt like with every passing second, Nolan's fate in the other Morley grew more sealed.

Amaya changed the subject. "I brought you some homework," she said. "*If* you want to do it. You have the perfect excuse not to."

"I could use a distraction," I said, and she nodded knowingly. "I wish I could go back to school now. But I don't even know when I'll be allowed to leave the hospital."

"Harlow," Amaya said, "you should stay as long as you need to. I'll visit you every day."

We talked a while longer until Topher and Cate had to leave for the airport.

"We'll keep in touch," Cate said. "Call or text me anytime."

"Yes, call us if you need anything," said Topher. "And if something comes up . . ." He gave me a pointed look. "I'm only a flight away."

I'm only a flight away. Those were the same words my mom always said to me when she flew home after her annual visit. She'd called earlier today, but I hadn't wanted to talk. If she really was just a flight away, why wasn't she here? For some reason though, I believed Topher when he said it. If we needed help, he'd come back.

Amaya left shortly after, and then it was just me and my dad. He was planning to spend another night here on a rollaway bed. I kept telling him I was fine and that he could go home, but he insisted on staying. I was glad he did.

His phone rang. "Harlow, it's your mom again."

"No," I said. "I'm not talking to her."

"Are you sure? She's going to try to fly out here this weekend."

That made me pause. I was mad that she wasn't here already, but maybe she deserved a little more credit than I was giving her. Still, the only reason she was thinking of making a special trip was because something was really wrong. Not because she just wanted to see me. "Tell her not to. I don't want to see her."

"Harlow—"

"No!" I'm sure I sounded like a petulant child, but I didn't feel like being reasonable. I was too bitter and in too much pain. His phone finally stopped ringing.

"I'll call her back later. She's worried about you."

"Did you tell her the story about the camping accident?"

"I did."

"She's probably going to blame *you* for this," I said, tears springing to my eyes. "That's not *fair*. It's not fair!" I cried harder and my dad carefully put his arms around me.

"I know it's not."

⌇

A few days passed. I spent as much time catching up on schoolwork as I could, but the pain, and the drowsiness from the pain medication, made it hard to focus. Thoughts of Nolan made it nearly hopeless. On Saturday night, Nole came to see me. He'd fully "recovered" from his illness and he walked into my hospital room, head hanging down, behind Amaya.

"Hi, Harlow," he said.

"Hi."

Sensing the awkwardness, Amaya got to talking, turning back and forth between me and Nole. "Nole's feeling better and he's going to come to school Monday. I know you won't be there yet, Harlow, but Nole, I'll help you get used to everything. Or maybe I should start calling you Nolan since—"

"No," I said, automatically. "Don't call him that."

Amaya sat down on my bed. "But we have to, Harlow. From now on, Nole *is* Nolan."

"No, I'm not."

Amaya and I looked at Nole in surprise.

"*Okay*," Amaya said slowly, "but 'Nolan' is who everyone will think you are. It'll work out. Topher got used to life here; I'm sure you can too."

"Maybe I *can*," he said, "but I don't want to."

I leaned forward, at once extremely curious about where this was going. "Nole, are you . . . are you thinking about going home? Because if you do, the Governor will kill you." I looked into his eyes, and he didn't turn away.

"I don't want to stay here," he said.

"You'd rather *die?*" Amaya asked.

I never would've asked Nole to consider going to his death just so I could have Nolan back, but here he was, offering the idea up himself.

"What are you going to do?" I asked.

"I'm going to go back." He didn't sound afraid; he sounded sure of himself. Still, I wanted him to fully understand the implications of what he was saying.

"Even though you'll be tortured? *And* after the deal you made with Lolo?"

"Yeah," he said. "Earlier this week, I talked with Topher about switching places with Nolan and he warned me that my life might not be the only one at stake. Governor Matthias could retaliate against others if I return." He shifted his weight back and forth. "But I just keep thinking about that phrase, '*could* retaliate.' He also could decide *not* to. The Governor has got to be getting tired of this chase between worlds. So, while the risk to others is there, the only person *guaranteed* to be in danger is me. And maybe Lolo. I can accept that."

I felt a sort of awe for him then. "That's . . . really brave," I said. It sounded lame, but I couldn't think of anything better in the moment.

"Yeah," Amaya said. "Seriously."

"And I don't want to keep waiting," Nole said.

"Then I'll go with you tomorrow," said Amaya. "I'll make sure you get to the pond, and I can help Nolan get home."

I reached for Amaya and she came closer to give me a light hug.

"I couldn't ask for better friends than you two," I said.

"You mean Nolan?" Nole asked.

Amaya stepped back and I looked at Nole. "No, I mean you."

41

NOLE

I stayed up almost all Saturday night worrying. It wasn't that I doubted my decision to leave, but I kept picturing Harlow's wounds and wondering if something similar was in store for me. Only, I wouldn't be taken to a hospital afterward.

In the morning, Amaya knocked on my door.

"Hey, Nolan," she said brightly. "Is your uncle still up for taking us to visit Harlow?"

"Um, wh—" I started, but she flashed her eyes at me and subtly nodded toward her mom, who was standing several feet behind her. "Oh, yeah, he is," I said.

"Cool," she said, then turned around to wave. "Bye, Mom. See you later."

As soon as the door shut, she dropped the act.

"Thanks for covering. I'm technically not allowed to go into the woods right now. Anyway, Harlow texted me a list of things we should take to the pond. I've got a first-aid kit and some snacks with me, but you'll need to grab a towel and change of clothes for Nolan—something warm."

"Okay," I said. "Does Matt know I'm leaving?" Once I'd gotten over his resemblance to the Governor, I discovered I really liked Matt. He'd been nice to me as both Nolan and Nole.

"Yeah, Harlow told him this morning. He said to say goodbye and that he thinks you're a 'very impressive and admirable young man.' That's high praise—especially coming from him."

I blushed, unaccustomed to hearing such words used to describe me. I remembered too that Harlow had called me brave last night. Their opinions made me determined to follow through with my plan. I would make them proud of me.

Once we'd filled a backpack with supplies, we set off for the woods. As we walked, Amaya fretted about the million different states that Nolan could be in when he returned. "I might have to call for help again," she said. "What if Nolan can't walk? Who knows what's happened to him."

Not too eager to think about the death trap I was probably about to fling myself into, I repeated Matt's and Harlow's words to myself, hoping they would be motivation enough, but they were little match for my anxiety. The closer we got to the pond, the slower I found myself moving.

Amaya, noticing this, put her hand on my arm and stopped us. "Hey," she said, "are you sure you want to keep going?"

I *had* been sure, but as I looked into Amaya's concerned eyes, I realized I was more afraid than I'd ever been in my life. "No," I said.

I thought she would tell me that I wasn't allowed to change my mind, or that I absolutely had to do this. Telling me what to do is basically the only thing the people in this world had done since I'd arrived. Instead, Amaya said, "Okay. That's what I thought."

She was actually going to let me decide. I could have given up right there, and I was about to, but then I pictured walking back into Harlow's hospital room and hearing her say those same words, her voice thick with disappointment. *That's what I thought.* I'd feel like more of an imposter here than I already did. So maybe I *could* be brave. And impressive, and admirable. Maybe my life, short as it was going to be, would still matter once it was over.

Amaya started to turn around.

"Wait," I said, "if there's one thing I learned growing up in Morley, it's that sometimes you have to do things you don't want to do."

"Like what? Civic duties or sacrificing yourself for the sake of the Governor?"

"Sort of," I said. "But at least I'll be sacrificing myself for somebody who sounds like he's a pretty good person."

Amaya threw her arms around me. "If they kill you, then they're unbelievably stupid. The world could use more people like you. *All* the worlds, actually."

Here were more words I would hang on to. After a moment I said, "Then let's make sure Nolan gets back to this one."

When we got to the end of Mountain Pass Trail, Amaya asked if I was hungry.

"No," I said. If I ate something, my churning stomach probably wouldn't keep it down.

Once we were at the pond, I took off Nolan's jacket and set it on the ground with his phone on top. I was wearing the clothes I'd come in originally. Nolan would return home to find nothing missing.

I concentrated on the still pool of water before me. Like all lower-class citizens of Morley, I didn't know how to swim. It was possible I'd drown before the guards had a chance to arrest me. Maybe that would be easier. But the thought of letting the cold water rush into my lungs and drag me down into darkness made me squirm. I'd fight for every last moment I could get.

Amaya's hand on my shoulder made me jump.

"Sorry," she said. "I just wanted to say goodbye."

I let out a shaky breath and turned to her. "Thanks for walking out here with me."

"Don't mention it," she said. "I hope everything goes . . ."

Worry lines appeared on her forehead. She pulled me closer for one last hug.

"I hope so too," I said when she released me. What exactly we were hoping for was unclear and most likely impossible, but we hoped all the same. I wouldn't have been able to dive headfirst into the pond's center without believing I had at least a sliver of a chance.

42

NOLAN

was wondering if it was possible to forget what the color red looks like. And orange and blue and green. In my cell there was only white. Technically, I don't think that even counts as a color. It's just a trick of light.

Then, all that light was gone. There was only darkness. And water.

Maybe they were drowning me. Lolo was taking too long to kill me herself and so Governor Matthias was finally taking action. I kicked furiously and reached upward.

"Nolan!" Someone called my name as I broke the surface. A girl's voice, but not Lolo's.

"Nolan, hang on!" she yelled.

Amaya?

My eyes darted around my new surroundings. Trees, bushes, dirt, and yes, Amaya. She was standing knee-deep in the water, her arms outstretched. Only as I struggled to move through the water did I realize how weak I was. I took hold of Amaya's hands and practically collapsed onto the shore.

"Nolan, oh my god, are you okay?" Amaya said, kneeling next to me in the mud.

I was breathing too hard to answer right away. "Yeah," I said eventually. "I think so." It didn't seem possible for me to be back.

Amaya looked me up and down, examining my legs in particular.

"What is it?" I asked.

"Oh, nothing," she said, quickly looking away. "I brought you some clothes to change into." She got to her feet. "What is that you're wearing anyway?"

"A hospital gown," I said, following her to a backpack, *my* backpack, that lay near the tree line. "I've had it on over my shirt and boxers for . . . I don't know. How long was I gone?"

"Just over a week," she said. I would have guessed a month.

Amaya handed me clean clothes and a towel. I stepped behind a tree to change. It was a relief to put on jeans again, but a part of me doubted I was really here at all.

I handed the wet towel and clothes to Amaya.

"Do you feel okay to walk back?" she asked.

"Yeah." But even as I said it, I felt I didn't have the stamina for a two-hour walk.

"Okay, good. I'll try not to ask too many questions. Otherwise, you'll have to repeat your story a million times."

"I have a lot of questions too," I said, feeling more whiplashed by the minute.

"I bet," Amaya said as she fished through the backpack. "But before we get to all of that, here are some snacks. I can only guess what kind of stuff they were feeding you."

"It wasn't much," I said, taking a bag of chips from her. "Thanks."

"Don't thank me. Thank Harlow when you see her."

I was about to open the bag but stopped. It felt like my brain was just starting to register what was happening, and all the thoughts I should have had were catching up.

"Wait. Why isn't Harlow here? Is she okay? What did the Governor—"

Amaya placed her hands firmly on my shoulders. "Hey," she said. "Harlow's okay. You'll see her soon."

"But where is she? Why isn't she here?"

"She's in the hospital. She's been there all week."

A spark of anger shot through me, replacing the worry I'd felt. "The hospital?" I said, twisting myself out of her grip. "Why? What's wrong with her? What did the Governor do to her?" I shouted.

Amaya backed away from me, her eyes fearful. She'd never seen me so upset before. No one had, except my mom.

I exhaled slowly. "Sorry," I said.

"I know. It's okay," Amaya said. "But we should get going."

The long walk gave Amaya plenty of time to explain everything that had happened in my absence. She told me how she, along with Topher, Cate, Nole, and Matt, had discovered Lolo and foiled the Governor's plan. I learned that my aunt and uncle would be watching me more closely. They thought I was skipping school and faking illnesses. It was hard to keep up with everything Amaya said. The only topic that she seemed to hold back on was Harlow. Probably, she didn't want to risk setting me off again.

"Can we call Harlow?" I asked.

Amaya hesitated. "Honestly Nolan, I think it would be best to wait to see her in person."

"Can we see her today?"

"Of course."

〜〜〜

We arrived in Morley at two. I texted Bailey that I was going to visit Harlow in the hospital. He asked if my homework was done. "Yes," I responded. Like usual, we had very different priorities.

Amaya called Matt to let him know we were back and ready to be picked up.

"What does Matt think of me coming home?" I asked, a little uneasily. After all, Harlow was in the hospital because of a plan I'd played a role in.

"He's happy, of course," Amaya said. "But it was Harlow, Nole, and I who planned your rescue last night."

Nole. He could have lived here forever and left me to die, but he hadn't. Whatever his motives may have been, he'd saved me. Nole must be the better version of me after all. He never let the Governor scare him into betraying people he cared about.

"And Nole was really okay with going back?" I asked.

"He was," Amaya said. But she kept her gaze down at the sidewalk. "I mean, it wasn't easy for him to go, but he said he never would've been happy here."

"Why? We've got plenty of problems, but the other Morley is on a completely different level. Trust me."

"Yeah," Amaya said, "but the other Morley is Nole's *home*. That's where his mom is, and his friends." She looked up at me. "Do you think you'd ever have felt at home there? If they'd let you go?"

I stuck my cold hands in my pockets and thought for a minute. "No," I said. I remembered the first time I saw Topher in the woods, when he'd talked about his ID and wanting to get home. Now his desperation made more sense to me. "Are Topher and Cate still in town?"

"No, they left," Amaya said. "But we can call them any time."

I nodded. There weren't many people I'd be able to talk about all this with, and Topher knew better than anybody how disorienting it is to travel between worlds.

"You know," I said, "while I was imprisoned, I told myself that life as Nole would be fine because I'd be with some version of my mom again. But I think I just needed something to keep me going. My mom's double isn't the person I remember."

"So, you can kind of understand why Nole went back?"

"Yeah . . ." I trailed off.

"What is it?" Amaya asked.

I kicked a small rock across the pavement. "I just feel guilty is all. And I want to know if Nole is okay. It doesn't seem fair."

"None of this is fair."

<p style="text-align:center">~~~</p>

I got nervous when Matt's car pulled up along the sidewalk, but he rushed over to me with a smile. "Nolan!" he said, clapping me on the shoulder. "How are you?"

"I'm good, thanks."

"It's great to have you back. Harlow can't wait to see you."

Harlow had been burned; that's all I knew. Matt said it was best not to ask her about how long the recovery was going to be, or what her legs might look like afterward. "Focus on the positives, okay? You're together again." When we reached her room at the hospital, Matt tapped lightly on the door a few times.

"Hey, Harlow," he said, "look who's here."

My heart pounding, I stepped out from behind Matt.

"Nolan?" Harlow sat up as much as she could and looked at me with big, hopeful eyes. "Nolan, it's really you?"

"Yeah, it's me," I said. I ran to her but stopped short of throwing my arms around her. I didn't want to hurt her. But Harlow wasn't afraid of that. She pulled me close and wrapped me in a hug. For a moment, neither of us said anything. We just held each other tightly.

Eventually, Harlow loosened her grip and lay back against the pillows. I sat on the edge of the mattress, keeping one of her hands in mine.

"I missed you," I said. "I missed you so much."

"I did too," she said. "I didn't think I'd ever see you again."

I glanced down at her covered legs, trying to hide my concern. "And you're . . . feeling okay?"

"I'm fine," she said. "But how are you? What did he do to you?"

I felt angry again as I thought back on everything he'd done. "He kept me in a tiny cell. They barely fed me. He and the guards were rough sometimes, but mostly, I was totally alone."

"Solitary confinement?" she said, clutching my hand tighter. "That's absolute torture."

It was so like Harlow to focus on me when she was the one lying in a hospital bed. "Yeah," I said. "I thought I was going to go insane."

"Me too," she said quietly. She looked at her legs. "That time you were speaking to me, when you told me I had to return home without you, that was just after they did this."

"I'm so, *so* sorry, Harlow. I didn't know, I—"

"Of course you didn't," she said. "But he knew his message would be better received if it came from you. It worked. I want to make sure no one ever goes near that pond again."

"I do too, but listen," I said, needing to absolve myself in some small way. "I'm sorry I ever talked to the Governor and Lolo. I shouldn't have told them anything about you. I should've been stronger." I started to pull my hand away, but Harlow held on.

"Nolan, what choice did you have? You were trapped."

"I guess so," I said.

She gave me a small smile. "It's all over now."

That's when Amaya spoke up. I'd forgotten that she and Matt were in the doorway. "I'm not sure it *is* all over," she said.

"What do you mean?" Harlow asked. "We've got Nolan back."

"Yeah, but do you think the Governor is just going to let it go? I know that's what Nole is hoping for, but the way you all talk about him, it sounds like he'd do anything to crush a threat."

Harlow looked frustrated. She rubbed her eyes with the hand that wasn't in mine.

"Sorry," Amaya said. "I'm not trying to be a downer, but I'm kind of worried."

"No, you're right," Harlow said. "I'm not mad at you, I'm mad at *him*."

"Same," I said. "I've never truly hated anybody before him."

"I hate him too," said Amaya. "And it sounds like the guy might snap and just jump through the pond himself."

At that, the three of us looked over to Matt. His face was stern and his arms were folded across his chest. "It's a possibility," he said.

Harlow let go of my hand. "Dad," she said. Immediately, he was on the other side of her bed. "What if . . . what if he—" Her voice broke.

"It's okay," Matt said. "We're not going to let that happen."

"How?" she wondered. I had the same question. As I watched Harlow cry into Matt's shoulder, I felt powerless to make it better for her. Even from another world, the Governor was ruining everything good in my life.

"Yeah, how?" I said, my indignation rising by the second. "As long as he's alive out there, we can never be sure that he'll leave us alone. He could show up here any time. It'll be like he's hunting us."

Matt stood up. "Then we'll just have to get to him first."

"What?" Harlow said, like she was afraid of where this was going. But I stood up too, eager to join in whatever plan Matt was forming. *Send me back there!* I thought with all the courage of someone who isn't currently facing any danger. *I'll make him sorry for what he did.*

"What you've all said is true," Matt said. "No one in either world will have true peace while Governor Matthias lives. Even if he doesn't come here himself, he could send any number of lackeys after us."

Matt was being so reasonable about it. But I was far too impatient to keep circling the idea I knew we both had. I was ready to attack. "Then we have to kill him," I said, excited by the thought of vengeance. "For the sake of both worlds, he has to die."

"Nolan!" Harlow said. "You *can't* be thinking of going back there."

"He won't be going," Matt said. "I will."

Harlow, Amaya, and I all protested: "What are you talking about?" "Are you crazy?" "How would that help?"

"Hey, hey, listen," he said, holding up his hands. "Just hear me out." Matt's voice was loud, but not demanding like Governor Matthias's. He sounded confident. I stopped arguing. Harlow and Amaya did too. Matt looked back and forth between the three of us and nodded when it was clear he had our attention.

"I won't have to be in the other Morley for very long. As soon as I switch with the Governor—" He spoke softer, eyeing the open door. "Someone will be waiting there—"

"To kill him?" Harlow finished. "Then you'll be stuck in the other Morley!"

"No, not to kill," Matt said, "but to mortally injure. He'll be placed back in the pond while he's still alive, allowing us to trade places again."

"And you don't think his guards would jump through to get revenge?" asked Amaya.

"I don't," Matt said. "They'll be far too occupied with the death of their dictator and terrified of whatever powers beyond the pond were able to destroy him."

It was quiet as we each considered the plan. Harlow and Amaya both looked uncertain, but I was feeling bolder than ever.

"I'll do it," I said, and everyone looked at me in surprise, probably taken aback by my obvious bloodlust. "I'll kill him."

"No, Nolan," Matt said. "I think getting Topher back here to do it would be more appropriate."

"It *has* to be me," I said, both impressed by and afraid of my own brazenness.

I looked at Harlow to see if she approved. But I found no answer on her face. Instead, her eyes were full of questions.

43

LOLO

Once the darkness fell over my cell it didn't leave. Light was only a memory. I spent my endless night sleeping, pacing between the door and the cot, and nibbling on stale bread. I was alone with my regret, just like my father wanted.

But did I actually regret sparing Nole and Nolan's lives? Of course I was upset about being imprisoned, but looking back, I don't think I would have done anything differently, even if now I felt utterly powerless. I kind of understood why my father hated the feeling. Still, I didn't see what good all my father's power actually did him. It certainly didn't make him happy.

I used to think it was the pressure of being governor that made him so temperamental, since he took his responsibilities very seriously. I'd heard him say that his power was the means to an end—the end being the citizens' safety. It seemed obvious to me now that this was never true. Power itself had always been his end. My father spent so much time and energy trying to protect this power that there was little room for anything else in his life. I didn't know what end I wanted to reach in my own life, but it definitely wasn't absolute power.

~~~

I was sleeping when the door opened. The sudden light burned my eyes, and I turned my face to the wall. Footsteps approached my cot. I recognized the cadence of his heavy-soled boots.

"Lolo," my father said in a voice barely above a whisper. It was unsettling, and I huddled closer to the wall. I'd rather he just yell at me and get it over with.

"An opportunity has arisen; one that may allow you to redeem yourself."

I lifted my head a bit. Since it was clear I was listening, he continued. "Such opportunities, as you well know, are rare."

I sat up all the way, afraid he was going to send me back to kill Nolan. I wouldn't do it.

"Nole Fredericks is a foolish boy, even for someone so low-born. You offered him a chance to escape, and yet, he's returned to our world."

"Nole is here?" The words cracked in my dry throat. I couldn't help but feel betrayed. Nole knew I'd pay the price if he ever returned. "He really came back?"

"Indeed, he did," my father said. "He's in our custody and awaiting your visit."

"My . . . my visit?" I didn't like that my father insisted on explaining everything in such obscure terms. It felt like yet another power move.

A second later, he was standing over me, his forearm pinning me to the wall. "You won't make the wrong decision again," he said. "Give him the arsenic. Prove your loyalty or suffer the consequences." He pulled me forward a few inches and then knocked my head backward. It smacked the wall and began throbbing immediately.

My father left the room and the lights shut off, returning me to the darkness. I traced my fingertips lightly o'er the spot where my head had hit the wall. Then, for the first time since I'd been locked away, I started to cry. I didn't stop until I fell asleep.
~~~

More time passed, although I didn't know how much. I spent nearly every minute arguing with myself about what to do.

At first, I tried to be purely practical. Maybe I'd been wrong earlier and I really *did* have it in me to kill somebody. Nole was going to die regardless, so by not killing him myself with the arsenic, I might be condemning him to a crueler death. Plus, once I did it and my father was satisfied, I'd have "proven my loyalty" and life could return to some sort of normal.

But how could anything ever be normal again? If Nole was here, that meant Nolan was in the other world. My father wouldn't like an escaped prisoner roaming free. I could be recruited to hunt down Nolan next.

Fine. After *that*, things would return to normal.

No again. Even if my life returned to what it was before we discovered the other Morley, *I* wouldn't be my normal self. I'd have killed two people.

Then my thoughts turned to the future. My father had taught me that purging undesirable citizens is part of the job of being governor, but maybe when I became the governor, it wouldn't have to be. I could do away with his violent policies. If I didn't kill Nole now, I might not ever become governor and be able to make life better for everyone in Morley. This was a question of the one versus the many, and I should choose to save the many. It was for the greater good. Right?

And yet, it wasn't so simple. I wasn't going to be killing a random person, but someone I knew. Nole. It was harder to think in abstract terms when I had his face in my mind. He was real in the here and now, whereas any good I might do in the future as governor was mere speculation.

As I considered disobeying my father again, I forced myself to confront the possible "consequences" he mentioned. No doubt he would come up with something more creative than this dark cell. There would be no more chances for me.

If I thought I'd felt powerless before, it was nothing compared to the turmoil I was in now. Worse than having no choices at all, I was being offered two horrible choices. Either way, Nole was going to die, and either way, it would be my fault.

44

HARLOW

On Monday, I was allowed to go home. My dad worked it out so that a nurse or physical therapist visited every few hours. I even had a hospital bed set up in the living room. The doctors were vague about how many months it might be before I could resume my normal activities, but this was a "step in the right direction." Those were my dad's words to me, spoken in his best hang-in-there-kiddo voice. I knew he meant them sincerely, and I knew I was lucky to be going home so soon, but it was getting harder not to be cynical. Judging by Nolan's demeanor the day before, it was clear he was feeling similarly.

Nolan came over after his first day back at school. My dad let him in, and when he walked into the living room, he stopped to observe the many changes.

"Wow," he said, coming over to the chair next to my bedside, "this is intense."

I glanced at the stack of medications on the coffee table and my bandaged legs. "Yeah," I said, sighing. I knew I didn't need to hide how gloomy I was feeling from Nolan. We were quiet for a moment.

"I still can't believe any of this happened," he said.

"I can't either," I said, grateful that we understood each other.

"Just look at all of this," Nolan said. "You're the last person to deserve something like this."

"No one deserves it."

"*He* does. Governor Matthias deserves it. Along with all the guards who blindly follow his orders." Nolan's face hardened and the wiry muscles in his arms grew tense. It was the same way he'd looked yesterday when the subject of killing the Governor came up. I thought then that maybe we *didn't* understand each other. We were both frustrated, but while I was sinking deeper into self-pity, he was rushing head-on toward revenge.

"Nolan, I get how mad you are, really. But—"

"What?" he said sharply. "Are you saying you *don't* want to kill him?"

"No, I want the Governor to die, but—"

"It's okay," Nolan said, cutting me off again. "You won't be the one to actually do it."

"And neither will *you*," I said. "My dad talked to Topher already, remember? He's flying here tomorrow, and he'll take care of it."

"There's no way I'm letting Topher do this without me."

"Nolan!" I said, angry that he wasn't seeing what was so obvious to me. "I don't care about the Governor dying, but I do care about what killing him might do to you."

"Me?" Nolan said, taken aback. "I'll be fine. The Governor won't realize what's happening until it's too late."

"You're missing the point!" I said. My patience was draining even faster than normal. "Look at yourself right now. I've never seen you like this and it's *scaring* me."

That softened Nolan's harsh expression. "Scaring you?" he asked. "How?"

I paused. I didn't like this confusion between us, and I needed to say just the right thing. "I don't want you to . . . lose sight of the person you were before all of this. I mean, I know we'll never be the same again. It's impossible to forget or undo the damage." I gestured to my legs. "But despite all that, I don't want to stay bitter forever. And more than anything, I don't want us to be bitter toward each other."

Nolan took my hand in his. "That won't happen, Harlow. I promise."

"But it *could*," I said. "If we both have all this built-up resentment, then every time we see each other, we'll just be seeing the past."

"Once the Governor is dead, that won't be a problem. We'll have won."

His blue eyes were shining with determination, but I shook my head, still feeling like we weren't quite understanding each other. "Nolan, if this breaks us apart or turns us into vengeful people, then it won't matter that the Governor's dead. We'll be living proof of his victory. And you'll . . . you'll have actual blood on your hands."

Nolan sat still for a moment. He looked like he didn't know what to say. Then he rose from his seat and kissed me. I was surprised for only a second. The tears that had been forming in my eyes evaporated as warmth coursed through my entire body. When he stepped back and looked at me, his hand on my cheek, I felt I didn't need words to understand what he'd just told me.

45

TOPHER

As soon as Jojo, Cate, and I returned to Arizona, life resumed its usual hurried pace. Cate was busy catching up on the schoolwork she'd missed, and Jojo took a few late shifts at the hospital. I had plenty of projects to occupy me, but my mind was wandering more than it had before my trip to Morley. It was like my life in Arizona had been paused while I was away, but now that I was back, it was playing forward without me. I was stuck in limbo between two states, two worlds, two realities.

It helped that at least now I could talk to Jojo and Cate about it.

On Sunday night, I made us dinner and we were eating together when my phone rang.

"Hang on," I said, putting my fork down. "I need to take this."

"Who is it?" Jojo asked.

"The mayor of Morley," I said. "I'll be right back."

I got up from the table and slipped into my office. "Matt?" I answered. "What's going on?"

He proceeded to tell me about Nole's decision to leave, Nolan's homecoming, and the plan they'd begun to form concerning Governor Matthias.

"Our options are limited when it comes to taking care of this," he said. "Nolan is fixated on the idea of taking the Governor down himself, but I just can't let him bear the weight of that responsibility. Even if he thinks he's ready for it, he's not."

"I'm in," I said at once. "It should be me, not Nolan."

Matt told me he was thinking a lethal injection would be the most efficient way to do it. I agreed, and I knew exactly whom to ask for help in securing the right drug.

By the time I hung up with Matt, Jojo was washing the dishes.

"Is everything okay?" she asked.

"No, not exactly," I said, leaning against the counter.

Jojo turned the water off and looked at me, her eyes worried.

"The mayor needs my help," I said. "We can end this for good." I thought she might ask me what I meant by that, or how I could be sure, or even tell me not to go, but she didn't.

"When do you leave?"

"Day after tomorrow," I said. "But Jojo, we could use your help, too."

I told her about our plan to get rid of the Governor. At first, Jojo balked at the idea of taking a drug from the hospital where she worked as a nurse practitioner, especially for the use of killing someone. I didn't think I was going to be able to change her mind until she said, "Wait. This is the same man who was governor sixteen years ago?"

I nodded, watching as she made the connection.

"That's when Chris . . ." she said, her voice suddenly small.

"Yes. Governor Matthias is responsible."

Jojo looked out the kitchen window for a moment. Then she said, "Okay. I'll do it."

〜〜

Having Jojo's support emboldened me. I wanted to start packing right away, but then I thought I should get Cate's support too. No more secrets, I reminded myself.

I tapped on her bedroom door, and she told me to come in.

"What'd Matt say?" she asked, sitting up on her bed. "Is Harlow okay? I texted her a few days ago and she was feeling all right."

"Yes," I said. "Harlow is fine. But something else has come up."

I sat next to her and explained Matt's plan and the rationale behind it. Cate interrupted me several times. I didn't always have the answer to her question, or an answer she liked.

"So basically, you're going back out there to murder someone?" she said. "And Mom is going to help?"

"'Murder' is a strong word," I said, "and not the best one for what we're doing."

"What's the best word then?"

"Think of it as a . . . political assassination."

"Right," she said, rolling her eyes. "Well, whatever it is, can I come with you?"

"No," I said quickly. "There's no need for you to put yourself in danger."

"I thought you said it wasn't going to be dangerous. You're taking the Governor by surprise."

"Yes, but I don't want you to witness it."

"You mean, you don't want me to be an accomplice to murder?"

I put my head in my hands for a moment. Her persistence, though understandable, was wearing me out. "Cate," I said, looking up again, "I'm protecting you. You just have to trust me."

~ ~ ~

Cate avoided me the next day as much as she could. But early Tuesday morning when I left for the airport, she was waiting by the front door.

"Bye, Dad," she said, giving me a hug. "Be careful."

"I will," I promised.

"And tell me everything that happens."

~

I tried to sleep on the plane, but nerves kept me awake. When Matt picked me up at 3:30, I was running fully on adrenaline.

"How are you on a mountain bike?" Matt asked, once I'd assured him the vial and syringe from Jojo were safely stored in my luggage.

"I should be okay," I said. "Why, are we biking to the pond?"

"Yes. At least most of the way until the path stops. We'll get there faster, and the bikes will allow Harlow to come with us."

"How?" I asked, surprised.

"Nolan used to work at a bike shop and so he knew about this attachable trailer big enough for her to sit in while we ride. Between the three of us, we can carry her the rest of the way."

"And you think it's safe to move her?"

His fingers gripped the steering wheel tighter. "No. But it's very important to her that she be there. I understand that."

I thought back to my conversation with Cate and wondered if I should have let her tag along. No, I concluded. Her situation and Harlow's were too different to compare. Amaya wouldn't be joining us either. Matt had told her something similar to what I'd said to Cate—that it was for her own good.

We talked through the logistics of the plan. Nolan would help me pin the Governor to the ground, but I would be the one to inject him in the neck. Jojo had shown me how. We'd need to put him back in the pond as quickly as possible.

"I'll make sure I'm the one who goes in the water," I said, trying not to let the gruesome nature of the task distract me from grasping my role in it. "If Nole is still alive, we don't want to risk losing Nolan."

"Yes, thank you." He shook his head. "Listen to me. I'm an elected offi-cial plotting to kill someone and cover it up. I wonder what the voters would think of *that*."

"I think they'd understand, if they knew all the facts." But even as I said it, I remembered Cate's accusing stare. "Not that it matters, though. The voters will never find out."

~~~

When we got to the house, Nolan was in the garage hooking up the trailer to a bike.

"It's good to see you again, Nolan," I said, holding out my hand.

He rubbed his greasy hand on his jeans before grabbing mine. His handshake was stronger than I'd expected, and as I looked at him, I thought there was little to remind me of the scared boy I'd met in the woods only three weeks ago. "Yeah, same," he said. "Good to see you."

Matt and I went into the living room to get Harlow. We lifted her off the hospital bed and moved her as carefully as we could. Even still, she yelped in pain a few times. Once she was settled in the trailer, Matt placed a duffle bag next to her.

"There are extra clothes in here, along with some lanterns. It'll be dark out there." Then he held up the vial and syringe. "These were the last things we had to pack," he said, tucking them into the bag. "I told Harlow's overnight nurse not to come until midnight, so we should have plenty of time."

We wheeled the bikes onto the driveway and Matt closed the garage door. The afternoon sunlight was fading as we made our way to the forest, and we turned on the bikes' headlamps before starting on the path.

Nolan led the way, but he peeked over his shoulder every once in a while, unsubtly checking on Harlow. I thought that she must be feeling as nervous as I was, if not more. She was about to come face-to-face with her tormentor while knowing her dad's life depended on whether or not two inexperienced hitmen could do their job properly. Though I was conflicted about killing another person, even Governor Matthias, that paled in comparison to my fear of what might happen if I failed.

After about an hour, we reached the end of the path. Nolan and I dropped our bikes and maneuvered Harlow's trailer through the thick foliage, each holding a side while Matt walked next to his bike and steered us forward, a single headlamp guiding our way.

We made it to the pond. Once we set Harlow down, Matt, Nolan, and I stood panting for a moment. The water was as still as I'd ever seen it. I set
~~~

up the camping lanterns then glanced at Matt, expecting him to instruct us on what came next. But he was looking at Harlow, who had reached up to lay her hand on his arm. He crouched beside her, his ear bent toward her. I suddenly felt intrusive and took a few steps away so the two of them could say goodbye.

46

NOLE

My cell was cold and lit by an obnoxiously bright light that hummed at a level just a little too loud to ignore. I hadn't been given a change of clothing, and it took ages for my pants and shirt to dry. As uncomfortable as it was though, the worst part of my captivity was having to guess at what was happening beyond the heavy white door.

Unsurprisingly, I'd been arrested at the pond and taken to this cell in a frenzy. But since then, no one had spoken to me or given me any clue as to what was going on. If it hadn't been for the water and scraps of food I received every so often, I would've thought they'd forgotten about me altogether. It seemed odd that the Governor wasn't trying to extract as much information from me as possible. I spent most of my time in the cell worrying about what that meant.

～

I was sleeping, my hands covering my face to try and block out the harsh light, when the door finally opened. I barely saw the guards enter the cell before a blindfold was tied around my eyes. They dragged me through hallways until I was shoved onto a metal chair and chained in place.

This must be my interrogation. The Governor would get the answers he wanted and then I'd be sent to die. I panicked as I heard footsteps approaching. *What have I done?* I should've stayed in the other Morley. What if by coming back I'd only made more trouble for my mom and Catherine and Jody? I'd been so unwilling to give the other world a chance that I might have condemned us all. Maybe they were already dead.

My blindfold was ripped off, and across the table sat not Governor Matthias, but Lolo.

In a way, that was even worse.

She stared at me, a scared expression on her hollow face. I stared back into the eyes of the person I'd betrayed by returning here. Finally, she looked down at the table. I noticed there was a cup, filled about halfway with some sort of liquid. That's when it became clear what Lolo was here to do. She was going to finish what she'd started.

I thought that since Lolo hadn't gone through with the Governor's plan once, she might not again. This was just my pathetic attempt to find something hopeful to hold on to; there was no one to stand in Lolo's way now.

"You came back," she said suddenly.

It was a statement, not a question. I didn't know how or if I should reply.

"I didn't think you would." It still wasn't a question, but she looked at me as though waiting for me to say something.

"I didn't think I would either," I said. "Not at first."

"What made you change your mind?" This was all so strange; she sounded genuinely curious.

"Well . . . a few things. It was obvious that I wasn't going to do a great job of impersonating Nolan. Their world is really different from ours. The main thing, though, was homesickness. I couldn't imagine living without my family and friends."

Lolo looked away when I said that, frowning slightly.

"Plus," I said, hoping to move on from whatever had upset her, "I was starting to feel bad for Nolan. He deserved to return. Harlow deserved that, too."

"And what about you, Nole? What do you think you deserve?"

I hesitated, afraid to say the wrong thing. "I um . . . I don't know. I guess—"

"And what about me?" she asked, her voice getting thinner. "What do you think *I* deserve?"

"You?" I said, not understanding why I was being asked this.

"Yes, me," she said, talking hurriedly. "Any other person in Morley who disobeyed an order like I did would've been killed immediately. According to the law, I deserve to die."

She was right, technically, but she wasn't just any person in Morley. "But won't *you* get another chance?" I asked.

"Only because I'm the *Governor's daughter*. He needs me to be his heir. Otherwise, I'd be expendable."

I was surprised by the amount of disdain in her voice. It made me wonder what the Governor's reaction had been when he'd realized her lie.

"I'm sorry I got you into trouble," I said, finding it weird that I had an impulse to comfort her even though I was the one who was truly expendable here.

She bit her lower lip, and her eyes grew red. "You didn't get me into trouble," she said. "I told my father I didn't go through with killing you before you got back."

That stunned me. "What? *Why?*"

"He ordered me to poison Nolan, but I couldn't do it. When I was talking to Nolan, the truth just sort of came out." She glanced nervously at the guards who were standing against the wall, then at a camera that was trained on us from the corner of the room. "I know the other world is confusing, but going there and coming back made me realize how *empty* it is here. At least, empty for me. My father already has my whole future planned out. It's just an endless list of tasks that I won't be able to bring myself to do."

The guards started whispering, and Lolo stared intently at the cup on the table. Suddenly, she picked it up.

"What are you doing?" I asked, scared she was about to force me to swallow its contents after all.

"A change of plans," she said, and raised the cup to her own lips.

"Wait!" I blurted. "Lolo, you don't have to do that."

She looked at me resolutely. "Nole, I'm glad you saved Nolan. I'm only sorry I couldn't save us."

The door swung open with such force that it bounced off the wall and almost hit the person charging in.

Governor Matthias.

He flew straight to Lolo, knocked the cup away, and picked her up from the chair, the veins in his neck bulging. "If you won't do this," he shouted, "then I'll do it myself!" He slammed her back down and turned his attention to me. This was it. I closed my eyes, hating that the Governor, his fingers curling into a fist, was going to be the last thing I ever saw. Was he the last thing my mom saw?

But nothing, no blow, no kick, or shove, came. All at once the room was quiet. I blinked my eyes open, unsure of what the delay was. Lolo was sitting in her chair, looking back and forth across the room. The guards seemed just as confused. Governor Matthias had vanished. For a moment, none of us said anything. Then, Lolo's face lit up. "Harlow's father," she said. "This has got to be his doing."

"Matt . . ." I said, still dazed. "Why would he—"

Lolo shushed me before I could say anything else. She stood up and faced the guards. "We need to go to the pond right away."

"We don't take orders from you," one of them said.

"Then let's find my father. Please, we need to hurry."

The two guards shared a few uncertain glances. I was afraid they might radio for backup.

"This is about the other world," Lolo said, with a confidence I hadn't heard from her before. "Nole and I know more about it than anyone. You've got to take us both to the pond."

One of the guards grabbed her wrists. "Fine. But we're not letting the two of you out of our sight." The other guard released me from the chair, and we were led out to a helicopter. Lolo dared to speak to me only once. She leaned over and said, "Until we know more, let me do the talking." I nodded, glad I hadn't been left behind in the interrogation room.

As the helicopter took off, I wondered what, and who, we would find at the pond. Why would Matt risk his life to come to this Morley? Were all of them, Harlow, Amaya, Topher, Cate, and Nolan, in on some plan? If they were, I wanted to do anything I could to help. This was now the second time they'd saved my life.

47

NOLAN

I waited by the pond as Matt said goodbye to Harlow. They held on to each other for a long time. I found myself thinking about the last time I saw my mom. She'd been lying limply in a hospital bed, unaware that I was there. I'd given her a weak hug, all the while wishing my final memory could be of something else. I wondered what my mom would say if she could see me right now. I hoped she would understand why I had to do this.

I heard Matt say "I love you" before he walked toward me.

"Ready?" he said. I nodded, but my heart was thudding loudly. Was I ready?

Topher was already knee-deep in the water, the syringe in his hand. Matt turned around one more time to look at Harlow, then he waded in and dove beneath the surface.

My eyes were glued to the spot where Matt had disappeared. I could feel the painful tick of each second as I waited for the Governor to emerge. I thought I was going to burst from anticipation when all at once, Governor Matthias came barreling out the water. His thrashing, outstretched arms nearly hit Topher in the face. As Topher wrestled him to the shore, he fought back with a vengeance. I'd expected the Governor to be fierce, but not right away. It was like he instantly knew where he was and what was at stake for him. He'd probably been preparing for some kind of ambush his whole life. Maybe all that paranoia was finally paying off. He was pure anger and action.

I, however, was paralyzed. It was one thing to want to kill the Governor in my head, but another to kneel down in the mud where he and Topher were struggling to get the upper hand.

"Nolan!" Topher yelled. He had managed to get the Governor on his back and pin one of his arms down. "Nolan!"

His plea for help snapped me out of my shock. Without another thought, I hurled myself into the mud. The Governor's attention was on Topher, and so he wasn't prepared for me to grab hold of his free arm and push it to the ground. I was able to get my knee on his chest, and for a few seconds, it seemed like we had him. Then, as Topher moved the hand with the syringe closer to the Governor's neck, the Governor broke free. He shoved me off and was suddenly on his feet. He panted as his eyes darted back and forth between me and Topher.

I was still on the ground, and again, fear kept me frozen in place. I didn't want to anticipate the Governor's next move and get it wrong. Topher lunged at him, but the Governor reacted quickly. They grappled with each other until the Governor kneed Topher in the stomach, which made him let go of the syringe. It dropped into the mud and Topher crumpled forward. The Governor stood over him with the same cruel smile that had taunted me when I was his prisoner. That got me going. I jumped to my feet and ran at him with fists swinging.

He was ready for me. The Governor caught my right wrist and yanked it up high above my head. I swung at him with my left fist and hit him a few times in the chest, but then he pulled his arm back and socked me squarely on the jaw. I thought he might have knocked a tooth out. Then, he did it again. My head was spinning.

Harlow begged for him to stop, her piercing screams reverberating through the trees. It took me a few seconds to register what was going on, for my stomach to sink with worry. She shouldn't have let him know she was there.

The Governor, startled by her voice, stopped and turned his head toward Harlow, keeping his grip on my wrist tight. Slowly, he began to approach her, dragging me along. I was too dizzy to resist. I looked at Topher, desperate for him to intervene. He had the syringe in hand and nodded, quietly getting to his feet.

"Lolo?" the Governor said, his voice more concerned than I'd ever heard it.

"Yes?" Harlow, having composed herself, said innocently. She was brilliant in that moment.

"Lolo?" he asked again. "It's you?" He sounded tired, and maybe even a little afraid. "How did they get you? Are you—"

He didn't hear Topher creep up behind him, and so he had no warning before the needle was plunged deep into his neck. The Governor buckled over and fell to the ground.

"Hurry," Topher said. Together, we grabbed hold of Governor Matthias's arms and hauled his twitching body back to the pond.

When the water came to my knees Topher told me to stop. I immediately sat down on the shore, exhausted. The Governor was on his back, squirming and moaning softly. It bothered me that for a minute, I actually felt sorry for him. I watched, with a strange mix of pity and hatred, as Topher guided him to the center of the pond. Then, using his full strength, he pushed the Governor all the way underwater.

48

LOLO

As soon as the helicopter landed, I climbed out and sprinted to the pond, a guard following me closely. Though I had little expectation of what I would find, I wasn't prepared for the sight that awaited me. The pond was illuminated by a few lanterns, and a large object bobbing in the deepest part of the water caught my eye. I peered at it closely. Then, I screamed.

The guard looked at where I was pointing and ran into the water to retrieve my father. Nole's guard, the helicopter pilot, and another guard who'd been patrolling the woods raced to help. "Careful! Be careful!" I called after them in a panic. Whether I meant they should be careful not to fall in the pond or careful with my father, I wasn't sure.

Nole appeared at my side and together we watched as my father's limp body was laid upon the shore. The guards crowded around him, arguing about what to do.

"Back away from him!" I said. "Radio for medical help!"

One of them nodded, a look of fear on his face. The others watched as I knelt next to my father. His breathing was labored and his eyes were closed. I knew then, as foam spilled over his blue lips, that there was no saving him.

I started to cry, and my tears confused me. I'd never felt close to my father. There'd been plenty of times when I'd wished he would disappear forever. Not because I wanted to be governor, but because I was sick of him and his rules. This was the man who had spent my entire life ignoring me, critiquing me, or controlling me. And more lately, torturing me. Today, I'd been so desperate to escape from him that I almost ended my own life. He didn't deserve my tears.

My father whimpered softly. I wasn't sure if he deserved *this* either.

I took his cold hand in mine. If I was going to tell him that I forgave him, that I would always cherish his memory, or that I loved him, now was the time. But none of those things were true. And if there was one crime I knew my father hated, it was lying.

"Morley will live on," I said. It was at least one thing I could promise him. "I'll protect the citizens, Father. I'm just going to do it in my own way." I don't know if he heard me or not. A minute later, he was gone.

The medical team's helicopter whirred in the air above us.

"Tell them it's too late," I said to the guards. I didn't know if I was allowed to give them orders, but they didn't argue and began to walk away.

Nole stayed behind. "Lolo?" he said. When I didn't answer, he joined me on the ground. I couldn't bring myself to let go of my father's hand.

"I didn't do this right," I said, suddenly ashamed, like this was yet another test I had failed.

"Do what right?"

"Say goodbye."

Nole considered that. "I don't think there's one right way to do it."

"Maybe," I said, still feeling guilty. "But what if I end up forgiving my father later on? I'll have no way to tell him."

"You think you'll forgive him someday?"

"I don't know." I finally released his hand.

"Lolo," Nole said, as if a new thought had popped into his head, "will you forgive the people back in the other Morley? After . . . what they've done?"

I looked down at my father's lifeless form. Just minutes ago, he'd been about to kill the kind, gentle boy kneeling beside me. And I might have been next on his list. That list was long, maybe never-ending, and it likely included the names of all the people who'd had a hand in stopping him.

More tears filled my eyes and I tilted my head back to stare at the cloudy night. "The people in the other Morley knew what my father was capable of. While he lived, they were never going to have peace. None of us were, really." Slowly, I turned to Nole and our eyes met. "So yes, I'll be able to forgive them."

"I'm sorry, Lolo," he said, his gaze steady.

"Thank you." I wanted to say something more, something that would keep Nole's blue eyes locked with mine, if only for a few seconds. But the medical team rushed in from the trees with a stretcher and we had to stand up and face whatever came next. Nole and I followed behind the long train of guards and doctors to the helicopters.

"Nole," I said, "I meant what I said to my father, about protecting Morley."

"I have no doubt."

"No, listen," I said, stopping him with a hand on his shoulder.

That touch, however brief, made him flinch. *Is he still afraid of me?* The thought was disappointing and made what I had to say all the more important. "What I mean is, my father only cared about the 'city-state.' And that was just his way of saying he only cared about himself. But I'm going to do things differently." I spoke faster as I felt an unexpected surge of hope. "The city-state doesn't just belong to the governor; it's the citizens' too. I'm going to do right by the people of Morley. Starting with you."

"Me?"

"Yes," I said. "Nole, you are free."

Slowly, the pensive look on his face was replaced with a smile. "I am?"

"You are," I said. "*We* are."

49

HARLOW

The wood was eerily quiet after the brief flurry of violence. As I stared at the water, willing my dad to appear, images of the scene I'd just witnessed flashed before me, searing themselves into my memory forever: the scuffle in the mud, the syringe dropping out of Topher's hand, the Governor hitting Nolan with all his might. When I'd screamed, the Governor had turned to me with a wild look in his eye. Then, his face softened into something like vulnerability. "Lolo?" he asked. In that moment, the Governor's resemblance to my dad was clearer than it had ever been before. I looked away when Topher stuck the needle in his neck.

The water stirred and my dad broke through the surface. I called out to him, and he swam quickly across the pond.

"Dad," I said with a breath of relief when he reached me. "Are you okay?"

"Completely fine," he said. "Cold, yes, but otherwise unharmed."

"What did you see there?" I asked, handing him a towel.

"Not much. There was a guard patrolling the area, but I surfaced quietly and hid among some plants. But tell me," he said as Nolan and Topher joined us, "what happened here?"

Nolan, who still looked a little petrified, didn't say anything.

"Well," Topher said, "the important thing is that, as far as I can tell, our mission was accomplished."

"Good," my dad said. "But what else? Are you two all right?"

"Yes," Topher said, "we're fine. But the Governor was formidable. It took more than the two of us to finish the job."

"What?" he said anxiously, glancing at me. "You mean Harlow?"

"Dad, it's fine," I said. "It was hardly anything."

"But it was something," he said, kneeling.

I shrugged, feeling self-conscious about the spotlight I was under. Nolan and Topher were the ones who had just been in a fight. "All I did was scream," I said. "But I guess that provided just enough of a distraction."

"A distraction?" my dad said. "Harlow, you were utterly *defenseless*. Why would you draw attention to yourself?"

"I wasn't *trying* to. I didn't really think about it." I sighed and looked at my legs. "I just couldn't bear to see him hurting Nolan."

My dad, his protective nature at full force, continued. "So, you endangered yourself?"

"I wasn't in danger; not really. When Governor Matthias noticed me, it wasn't *me* he was seeing, but Lolo. It broke him out of the frenzy he was in."

"It's true," Topher said. "That lull in the fight was exactly what we needed."

My dad's frown loosened. "You're sure you're all right?"

"Yes, I'm positive."

He nodded. "You're all very brave." He stood up to acknowledge Nolan and Topher. "Thank you."

~~~~~

While my dad changed and Topher collected the lanterns, Nolan stole a moment alone with me.

"Hey, Harlow?" he said.

"Yeah?"

"Thanks for what you did. Things might have ended differently."
~~~~~

I shook my head, not wanting to consider alternate endings. "Like I said, I had to. It was automatic."

Nolan sighed. "*Nothing* during the fight felt 'automatic' for me. I had no idea what I was doing."

He was clearly frustrated with himself. I reached out my hand and he took hold of it. "I even sort of felt *bad* for the Governor at one point," he went on. "I mean, we're talking about the guy who made our lives a living *hell* and—"

"I felt bad for him too," I said, giving his hand a little shake.

"Really?"

"Yeah. I wavered a bit."

He lowered his voice. "Do you think that means we should've done things differently? Like, not killed him and figured out a way to reason with him?"

Slowly, I shifted my gaze from Nolan to the pond. "I don't know," I said. "Reasoning with him never seemed like an option. At least, not until I saw him walking toward me, looking so weak and . . . forlorn."

"But by then it was too late," Nolan said.

"I guess it was." And that's when I fully understood what we'd just done. I let go of Nolan's hand and wiped the tears that trickled down my face.

"Are you okay?"

"No," I said. "Maybe later I will be, but not right now."

Tears shone in Nolan's eyes too. "I know what you mean."

I didn't want to cause my dad worry by allowing him to see me cry, so I dried my eyes as best I could. "It's too late for the Governor," I said, "but it might not be too late for everyone else in the other Morley." I remembered what Nolan had told me about his last meeting with Lolo, how she'd shown him mercy even though it had gotten her arrested. "If Lolo wasn't willing to kill you like her father wanted, then she must be pretty different from him. Maybe she can change things for the better."

"Yeah," Nolan said, brightening a little. "I think she can."

We couldn't know for certain though. All I could do was speculate, and hope.

50

NOLE

When we arrived back at the Governor's manor, no one seemed to notice Lolo and me. A team of doctors immediately surrounded Governor Matthias to see if he could be saved. Guards and other staff members hustled about the large, open room we stood in, everyone trying to occupy themselves while the unthinkable happened. Their restlessness must have affected Lolo, as she didn't seem as confident as she'd been at the pond.

"Lolo," I said, "should I go home now?" And, more importantly, would anyone be there waiting for me?

"Yes," she said. Then, somehow sensing the question I'd left unspoken, she added, "Your mother was released last week."

I almost laughed from relief, but stopped myself, remembering that Lolo had just lost her father. She was looking more stressed with each second. "We should hurry, before any of my father's advisors has a chance to question you about your involvement in his death."

"Aren't they *your* advisors now?" As I said it, I realized the changing of power may not be so simple.

"I'm not actually sure," Lolo said. "But right now, they're more likely to be loyal to my father's memory than to me. They won't like that someone out there knows the truth."

Lolo led us out of the busy room and into a hallway where a lone guard stood watch.

"Your attention," she said, assuming a commanding tone. "This citizen needs to be escorted home. Please prepare a car."

The guard looked at her skeptically, but Lolo kept her composure, like it was natural he should listen to her.

"Now."

"Yes, miss," he said with a deferential nod. We followed him through more halls until we reached a high-ceilinged room full of cars. Whenever the Governor drove through the city in a black car, I'd assumed he used the same car each time, not that he had an entire fleet of nearly identical black vehicles. I thought about all the people I knew who walked miles to work whenever the trams weren't running, which in our neighborhood, was often. How much good could a few of these extra cars do?

The guard went to start one of the cars. Lolo wasn't about to waste our final minute together. "Nole," she said, "don't tell anyone about what really happened with my father today. Okay? Or, at least no one outside your family."

"I won't," I said.

"Whatever story my father's advisors decide to tell the public, it won't be the truth."

"I understand," I said, trying to reassure her.

"It's not that I don't *want* to tell the citizens the truth, but it could be the eight advisors versus me. Plus, what if the truth scares everyone and I cause another Chaos? With my father gone, maybe people will take drastic measures to make sure Morley changes."

"Lolo, you don't have to explain it all to me. I get it." But she didn't look convinced. She crossed her arms, breathing unsteadily. "Look," I said, "on your first unofficial day as Governor, you've already helped one person. Two, if you count my mom. She's not going to believe it when she sees me."

Lolo smiled halfheartedly. My mom also wasn't going to believe it when I told her I was on a first-name basis with the Governor's daughter. Just then, the guard drove up in the car. He got out and opened the door to the back seat.

"Well, goodbye, Lolo," I said, not moving from my spot next to her.

"Goodbye, Nole. I'm sure we'll see each other again?" She sounded scared. While I was going home to my mom and Catherine, who did Lolo have to confide in? It struck me that I might be the nearest thing she had to a friend.

"Yes," I said, "we will." I was surprised at how sincerely I hoped it was true.

~~~

When I told the guard where I lived, his eyebrows jumped up to his hairline. He'd likely only taken people *away* from that area, not back to it. We drove in silence, and he dropped me off in front of my building unceremoniously. As I stepped onto the sidewalk, I noticed a few window curtains being drawn closed. Everybody around here knew what that black car meant. I waited until the guard drove off before jogging upstairs to my apartment. I was considering the best way to announce myself when I heard my name.

"Nole? *Nole?*"

"Catherine!"

She dropped the bag of groceries in front of her door and raced toward me. We threw our arms around each other.

"I thought I'd never see you again," she said. "I thought you were dead."

"It's okay. I'm back now. I'm not going anywhere."

Just then, her mom opened their door.

"Shh, Catherine, what's—?" she started, but when she saw what the commotion was about, she stopped. "Nole . . ." Jody breathed. "You're alive. But—" She looked left and right as if she was sure something was amiss.

"No one's following me. It's all right. I can explain everything."

She ushered us both inside.

"Is my mom home, or is she at work?" I asked.

"She's at work," Jody said. "But she should be back soon."

"You can wait for her here," Catherine said, clinging to my arm.
~~~

"Nole, are you hungry?" Jody asked, clearly still a bit dazed. "Would you like anything to eat?"

"Of course he's hungry," Catherine answered for me. She went out and retrieved the spilled bag of groceries. Jody made us some toast while we waited for my mom. Catherine filled me in on what had been happening here during my absence. With my mom and I both gone, the neighborhood had been even quieter than usual. People looked at one another with hostility and suspicion.

"I'm sorry, Catherine," I said, "that sounds awful."

"It was," she said. "But it's over now."

I nodded, but what I didn't say was that it may be even more over than Catherine thought, so long as Lolo was able to take her place as governor.

<center>~~~~~</center>

About an hour later, we heard my apartment door opening and Jody went to get my mom.

I stood up, trembling slightly. When my mom walked through the door and saw me, she started to fall to the ground. Jody caught her just in time. We sat on the couch, holding each other tightly, and she cried over me. I didn't mind. I didn't want her to let go.

Eventually, she was calm enough to listen to my rambling story. I started with that first shocking moment when I'd found myself submerged in a forest pond. I told them about the portal, the other world, and our doubles. Jody and Catherine looked at me doubtfully, but my mom remembered the boy who had been interrogated with her at the pond. "He could have been your twin," she said, "but I *knew* he wasn't you." After that, they listened with less skepticism.

"When I arrived in the other world," I said, "I met three people right away, a man and two girls. They were at the pond looking for something the man had lost there a long time ago." I paused and looked at Jody. "His name was Topher. Topher Collins."

She frowned. "What? That can't—He was killed years ago."

"His *double* was killed. Topher made it out. He's alive in the other world."

Jody was silent for a moment, then, quietly, she began to weep. Catherine wrapped her arms around her mom, but her eyes pleaded for help. Quickly, I told them everything I knew about Topher's life in the other world. "He's doing fine," I said. "He's safe."

Jody kept crying. It reminded me how Topher had cried when he first heard that I knew his family. "He's never forgotten you," I said. "He thinks about you all the time. And he misses you."

Those words, instead of soothing her, made her more agitated. "But he's out there living some alternate life? With another family?"

"Sort of," I said. "With your doubles."

"Why didn't he come back? *You* came back."

"I could come back because my double, Nolan, didn't die here. But Topher's double was killed in his place. He tried to come back, but he's stuck."

Jody put her face in her hands. I decided there was nothing I could say to make it better.

"So, my dad's out there somewhere, but I'll never meet him," Catherine said, a bit mystified. She thought for a minute then said, "What was my double like?"

"She was really nice. But seeing her only made me miss you more."

Catherine smiled at that.

"Nole," my mom said, "what else happened? I want to hear everything."

Going in order as best I could, I told them the rest of the story leading up to the minute I'd gotten in the car with the guard. As expected, one of the hardest parts for them to believe was how different Lolo was from the Governor.

"I always thought Lolo would be just like her father and grandfather," my mom said, amazed. "Do you really think things are going to start changing?"

I nodded. "Yeah, I do."

"And do you think you and Lolo will ever talk again?" Catherine asked. Worry lines etched into her forehead. I didn't blame her. She knew now that our doubles were together in the other world. It was clear, even from a few conversations, that Lolo and I got along very well. I tried not to think about the moment when she'd reached out and touched me on the shoulder.

"Yes, we probably will," I said. "But I know better than ever before *where* and *who* I belong with."

Catherine smiled again, but I felt unsettled, like what I'd said to her wasn't entirely true. It was actually sort of sad to think that I would never see the people in the other Morley again, even if we were all back where we belonged. I would miss them. As I followed the thought deeper though, I realized the person I would miss most of all was with me in our Morley. And I think Lolo might miss me, too.

51

LOLO

As Nole was driven away, I felt my heart begin to flutter in my chest. It was subtle at first, but as I watched the car disappear beyond the gates of the manor, the beating became louder and more rapid. I could hear each pulse thundering in my head. My chest tightened and soon my breaths were short, shallow, and sharp. I leaned back against the wall and sank to the floor. Shaking all over, I gripped my knees and waited for everything to go back to normal, but it didn't. That scared me. I started to cry as my body continued to disobey.

Eventually, a guard made his way into the garage. When he saw me on the ground, he radioed that I had been found.

"Miss Stevenson?" he said, looking at me nervously, but I had no time in between breaths to speak. "We're going to need a few nurses in the garage," the guard said into his radio.

While we waited for the nurses to arrive, my heart finally relented, and I could breathe normally again. Usually, I'm able to brush away bad feelings, but this had been something altogether more forceful. I could barely fathom everything that had just happened: the dark cell, the poisoned drink, watching my father die, making and then immediately losing a friend. The shock faded, but I was left feeling as anxious as I'd ever been.

By the time the nurses were by my side and checking my vital signs, there was little to suggest that I was in any kind of medical danger.

"Her fit seems to have passed," one of the nurses observed, scribbling notes onto her clipboard. As soon as he heard that, the guard said we needed to go; the Advisory Board had requested my presence. *Requested.* I couldn't refuse this meeting any more than I could have refused the "fit."

I was escorted back inside the house, which was even more abuzz with activity than before. Still, I was immediately able to pick out my mother's voice.

"Lolo, there you are!"

I looked up, eager to see her, despite hardly thinking about her during my captivity. The sight of her familiar face, now alight with concern, drew me toward her.

"Mother," I said, but she put out her hand to stop me.

"Where have you been? It's urgent that we talk to the Advisory Board. Your father is dead."

She said it so matter-of-factly that I thought her only worry was what would happen to her with my father gone. I don't know why I expected anything different. I assumed a practiced air as detached as hers as I followed her to the meeting room where the eight members of the Advisory Board were waiting impatiently.

I listened as they explained the emergency succession plan. It had been written when my great-grandfather was the governor, but I'd never heard it before. Probably because no one thought it would be needed.

"In the event that the governor dies before his heir reaches the age of twenty-one, the Advisory Board will continue to rule in the name of the deceased. During that time, the heir will continue his education and training to prepare for the responsibilities of the governor's office."

Various board members droned on about the law, but I'd heard enough to understand that my novel ideas for the future would be put on hold. I grew cynical as I realized life in Morley was going to remain much the same until I turned twenty-one. For almost five years, the Advisory Board would do all it could to shape me into my father.

Unless, a voice inside of me protested, *I don't let them.*

Even if I couldn't make sweeping policy changes, I didn't have to wait to do *something*. I could start small. I thought about what Nole had said to me before he left, that today I had made life better for two people. So, in a way, I had already started. I just needed to keep going.

For a moment, I felt as hopeful as I had when I'd freed Nole at the pond. Then, as the conversation moved to the official story that would be told about my father's death (a heart attack) and next to the plans for his funeral (an all-day affair followed by six months of mandatory mourning), I found myself growing irritated at all the lies and arbitrary rules. Why should the thousands of people my father ruled over be forced to perform their sadness? It made me furious, and soon I felt as angry as I did hopeful. Maybe I would need both to keep me going on the path I'd chosen.

When one of the advisors mentioned "that boy who came through the pond," I jumped at the chance to do something.

"That boy will remain unharmed," I said, cutting the advisor off mid-speech. They all turned to look at me, surprise and suspicion written across their old faces.

"Lolo," my mother whispered harshly, "that's not for you to decide."

"But I *have* decided," I said, raising my head high. "And there is no reason for him to be involved in this any further."

The members of the Board started arguing, but the Chief Advisor silenced them. "I want to hear your proposal, Miss Stevenson," he said. His stern eyes told me this was no act of charity, but a challenge. I wasn't backing down now.

"Nole Fredericks will not do or say anything to compromise the safety of Morley," I said.

"And what of the people he has undoubtedly told of his . . . travels?" asked the Chief Advisor.

"They are every bit as trustworthy. And I'm sure they would sign any document swearing them to secrecy that you asked them to."

There was some murmuring among the Advisors. While it wasn't totally unheard of for citizens to be bound to secrecy, it wasn't the preferred method.

"And what if a new person from the other world stumbles into the pond and finds themselves here?" asked the Chief Advisor. "What then? Do we keep swearing these unknown individuals to secrecy?"

"No . . ." I hadn't thought of that. Quickly, I began forming a solution. "But maybe we can prevent that from ever happening again. And Nole can help."

"Do go on," the Chief Advisor said, folding his arms across his narrow chest.

"Well . . ." I said, figuring out the plan as I spoke, "we want to ensure that no one ever goes through the portal to the other world again. This might be as simple as draining the pond from our side, but it might not. It could be that *both* sides need to be drained."

I paused for a moment, half expecting to be interrupted, but I had the room's attention. "We could send Nole to the other world one more time. His task would be to inform the people there that the pond *must* be drained. No travel between worlds is to be permitted. When Nole comes back, he and his family will be repaid for his service in the form of a pardon."

The Advisors talked quietly among themselves. I tried to ignore the sound of my mother's hands tapping nervously on the table.

"Very well," the Chief Advisor said at last. "We'll try things your way, Miss Stevenson. However this little experiment plays out, it will undoubtedly provide an important lesson for our young governor-to-be."

My heart was racing again, but now I felt energized, not afraid.

~

The next afternoon, Nole, his mother, and Topher's family were escorted to the manor. They were seated in straight-backed chairs and surrounded by a team of guards. The Chief Advisor explained the plan to them. Although we weren't permitted to speak to each other, I managed to give Nole a half-smile. He smiled back, so faintly I almost missed it. But it was enough. He would do it.

52

NOLAN

never used to remember my dreams. But every night since coming home, I'd woken up sweating and panicked. I would pace my bedroom, afraid to fall asleep again. My nightmares seemed real, like I could feel the cold metal of handcuffs against my skin. Tonight, though, there was no mistaking the sensation of really and truly being submerged in the pond.

"No!" I screamed underwater. "Not again!" I broke through the surface, not sure if I was more scared or angry.

"Nolan!" a voice like Harlow's called out. Frantically, I turned and peered at the shore. It was Lolo. "Don't worry," she said. "Everything's okay."

"*Okay?* Why am I back here?"

That's when I remembered her father, and what I had done to him. I grew still in the water. But Lolo didn't seem upset.

"Come on, let's get you cleaned up," she said. She held a towel open for me. I looked at it skeptically.

"What's to stop me from diving back through the portal right now?"

She lowered the towel. "Nothing, I suppose," she said, a little sadly. "I was hoping you would want to talk."

It struck me that Lolo could have sicced her guards on me the second

I got here. The fact that she hadn't made me curious as to what this was all about. I reminded myself that Governor Matthias was gone, and if Lolo was in charge, things could be a lot different.

I trudged through the pond and accepted the towel.

"Thank you, Nolan," Lolo said, giving me a genuine smile.

"So, are you the Governor now?" I asked, skipping the formalities.

Her smile fell away. "Not exactly. But please, let me explain."

<div align="center">~~~</div>

Once we were back at the Governor's place, I was handed a fresh towel and a change of clothes. "In there," a guard said to me, pointing to an open door. Still a bit suspicious, I peeked inside. It was a normal bathroom. I went in, closed the door, and took off my wet pajamas. Even though the warm water was comfortable, I was nervous the entire time I showered, thinking the temperature might jump to scalding at any second.

After I was clean, the guard escorted me to a large meeting room with a circular table. Lolo was sitting there with three other people. Of course, I recognized Liza. Seeing her was sort of eerie, and I had to look away. Next to her was a curly haired girl.

"Cate?" I said. "Or no, you're . . ."

"It's Catherine," she said. "You must be Nolan."

"Yeah, hi," I said as I took a seat.

"And this is Topher's wife, Jody," Lolo said, gesturing toward her. I felt guilty that I was the one getting to meet these people.

"Um, hi," I said, feeling a little awkward. "I know Topher, he's a . . . he's a good guy." Jody looked down at her lap and Catherine laid a hand on her back.

"So, Nolan," Lolo said, sounding businesslike, "we brought you to Morley one more time in order to reach an understanding about what is to be done with the pond. I'm sure you'll agree that it's caused quite a bit of harm to our worlds."

"Yes."

"We, my father's Advisory Board and I, believe the only thing we can do to prevent further mishaps is to drain the pond. On *both* sides."

"Drain it?" I said. I'd rather just never go anywhere near the pond again. Plus, I wasn't sure how we'd even pull something like that off. "How are we supposed to—"

"Yes, drain it," Lolo cut in, flashing her eyes at me. "And fill it in so water won't collect there again."

"Right," I said. "Matt is the mayor; if anyone can figure it out, it's him."

"Yes, very good," said Lolo. "So, you swear to enact this plan as soon as you return? It's important we don't miss this opportunity."

"I swear. It's for the best."

The room was quiet for a moment except for Jody's soft sniffling.

"So, is that it?" I asked. "Can I go home now?"

"Not quite yet," Lolo said. "Nole will be the one to initiate the switch. His job is to explain the plan to Harlow and her father. Since he has to walk all the way to the city and back, it could be a while."

"Oh, right," I said. Even if I wasn't in any danger, I was still anxious to get out of here.

"But we can wait someplace else," she said. I noticed her looking at a camera in the corner of the room. "The Advisory Board has your promise to drain the pond, and that's everything they need."

"Can we wait by the pond?" I asked, hoping to get as close to home as possible.

"Yes," Lolo said. Then she turned to Liza and the Collinses. "We all can. We'll be there to greet Nole as soon as he's back."

Before we left for the pond we were treated to an elaborate breakfast, but I barely ate anything. It was too early, and I kept thinking back to the time I'd spent starving in this very building. Maybe there were still prisoners starving in their cells right now. After a long, mostly silent meal, the five of us were helicoptered to the pond at 7:30. Bailey and Trish were going to notice I wasn't getting ready for school, but there was nothing I could do about it now.

A few guards set down blankets for us and we settled in for what could be a long wait. Since this was my last chance to talk to these people, I decided I should try to make it count. Lolo must've had the same idea, because as soon as the guards were out of earshot she said, "I found out something that the Collins family in your world may want to know."

"What is it?"

"I read Topher's file. He was right; his double was executed in his place," she said. "After Topher took the illegal photo of me and my father, he escaped into the woods. The guards chased him here to the pond where he was arrested. Only by then it wasn't Topher they had; it was his double. The double told my father a story that made no sense. The notes in the file say it was like his memory had been warped. Topher's camera was never found, so the guards figured it was lost in the pond." She paused, like she had to prepare herself for whatever was coming next. "My father ordered that as punishment for treason, Topher's double be drowned."

I sighed. "Actually, the Governor told me about the drowning at one point."

"I guess I'm not surprised," Lolo said. "He liked to brag about that kind of thing." She shook her head slightly. "Have you told Topher's family?"

"No. Maybe they wouldn't want to know that particular detail. I don't know."

"I think they would." It was Catherine. She was leaning against her mom, looking at the pond thoughtfully. "It's better than having to guess forever."

"Yeah," I said. But I wondered if this new piece of information would just tear open an old wound. It could destroy any peace the Collinses had managed to scrape together over the years. Maybe I'd just tell Topher the truth. He could decide what his family could and couldn't handle.

"How is Amaya doing?" Lolo asked, changing the subject.

"She's good," I said. "I mean, she's been crazy worried about Harlow, but she's hanging in there."

"And . . . Harlow?"

"It's been a tough recovery," I said, "but Harlow is strong."

Lolo wrapped her arms around her knees. "I read Harlow's file too. I . . . I can't imagine." She was on the verge of tears. "I'm sorry."

"It wasn't your fault."

"I know. It was my father's."

"Yeah," I said, feeling suddenly queasy at the memory of Governor Matthias twitching in the mud. "Actually, I feel pretty guilty about what we did to him."

Lolo wiped her eyes. "Nolan?" she said softly. "Would it help to know that I forgive you?"

"What?" I said, surprised.

"I do," she said. "I forgive you." She seemed totally sincere.

"Thank you," I said. It made me hopeful that I wouldn't have to drag my guilt around with me forever. "That means a lot, Lolo."

She nodded. I thought then about the guilt I still felt over my mom's death, and all the things I wished I'd done to help her. Governor Matthias's death served an important purpose, but my mom's hadn't. It was pointless. I think my mom would say that what happened to her wasn't my fault, and there was nothing I needed forgiveness for. Still, I wished I could hear her tell me as clearly as Lolo that I had her permission to move on.

We were quiet for a few minutes until Lolo said, "There won't be major changes in Morley anytime soon." I pulled myself out of my brooding, not wanting to miss what she had to say. "I won't officially be the governor until I'm twenty-one, and until then, I'm sure the Advisory Board will do everything they can to keep things as they are."

That was disappointing news, especially for the people of Morley. "I'm sorry to hear that," I said.

"But in the meantime, I'm going to do everything I can to start changing little things," she said. "I don't want to waste this time and end up with a bunch of regrets later."

That reminded me of something I'd heard Harlow say before, and it made me feel more comfortable with Lolo than I had been all morning. "I know what you mean," I said. "It sucks living with regrets." Again, I pictured my mom. "But this could be a fresh start."

"Exactly," Lolo said, her face brightening just like Harlow's did when she got excited about something. "It *is* a fresh start. I'd forget the past if I could."

I almost agreed with her. After all, I'd just been thinking how badly I wanted to move on from the pain of my mom's death. Forgetting, however, wasn't exactly the same as moving on. I thought it might be possible for me to let go of my regret without letting go of my mom. Hopefully it would be possible for Lolo to do something similar; to break her family's cycle without forgetting how it got started.

"Um, Lolo," I said carefully. "I'm not sure that's the best idea."

She gave me a puzzled look. "Why not?"

"Maybe," I said, trying to think of how Harlow might phrase it, "forgetting the past is why you've all been trapped in this present for so long?"

"We have history books," Lolo said.

I couldn't help but grin. "I'm no expert, but the books I read in my cell hardly seemed like 'history' to me. There was too much editing. It's like, if people don't know how they got stuck, they might not ever get free."

"Yes," Lolo said, as if what I was saying was starting to make sense. "Well, I *do* want to be more honest with the citizens of Morley."

"Yeah, maybe you could write some real history, starting with your own. A new era with a new leader."

"I like that," Lolo said, smiling. "But I think I might let other people write my history too. My father wrote his own history books and look how *they* turned out."

I laughed. "Yeah, fair enough."

I talked more with Lolo, Liza, Jody, and Catherine and learned how the pond was created as an accidental by-product of some energy experiment gone wrong. Since then, it seemed that very little had gone right with this pond. Except without it, I realized, Morley wouldn't have this brave young leader who was ready to take her city-state in a new direction. The fact that things were turning out for the better in this world was comforting in some way. It didn't make all the pain I'd endured here any less real, but it gave it a reason. It was pain I wouldn't regret.

53

HARLOW

On Thursday morning, I awoke to a faint tapping on the sliding glass doors. The heavy curtains blocked my view and at first, I thought it was the wind. But the sound persisted.

"Dad?" I called out nervously. He was in the kitchen making coffee.

"Yeah?" he said.

"I think someone's in the backyard." Again, I heard the knocking. For one irrational second, I feared it might be the Governor. Then, a voice outside said hello. It sounded like Nolan, but Nolan usually texts before he comes over.

My dad appeared in the living room and pulled the curtains aside. "What the . . ."

"Dad?" I said, sitting up as much as I could. "What is it? Who's there?"

He slid the door open and Nole entered the room, shivering and covered in dirt.

"No," I whispered. Maybe I was still asleep, and this was a nightmare. Lately, my nightmares had been vivid enough that it seemed almost plausible. "No," I said again, louder.

"Harlow," Nole said, "it's not what you think—"

"Why are you here?" I cried, too upset to listen. "Where's Nolan?"

"He's in the other Morley, but just for a little while."

"What? Why?"

"He's talking to Lolo. She wants us all to drain the pond."

"What?" I said again. Suddenly, I thought this must be revenge for killing the Governor. "Is she draining it now? While Nolan is there?"

Nole shook his head. "No, it'll be done once he's back. I can explain."

But I didn't have the patience to hear him out, not if Nolan might be in danger. I was about to tell Nole not to bother explaining when my dad laid a gentle hand on my shoulder.

"Let's hear what he has to say, okay?"

I took a deep breath. "Fine," I said.

Nole told us what happened after the Governor was declared dead. When he got to Lolo's plan to drain the pond, my dad focused mostly on the logistics.

"Draining the pond won't be easy," he said.

"But it can be done, right?" asked Nole.

"Being the mayor has its perks. I can call in a favor or two."

"Lolo and the Advisory Board will be glad to hear that."

I, however, wasn't concerned with how this feat would be accomplished. I was still wary it was only a trap.

"But Nole," I said, "you just said that the pond is to be drained 'as soon as possible.'"

"Yes . . ."

"What if that means *right now*? What if your visit is a trick?" My heart was beating rapidly, and I'd have run straight to the pond if my legs allowed me.

Nole looked surprised, like what I'd suggested was unthinkable. "No," he said simply, "it's not a trick. Lolo wouldn't do that."

"After what we did to her dad? She might."

"She won't," Nole said. "Harlow, Lolo has forgiven you."

"She . . . what?" Over the past few days, I hadn't been able to stop reliving the moment at the pond when the Governor's wide, searching eyes had locked with mine. Though in my head I'd built him up to be a monster, in that instant, he'd been unmistakably human. Unmistakably like my dad. Our plan had worked and the Governor could no longer hunt us like we'd feared, but I wondered if the way he was haunting me now wasn't worse. I might always carry a certain amount of guilt about my role in his death. Since I hadn't forgiven myself, it seemed impossible that Lolo already had.

"She told me so herself," Nole said. "Lolo understands why you did what you did."

I felt tears start to roll down my cheeks. "I keep telling myself that killing Governor Matthias was the moral thing to do because it was for the greater good. But anyone can use that as an excuse."

"I think you did the right thing," Nole said, "and Lolo does too. But anyway, draining the pond isn't about fixing the past. It's about securing the future."

"I guess so," I said, feeling pessimistic. "But if you have to wait five years for Lolo to become governor, that future is a long way off."

"Changing Morley is probably going to be a long process," Nole said, "and the changes will be small at first. But Lolo has already gotten started."

Still frustrated, I reached down to scratch my bandaged legs. They were itching and hurting more than ever. "Pain is part of the process," the nurses kept informing me. "It's a sign that you're healing." Each time the bandages were changed, I would glimpse down at my uncovered legs, always upset by how strange and blotchy they appeared. I wanted to skip past the bandage changes and bedrest and physical therapy to get to the end, whatever that was. This recovery was proving just how impatient I can be. I don't like unknowns and in-betweens. But, if Lolo could be satisfied with starting small, then maybe I could be too.

"You know," I said, after a minute, "maybe it's a good thing that Lolo won't have to rush into her new role right away. There's something to be said for slow and steady change. I'm learning that the hard way now."

Nole nodded. "There's probably not an easy way to learn."

"Yeah," I said, "but it seems like Lolo's whole life has been a long test of patience. It just makes me wonder what I would've done in her shoes."

"I've been thinking that too," Dad said. He was gazing out at the backyard, a pensive look on his face. "What makes me different from Governor Matthias? Under those circumstances, what would I have done?"

He sighed, and I got the feeling we were only scratching the surface of what would be a long, difficult conversation. But then Nole shifted back and forth on his feet, and I realized that now wasn't the time.

"Nole! I'm so sorry. Do you want to shower? Or a change of clothes?"

"No, that's okay," he said. "I'll just get all wet again when I go through the pond."

My dad pulled himself away from whatever thoughts had been keeping him captive. "We're going out there with you, Nole," he said. "Topher's in town until this afternoon and I'm sure he'll want to come too. We'll take bikes; there's a special trailer for Harlow and everything."

"Thank you," Nole said.

"If you don't want to change, will you at least have something to eat?" I asked.

That was an offer Nole didn't refuse.

<p style="text-align:center">~~~~</p>

My dad went to prepare the bikes and let the morning nurse know that we would be going on a little outing. "She thought a bike ride to a parallel world sounded like a ton of fun," he said as he closed the garage door.

"You *told* her?" Nole said.

"No, he didn't," I said, rolling my eyes. "It's just a joke. And a *bad* one." I laughed, and my dad did too. That hadn't happened in a while.

Then, I realized it was a school day and we would need to cover for Nolan. We quickly left the driveway and Dad texted Bailey to tell him that Nolan had come over to visit me before school, and he was happy to give him a ride. After that, he pretended to be Bailey and called Cardiff Hall to excuse Nolan for the day. When he hung up, the pensive look on his face was back. He hated lying as much as I did.

"Dad," I said, "it's okay. It's for the greater good."

He smiled. "You're right."

~~~

Topher met us at the beginning of Mountain Pass Trail and we got to the pond at nine. I was sufficiently bundled up, but the weak autumn sunlight barely touched the forest floor. The pond looked cold and uninviting. My dad opened his backpack and took out a sealed plastic bag.

"Topher," he said, "your photo is in here. It was left at our house. I don't know if you'd like it back, but I was thinking Lolo might want it."

"Yes," said Topher. "It belongs to her."

My dad handed the photo to Nole.

"Take this too," Topher said, reaching his hand into his pocket. He pulled out a plastic bag with a sheet of paper folded inside. "It's a letter. For my family."

I thought that if I were writing a final letter to my family, I might end up with an entire book. I'd be so afraid of forgetting to say something that I'd say everything. Topher's letter fit onto a single sheet of paper. The way he handed it to Nole though, like it was something heavy and breakable, gave me the sense that if the words weighed any more, they might drop right off the page.

"Well, I . . ." Nole's voice trailed off. *Goodbye* felt like too casual a thing to say, and I think all four of us sensed that.

"Nole," I said, "I'll never forget you."

He looked back at me with solemn eyes. "And I won't forget you. I won't forget any of this."

My dad patted him on the back. Then he entered the pond and was gone.

A few tense seconds ticked by before Nolan took his place.

"Nolan!" I shouted.

"Harlow! I'm back!" He came running out of the pond and hugged me, sopping wet. "Sorry," he said, letting go.

"No, it's okay. Tell me *everything*."

"He will," my dad said, forcing a towel into Nolan's hands. "After he's dried off."

"Right," Nolan said. Once he changed into the warm clothes we'd
~~~

brought him, he filled us in on his visit, his *final* visit, to the other Morley. I beamed with pride as he recounted his conversation with Lolo about her plans for Morley's future. Then, it was our turn to tell him about Nole.

"All that's left for us to do is drain the pond," my dad said. "Lolo and her Advisory Board will likely never know if we don't follow through with it, but I don't disagree with their idea. I think the safest way forward is to eliminate the chance of future contact between worlds."

"*Yes*," Nolan said emphatically.

I smiled and took his hand in mine. "I've got everything I need in this one."

54

TOPHER

kept my promise to Cate. When I came home from my latest trip to Morley, I told her the full story. She listened with rapt attention as I recounted the details of Governor Matthias's killing.

"So, that's it?" she asked. "It's really over?"

"I suppose it is."

Still, the bad dreams hadn't stopped, and I became nauseous every time I remembered the moment I'd shoved the Governor underwater.

<div style="text-align:center">~~~</div>

I was in my photography studio, trying to lose myself in work, when Matt called. I was hesitant to answer the phone, knowing that the more I indulged myself in thinking about Morley, the harder it was to leave behind. But curiosity prompted me to answer.

"Hi, Topher," Matt said. "How would you like some closure?"

Slowly, I lowered myself into my desk chair. "I'd like that very much."

~~~

That night, I brought up the idea of another trip to Jojo. I made us both a cup of tea and we sat at the kitchen table.

"I don't know," she said when I was done explaining the plan. "If killing the Governor and writing to Jody wasn't enough to bring you closure, will draining the pond *really* help?"

"Maybe not," I said. "But I want to try."

Jojo swirled a spoon around in her mug. "I think the real question is, are you sure you *want* closure?"

"What?" I said. "Of course I do."

Jojo didn't say anything, and I thought for a moment. "Actually," I said, feeling somewhat lighter at the realization, "you're right. I *don't* want closure. I'm tired of endings and goodbyes." I put my hand on her shoulder. "What I want is for you and Cate to come with me this time. I want us to stop putting our lives on hold."

Jojo nodded. "I want that too."

~~~

The three of us flew to Morley the first weekend of December, before the pond froze for the winter. Matt, Harlow, Nolan, and Amaya were waiting to pick us up at the airport. I was surprised, but also rather relieved, at how quickly we moved on from discussing the other Morley. Our families had only met each other a few months ago, but as we sat around Matt's living room eating dinner and chatting, it felt like being with old friends.

The next morning, we prepared to go to the pond. Matt had borrowed two all-terrain golf carts and an industrial-grade submersible pump from the city. It would take a few hours to drain the pond and disperse the water into small puddles that, come springtime, would evaporate. We'd finish by shoveling dirt into the empty space. It was as if we were erasing the pond from the forest's memory.

We let Nolan, Amaya, and Cate each take a turn at the wheel as we rode down Mountain Pass Trail. Harlow, although greatly improved, was still a ways off from having full mobility back. Not that it mattered. She seemed at ease with herself, like she had fully accepted the turn her life had taken.

We parked the golf carts at the end of the trail and walked the rest of the way, taking turns helping Harlow and carrying the equipment. The sight of the pond, its edges laced with ice, had a sobering effect on us. We quietly observed the glassy surface, each of us lost in our own memories and reflections. I thought about my old ID and how it would remain lost forever. That was okay. I'd gained much more by not finding it.

Matt leaned over to me. "Topher? Before we drain it, can you take a picture?"

I nodded. My camera was hanging around my neck.

The water was still, too still. There needed to be some movement, some sign of life. I scooped up a rock and tossed it into the center of the pond. The rock disappeared beneath the surface, as irretrievable as the ripples moving steadily toward our feet. I took the photo.

ACKNOWLEDGMENTS

First and foremost, a heartfelt thanks to my parents, Marty and Lady Gail, and my siblings, Brooks and Katie, for patiently reading every new draft. (I promise, the one you're holding is the last one.) This book would not exist without your insights, questions, and enthusiasm.

I cherish every moment I spent in the South Coast Repertory Conservatory, where I learned how to tell stories. Thank you to the brilliant Hisa Takakuwa, who saw long ago that I had "a heart to love" and gave me "courage to make love known."

I will always be thankful for the teachers who nurtured my love of reading and learning and supported me as a fledgling writer: Kathi Wingerd Jenness, Carol Lang, Coby Oviatt, LaVelle Johnston, Wes Bareford, Brent Rudmann, and Glen Worthington. Thank you to Dr. Ken Chase and Dr. Theon Hill for generously sharing your wisdom at countless office hours and pushing me to do better work than I thought I was capable of.

I am grateful for my incredible Reedsy editor, Rachel Stout. Thank you for so graciously balancing constructive criticism with positive feedback. I hope I get to collaborate with you again.

Finally, thank you to all my students. You inspire me with your passion, fresh ideas, and resilience. A special thanks to my Zoom cohort: Noosha, Lilly, Parsa, and Henry. Our classroom was unconventional, but our community was joyful. Remember, you're irreplaceable.

QUESTIONS FOR DISCUSSION

1. Compare and contrast Harlow and Lolo as characters. What do the similarities and differences between their personalities highlight about expectations placed on teenagers?

2. In the early chapters of the book, Nolan's biggest issues are adjusting to his new life and grieving his mother's death. How do the challenges he faces in his day-to-day life change after he discovers the pond? In what ways are they the same?

3. Consider the role of physical violence in the story. What is the significance of the torture experienced by the characters, particularly Harlow?

4. Think about the systems and government in place in the alternate Morley. While the city-state seems to be entirely different from our world, do you see any similarities?

5. How would you describe the relationship between Topher and Cate? How does his obsession with his old life affect her?

6. Both Nolan and Harlow have complicated relationships with their

mothers. Discuss the role each mother played in their respective lives, and how these maternal absences have shaped each of their worldviews.

7. Do you think Lolo will be able to make meaningful changes in her Morley and build a different legacy for herself? Why or why not?

8. The Governor's coldness and anger toward Lolo, his own daughter, grows more and more disturbing as the novel continues. Why do you think he has so little love for others? What drives him to do and act the way he does?

9. Jojo, the double of Topher's wife, Jody, plays a pretty small role in the book, but is still an important figure. How do you think she has dealt with the sadness of losing her original husband, knowing there is no hope for his return?

10. Even though they are immediately attracted to each other, Harlow and Nolan's relationship builds slowly from friendship into romance. How did starting from a place of friendship affect their ability to survive the tough circumstances they faced?

11. Nature plays an important role throughout the book. Discuss the symbolism of key elements like the woods and the pond.

12. Unlike Lolo and Harlow, who both share redeeming qualities, Mayor Matt and Governor Matthias seem to be total opposites. How does each of them use their positions of authority in different ways, for better or for worse?

13. Why do you think the photograph was such a big problem for Governor Matthias?

14. One of the book's key themes is family relationships and how they can be positive or negative. What are some other themes of the book?

15. What do you think about Nole's willingness to sacrifice himself so that Nolan can return?

16. What do you think about the morality of killing Governor Matthias? Were any choices available other than murder?

17. In chapter 26, we learn that only English is spoken in the city-state of Morley and that immigration is illegal. That means Amaya has no double. Discuss what this demonstrates about the other Morley's culture.

18. The chapters in the novel alternate between different narrators. What do you think of this choice by the author? How did it affect your understanding of the story?

19. What is the significance of the book's title? How does the title relate to the story?

20. Do you think nature or nurture is more important in shaping who you are? Does the book support one side more than the other? Give examples of nature and nurture you see in the story.

ABOUT THE AUTHOR

 **JASMINE O'HEA** is from Orange County, California. She graduated summa cum laude from Wheaton College in Illinois, with a degree in communication and theater. Jasmine has performed in nontraditional settings including jails and a living history museum. As a teaching artist, she has served as a director, acting instructor, and piano teacher. Jasmine currently works as a copywriter for nonprofit organizations. When she's not writing papers for her MA in leadership, she enjoys hiking, kayaking, and listening to Broadway cast recordings on repeat.